Human Sushi

By Saul Wheelock

Human Sushi is a work of fiction. Names, characters, places, and incidents are the products of the author's imagination or used fictitiously. Any resemblances to actual persons living or dead, events, or locales are entirely coincidental.

Table of Contents

But when dawn came up the next day, God appointed a worm that attacked the plant, so that it withered.
                    - Jonah 4:7

Prologue

"Transit Police to downtown B. All carriages, repeat, all carriages."

On the upper platform at West 4th, Sergeant Bernie Higgins dropped a *New York Post* to his thigh. In twenty years on the force, he'd never heard a call like that. Announcements over the station loudspeakers usually sounded like they were shouted down an air vent by someone standing next to a garbage truck. This one came through clearly.

His partner, Officer Silvia Aracena, glanced up from her phone, her thumbs hovering over the screen. "Some idiot pull the emergency brake?"

Higgins replaced the newspaper on a stack of *Post*s beside the vendor and waited for a bubble of regurgitation to rumble up his chest. He hadn't made twenty years on the transit police by panicking every time an idiot pulled the emergency brake.

"Let's find out."

They trotted down two flights of stairs, Aracena a step ahead. On the lower level, scattered straphangers crouched against the damp, holding newspapers open at their waists.

Higgins and Aracena followed protocol and went to the far end of the platform. Driver first, conductor second. Stop signals shot red arrows down the tiles. The announcement came through a second time.

They bent to peer down the tracks. Deep inside the tunnel, a spark of electricity flared blue, lighting up tracks, garbage between the ties, soot-frosted pylons, and grimy walls with sweeping arcs of graffiti. The light dissipated. Tracks sank into the gloom, pylons retreated into shadows.

Aracena tensed. "Here it comes."

The tunnel brightened, headlights shot into view, and a train with a cyclops eye 'B' resolved, ghostly then real. It rattled into the station, swerving before straightening.

The driver's window was fractured, cracks shining through the grainy window like a nineteenth-century photograph of a bolt of lightning. The wiper was bent forward, a skeletal finger pointing at them.

The commuter nearest the train backed away from the platform edge and dropped his newspaper, which was torn apart by the gust of the passing train. He shouted to the police officers, jabbing a finger at the train, then ran up the stairs in a whirlwind of newsprint. The rest of the commuters fled.

Aracena felt for the handle of her gun, reassured by the calm presence of her sergeant behind her.

"Mother of God," whispered Higgins. He pulled out his walkie-talkie: "Get me some friggin' back up, over!"

The walkie-talkie gave a noncommittal crackle in response.

Aracena removed her gun and bladed towards the train. The first carriage snapped past, its windows smeared red and black. She pointed her gun at the doors as they rolled by, and at the next, and the next. "What the fuck is on the windows?"

"Blood," hissed Higgins. He hadn't even unholstered his unit. The first carriage entered the tunnel behind them.

"It's not stopping," cried Aracena. "Bernie, it's not stopping!"

The last set of doors was shaking. She aimed her gun at the rear carriage. Fingers wormed between the rubber ridges, splayed them apart, and a man tattered with gore thrust his torso through. The doors snapped tight around his waist and he hung between them like a burnt figurehead. His mouth opened and closed, his teeth were crimson-stained. White eyes glowed in his muddy face and searched the ceiling tiles speeding overhead.

Higgins held up a hand as if instructing him to stop. Aracena dropped to her knees and lowered her gun.

The last carriage entered the tunnel, whisking the man past them. With a thwack, he was cut in two, his head and torso dropping onto the platform, his waist and legs remaining inside, part of the carnage that would soon be arriving at Broadway-Lafayette.

Part I: It All Began in New York

I.

"It all began in New York."

The kids in the classroom looked bored. No, they didn't look bored; they *were* bored. And they didn't have the grace to hide it. The ones in front doodled with brazen contempt, the ones in the middle blinked as their eyes rolled back in their skulls, the ones in the back snuggled into their arms. They weren't fighting sleep, they welcomed it.

The teacher watched from her desk. I think she was on their side. Somewhere in the wasteland of late middle age, she had an unhappy smile and the translucent skin of the long-forgotten paramour, a fragile surface any contact might break.

"I was working the midnight shift."

Fifteen years ago. The brats in front of me were still in diapers. Or weren't even born yet. Maybe they were gametes being generated in hot teenage crotches during an abstinence education class, maybe they were a microscopic hole in a condom in a deadbeat's wallet, maybe they were being conceived with the tender words, "I swear I'll pull out."

It took some effort to go on. "I began at dusk and closed at 4 a.m. Then I'd return to my apartment to write as the sun came up."

This was the part of my talk where I left out the lines of cocaine on the sink in the bathroom. By the end of my shift, the sink had a gelatinous sheen with globs of phlegm and curled pubic hairs adhering to the cracked porcelain. The bathroom stank of piss, beer, ejaculate, and vomit. And hot dogs on Hot Dog Nite. It was a grim Hot Dog Nite when I was hungry enough to choke down a few on my break. But I never figured out how people got their pubes into the sink.

These details would have been more interesting to the kids than anything else I had to say, but I didn't want to deal with the aftermath: the phone calls, getting blacklisted from schools, hearing about it in the press. I couldn't tell how old they were. Between twelve and sixteen, I figured. They were all experimenting with blow and blowjobs but if I were to mention those things, they'd go home, bat their eyelids, ask their parents what I meant, and I'd be forever blamed for taking their ersatz innocence.

"My first story was published in an East Village 'zine."

Did they even know what a 'zine was? Hadn't the 'zine craze been put out of its misery? It would have been the world's smallest book burning.

"The story didn't make a lot of waves but sometimes a ripple is enough."

I paused to let them appreciate my facility with words. One of the kids popped a piece of chewing gum, timing it to go off in the middle of the silence. There were a few snickers, and the teacher's eyebrows did a little jump of appreciation for her student's critical acumen.

"I got a copy into the hands of an agent who liked it enough to take me on. He farmed out my work and pretty soon I was able to quit bartending."

I wondered if I should tell the kids about Larry. He wasn't just my agent, he was a *mensch*, a mentor, the last of a dying breed: grizzled city veterans who teach young writers how to live in the big metropolis. He treated those of us in his stable like we were horses to be groomed and run around in circles, preferably after a trough of whisky. Under his tutelage, an old-school education of liquid lunches in midtown chophouses and blistering hangovers in the late afternoon, I cut my hair short on the sides and slicked my forelock back, my chin was clean-shaven, I donned navy blazers, white shirts, and pressed trousers over shoes as black and shiny as obsidian. Wherever I went, it was like I was on my way home from an all-night party that began in 1923.

Times were good. I drank fine wines and made passes at beautiful women, I read Proust and filled Moleskine notebooks with stories until it was time to head to Scheherazade's for a dusk Gibson and long conversations about the future of the novel, a future I was sure I would be writing. And just before dawn when the streets were empty and the sky was paling, I listened for my name and heard the sirens call back: Jack

Forbes, Jack Forbes, Jack Forbes.

"My next story got picked up by a magazine you might have heard of—the *New Yorker*?"

I waited for a flicker of recognition. Nothing. They hadn't heard of the *New Yorker*. I wasn't even sure the teacher had heard of it. When I was a tenth grader, we argued about who would be published there first. But back then we didn't have video games, unless you count chunky Space Invaders machines, so we had nothing to distract us from our ambitions. I envied these kids. Distracting kids from their ambition is the kindest thing you can do, especially if that ambition is literary. A lifetime massacring zombies and pillaging post-apocalyptic wastelands is a lot more rewarding than choking back disappointment after another rejection or, worse, the cosmic silence that follows publication.

"And that's one of the joys of being a writer," I said. "Seeing your name in print."

Christ. I was even boring myself.

When the talk was over, a girl came up to me. She had been nodding off in the back row.

"I hope I didn't keep you up."

"You didn't," she replied. She held out a collection of my short stories, *From Brooklyn to Babylon*. "My brother likes your books. Would you sign it?"

"What's his name?"

She told me and I wrote: "To Greg. Bedtime stories for your sister." And then I signed my name. Jack Forbes.

After talking to two more classes of fidgety and apparently sleep-deprived children, I was given a tour by the principal, a busty woman with an efficient demeanor that couldn't hide the toll the work had taken on her. Her hands flittered along the buttons of her blouse as if years of being mentally undressed by adolescent boys had finally gotten to her. We played the charade of being impressed by a creaky gymnasium, a cafeteria with inspiring banners, and a cabinet of trophies with gilded athletic fetuses swinging tiny bats and taking jump shots with gravel-sized balls. She knocked at doors and teachers leaned out with open mouths to meet me with unhidden impatience to get back to students whose reservoirs of attention to long division and the Reconstruction Era were rapidly evaporating.

As I left, hunched against the first drops of rain, the principal chased after me and unhappily purchased a copy of my most recent novel, which I signed. One sale.

I left the rest in a box in the trunk and got into my car, a grass-green beater with close to 150,000 miles on it. I sensed their eyes on me—the principal, the teachers, the students—watching from behind rain-speckled windows with the institutionalized curiosity and contempt most people reserve for foreigners and Americans reserve for failures. Before I switched the ignition, I offered up a prayer: *Please start, O holy car, O righteous tin can, you sonofabitch metal mother of my journey, don't humiliate me now.*

She cranked up. One prayer answered. That's about as much as you can ask for on any given day. I pulled out of the parking lot and hit the road.

And what was next? A night in a motel somewhere outside of Toledo and then home to Chicago. I'd shower and shave, head out to pick up an Italian beef sandwich, and then settle in for a White Sox game followed by a Western. You know what that's called? Heaven. Pure heaven.

Night was falling and the rain came down hard. Streetlights looked like neon palm trees. The wet road reflected signs for gas stations and fast food restaurants in a chaotic boiling stream like Las Vegas submerged under the Alpheus.

With my knee controlling the steering wheel, I phoned my only friend in New York, an alarmingly successful poet called Lance Hairoun who published heavily enjambed ditties about crows, death, and, for want of a better word, his penis. You couldn't open a magazine without seeing one of his poems dangling down the page. That was how we met. My work had been generating a lot of interest and Larry got me invited to the first and, as it turned out, last party for a glossy literary magazine called *SINcerity* or something, which was being held in Williamsburg back when Brooklyn was the next frontier, a chic place for literary superstars and their entourages to slum it outside of Manhattan's splendor. I was fondling a weak vodka tonic and searching for a kindred spirit in the crowd of badly dressed writers, editors reeling in a fog of cheap white wine, and publishers with faces crumpled like tissue paper.

A shaggy guy came up to me and said that I was too good looking to be a writer, I must be one of the drug-dealers.

"Nope," I said, "a writer."

Despite his disappointment, we hit it off. Plus, I had a little coke left. We repaired to the bathroom, and then returned to the party with dilated pupils, attending to our noses so nobody would think we had been blowing each other. Over more vodka tonics, we bonded over the existential quagmire of being successful writers, and laughed at the dinky canapés served by aspiring writers who looked into our eyes for a hint of recognition, and at the pompous dopes around us discussing the death and re-birth of theater, the death and re-birth of the Democratic party, death and re-birth of cuisine. Lance and I became friends, bound by the most powerful social adhesive known to man—the glue of disdain—and we stayed in touch even after I left New York, mostly so he could tell me about the parties I wasn't invited to anymore, which made my disdain more bitter and his, annoyingly, sweeter.

Something had happened that morning. In New York. I wasn't paying much attention to the radio but it sounded weird. A mass murder on a train. Dozens dead. Details still coming in.

Lance picked up on the second ring but didn't say anything. I could hear a television in the background.

"Lance? Lance? I know you're there, I can hear the TV."

"Jack?"

"What the hell's going on?"

"Holy shit, Jack, you wouldn't believe it. About 40 people were killed. On the B train, man. The B train! Nothing ever happens on the B train."

"Who did it?"

"No, man, what. *What* did it."

"Lance," I said as calmly as I could; my patience was wearing thin. "I'm in the middle of Nowheresville, Ohio, just tell me what's going on."

"It's all over the news." He faded away.

"Lance?"

"Jack, shit, they're saying a gorilla escaped from a zoo."

"A gorilla?"

"That's what's the newsman is saying—" He began to cut up.

I pulled over. I couldn't drive sober and talk on the cell phone at the same time. The wipers beat back and forth but didn't clear the waterfall pouring down the windscreen. I idled on the verge in a crossfire of bouncing white headlamps and sparkling red brake lights.

"Oh my god," said Lance, coming through clearly again. "They've got pictures."

"Of the gorilla?"

"Yes! The officials want to make it official! They don't want people freaking out—" His voice rose another octave: "Holy shit, man, holy shit!"

"What?"

"They just showed the picture, man. Holy shit!"

"What the hell, Lance!? What does it look like?"

"It's hard to describe."

"You're a poet, Lance, use your words."

"Okay, so it's big, as big as three men, but like three *big* men. Yeah, um, imagine like three Russian strongmen. Now glue them together."

"Okay, so it's big."

"No, it's huge. And a weird pale color—it's hairless!"

"A huge, pale, hairless gorilla? Isn't that just a huge person?"

"Its head is a gorilla head," shouted Lance, "but as big as a regular guy's body. And it has no hair." His voice sank a register and became huskier, more profound. I recognized the voice he used when he read his poetry in bookstores. "Its skin / is / moist / speckled / gray / and wrinkled / like the flesh / of an / enormous salamander.

12

"Hmm, no, not quite a salamander, not oily and green enough. A plucked chicken! Yes, its skin / is / moist / speckled / gray / and wrinkled / its flesh / is as / a plucked chicken's."

"Okay?"

"And, let's see, um, it has / huge paws / with / brown claws—no! Talons, it has talons / sharp as / nails—no, not nails—sharp / as / *knives*—hold on, Jack, I've got another call."

I heard a click.

"Lance? Lance!? You—"

Another click. "Jack? I'm back. It was just my mom. Anyway, this is the biggest hairless gorilla anybody's ever seen. Wait, wait—yes! Yes! They're confirming it was a gorilla, they've done DNA analysis and it's / gorilla / DNA."

"Why did a gorilla go on a rampage on a B train?"

"They're saying it got on south of 34th Street. The driver hit the alarm but it killed everybody before West 4th."

"Why?"

"I don't know but here's somebody who does!"

"Who?"

"The mayor. He's getting up at a podium in front of City Hall. It's raining, they've got an umbrella over him. The picture is blurry like footage from a History Channel film of the 1960s. White men / wearing / hats, / shaky / cameras / filming / them. Okay, he's unfolding his notes, he's stepping up the podium, now he's talking."

"What's he saying?"

"Blah, blah, blah, public safety, blah, blah, blah, no need to panic, blah, blah—terrorists! TERRORISTS! They think it's a terrorist-trained gorilla. That blows my mind."

"Hold on. Are you high?"

"No."

"You're high."

"At a time like this?"

"Are you high?"

"No, okay, yes, I smoked a pinch of weed, but it was weak shit, man, it was basically organic. I got it from a comic book artist in Bushwick. Jack, you should have seen him. He actually waxes his puny hipster moustache. Have you seen my 'tache? It takes/ a whole / candle / to wax / it. Yeah, uh, Bees work /overtime/ to make / enough wax / for my 'tache. Hey, did I tell you who loved my 'tache? Wanna guess? You won't guess, I'll tell you. Are you ready? It was Coetzee. That's right. We were at this shit party, I think it was in honor of vegetarian essayists or something, and Coetzee came over to me and admired my 'tache." He paused to let it sink in. "Hey, it'd be cool if it was a terrorist gorilla. Do you think it should be called Al Kong or King Qaeda?"

I hung up.

The next day, the *Daily News* went with Al Kong and the *Post* went with King Qaeda.

II.

It was dark, the rain was letting up, and I needed some sleep. I took an exit just past Toledo and drove past vacant lots and warehouses torn up by years of neglect until I saw a sign: SWEET PLAI. It was only half lit but that was enough.

The Sweet Plains Lodge: an ambitiously long, double-storied relic cast in a bronze glow, clunking up the corner of a strip mall with a shuttered pizzeria, an aikido studio, a Chinese take-away with neon signage insisting it was open despite the fact that it was dark inside, and retail stores selling cell phones, baubles, plastic beads, and tax rebates.

I parked beside the reception and got out. The air was greasy and cold. At the other end of the mall, a group of men came out of the aikido studio, wheeling and kicking and shouting. Drunken martial arts were the best thing this dead end world had to offer.

I hurried inside. The reception had a wooden counter cutting the room in half, a display rack with strings of elastic to keep nonexistent brochures in place, and an enlarged, framed photograph of people at a swimming pool, circa 1955. I gave the brass ringer a slap and was rewarded with a dull ting.

A pair of blue-veined hands crept like malformed spiders onto the counter. I let out a small male scream. The hands froze then steadied the rise of a woman, who glared at me like I was just another moron surprised that she had been waiting under the counter.

"Good evening," I said. "I'm wondering if you have a room for a weary traveler? I'm afraid I didn't make a reservation."

She puckered her lips like she was going to suck the sarcasm out of the air, and then, in a voice wrapped in sandpaper, said, "Yes, there's a room . . . young man."

Now, normally I'm pleased when somebody calls me a young man, although I'm aware that being pleased about this masks its own bitter acknowledgement of decrepitude's triumphant approach. But this didn't feel good any way you looked at it. It wasn't just that she was so old she probably called white-haired priests "young man" but because she said it like she was furtively communicating this information to someone hiding under the floorboards.

"Yes," she went on, "there's a room for you. Do you have identification . . . young man?"

I gave her my driver's license, waiting for her to be impressed by how well I'd kept my looks when she saw my birthdate. She took it with disgust as though I had removed it damp and fruity-smelling from my underpants.

"And a credit card?" she rasped. "Young man?"

"Definitely old enough to have one of those," I said, removing one from my wallet and letting her see that I had several more where that came from.

She floated into an adjacent office behind the reception desk. The room lit up with the lightening flash of a photocopier and then she returned, mumbling, "There's a young man . . . yes, a young man." She handed me a plastic keycard along with my driver's license and credit card.

"Room 232," she said, too loudly. "A young man in room 232."

I had no idea what to do. She was obviously telling a hatchet-wielding son-husband in an alcove with his collection of ladies' underwear and violated dolls where to find me when he had a midnight urge to chop somebody into pieces while singing selections from the American songbook in a falsetto punctuated by grunts of exertion. I was going to cancel the room but something on the floor caught her eye and she sank under the counter, followed by her spidery, blue-veined hands.

I may be young, I thought, but I'm too old to be freaked out by this shit.

I re-parked my car at the far end at the motel—as if spending the night in a forlorn corner of Ohio wasn't exile enough. I took my bag, leaving the box of books in the trunk, and made my way up a flight of stairs that had the extraordinary quality of being both open-air and cave-like.

Room 232 was on the corner. The keycard worked, I stepped inside and flipped on the light. The room was claustrophobically brown and bland, with a queen-size bed

16

bloated with a brown bed spread, a desk under a mirror, and a television with finger smudges on the screen like someone had been touching it longingly while watching porn. The air was fragrant with the lingering scents of diapers, cigarette smoke, and semen.

It was the kind of room where you didn't want to spend any time, unless you were waiting to be diced into pieces or planning on offing yourself, in which case it was perfect—you could accustom yourself to death, easing your way into the coffin.

I threw my bag on the bed, more hungry than morbid. I remembered a bright and relatively clean vending machine under the stairs and went to see what it had to offer, besides the diaphanous rubber laying in front of it like the shed skin of a cave-dwelling worm. I bought two caffeine-free sodas and used the rest of my dollar bills on Twizzlers.

The whole ape thing had piqued my curiosity. Back in the room, I settled on the edge of the bed, cracked open a soda, and turned on the TV.

With the exception of the sports channels, all the stations were carrying the story about the gorilla in New York. Experts in animal behavior, and large ape behavior in particular, were having a field day. A tough little guy with a blond crew-cut and a trim moustache, who had lived for a year with Macaques to study their mating habits, gave a terrifyingly vivid description of hormonal rage in monkeys. It was terrifying because he made the faces the monkeys make when going into a sexual frenzy: barking, gagging, snorting, baring his teeth.

I didn't want go to sleep with that guy's face imprinted into my psyche, so I changed the channel until I found another expert in simian behavior. She was mousy and unassuming but with excellent credentials: her research over the past decade was to teach sign language to gorillas, so she was the one person on television who had actually spoken with an ape.

"This is really unusual," she was saying.

The anchor was not impressed. It was obvious to the densest members of his audience that this was not your typical everyday occurrence.

"So what do you think happened?" he prompted wearily. "Rogue gorilla?"

"We've never seen anything like this before," she stammered.

I was about to change the channel to find the guy who made the cool monkey faces when she said, "It could be a herald event."

This caught me and the anchor off guard. By now, we both knew a lot more about gorillas, apes, New World monkeys and Old World monkeys than we had a few hours before, and we were expecting a synopsis from another expert who had trained his or her entire life for this moment and could rattle off a by-now familiar list: rabies, a pet that had been locked away in Manhattan, an animal from an underground circus, or even—here, people were only speculating—the beast had been trained by a nefarious ring of animal-fighters and put into battle with pit bulls and bears.

"What do you mean by 'herald event'?" asked the anchor. The look on his face said it all: my network got the worst damn simian expert in the country.

"I'm not sure," she said. The anchor may or may not have known he was on split-screen with her; either way, he grimaced. She got flustered. "It's just that this is so unusual."

"Thank you," said the anchor, searching for her name and then giving up. "And now we're going live to New York—"

I turned off the television. It was just after midnight and I had been watching the news for four hours. Lance's description had been pretty good. All the stations showed the same photograph of a large hairless gorilla with wrinkled gray skin like it had lived its whole life in a cave. Or the New York subway system.

I got up. With the back of my hand I opened the curtain to look out a window patched with the gray paisley of dried rain. Half the lights in the parking lot were lit, scrawny beacons sending out a waxy bubble of light; the others were slim needles vanishing into the mists. Beside my car was a beat-up BMW. I pressed against the window but couldn't see any lights in the neighboring rooms. There was a dull thump from next door.

I went back and lay on the bed.

Besides Lance, there were three people I knew in New York.

First, of course, there was Larry. But I wasn't going to phone him, not after he told me it would be good for my career to educate Buckeye youth about the life of the writer. The chances of him being awake and sober were miniscule and it was possible he didn't really remember who I was.

The second was my ex-wife. She lived in New York City or on the Jersey side of the Hudson. Or in Westchester. Maybe Long Island. She dumped me before my career hit its stride, predicting correctly it would only reach the slow boil of mediocrity, and went on to re-marry, hitching herself to a nice if effete dermatologist who left a moisturized smear across life's windowpane. I think they had a kid or two.

The third was my High School English teacher. He was probably a pederast and also one of my heroes. Mr. Chester. Mr. Something Chester. What was it? I stared at the ceiling, his first name on the tip of my tongue. I couldn't get it, I just couldn't remember. I had to think of something else, so I imagined my ex-wife having sex with her dermatologist husband and, bang, Mr. *Brian* Chester.

Mr. Brian Chester was a ruddy man with cigarette breath and what was then considered long hair—dandyish, dandruffy curls coming down over his shirt collar. He carried himself like a defrocked priest glad to be done with the ministry, in yellowed tweed jackets debauched with stains and leather elbow patches. Twain and Melville were his heroes. He insisted that only in America are the best novels written by older men for teenage boys. Ghost stories, he said, all of them.

Mr. Chester was the type of teacher who impressed about a dozen kids in his forty-year career and was forgotten by the scores of others turned off by his squinting effusions over novels they didn't read, disgusted by his yellow-toothed smile, and who laughed at him, even harder when he joined them, inaccurately assuming they were laughing *with* him. But he said I had talent. You never forget the first person who tells you that. Mr. Chester left the North Shore and retired to New York so he could live out his final days in a city where culture wasn't restricted to black tie events. Or so he said. I think he wanted to find a place where if former students avoided his eye in the street, it was because everybody was avoiding his eye. Even me, the one time I spotted him at Columbus Circle.

It was not without shame that I admitted I would only be sorry to learn that Mr. Chester was on the B train.

I stared at cracks in the ceiling, rooting out chunks of Twizzler from between my teeth and deciphering the creaks coming from the room next to mine. Out of the corner of my eye, I saw a gargoyle hanging bat-like from the ceiling with an eyeless, mouthless face. I flinched and turned to look: it flattened into a sharply edged polygon, claiming for itself the natural innocence of a shadow cast by the lightshade.

A dull thump came from my neighbor's room, and another, and another, until the thumps took on a mechanical rhythm: ba-thumpity, ba-thumpity, ba-thumpity. There were no voices, no muffled strains of music, no cries of delight; it was just the ghost train of desire chugging faster and faster out of the station until with a few fading chugs, it passed into the distance with a dying howl.

I got up, slouched to the chair at the desk and opened my laptop. It was time to write. My fingers played in the air over the keyboard like a concert pianist silently rehearsing a particularly hard passage. I wanted to get away from this haunted place, cursed with premonitions of murder. The one place I could go was writing, where the empty moonscapes of death bloomed with orchards and singing drunkards and swashbuckling adventures.

Or at least I used to be able to go there. When I started writing, I could materialize something out of nothing; it gave my early novels a precocious, life-affirming energy, what Bella Haughterrier at the *Times* called my "penchant for a vigorous masculine spontaneity" (at least that's what Lance thought he heard her say). It's what Mr. Chester saw in my short stories, it's what Larry tried to cultivate, it's what the publishers put their money into. But in my late-twenties, I lost that superpower. My ex-wife saw it coming. For a while, I blamed her. But she wasn't kryptonite, she just knew me better than I knew myself. There came a time when I was no longer able to wish life into existence. I couldn't just drink a glass of scotch, blink three times, and become Fitzgerald, Hemingway, or Kerouac, much less Proust. Nope, I was Jack Forbes. And that disappointed nobody more than me.

I checked my reflection in the mirror. A man with a head of thick black hair streaking silver over the ears, a solid chin shadowed with stubble, and hard gray eyes looked back at me; the man in the mirror had a lot more resolve than I did. He refused to accept that it was over. But I didn't believe him.

Almost a year had gone by since I hit rock bottom. Unable to write, blitzed by drink and failure, I faced my age, mortality, my descent into the pits where the has-beens can't distinguish themselves from the never-weres, and a last shot at redemption. Yes, there could be a second act for Jack Forbes. It began with three vows. I wouldn't drink again, I wouldn't fall in love again, and I would write a last novel.

It didn't occur to me that all three vows were about death. Death was never present to me, which is why my novels were so shallow, but it must have been there somewhere, because when I made the vows, ostensibly about how I was going to live, only death would see that I fulfilled them.

I closed the laptop. Two of the vows were being kept, the third—not so much.

I lay down with my arms behind my head, my mind spinning in the mud of white male fantasies, and wondered whether I should wait a few minutes or start masturbating right away.

III.

The night passed slowly. I woke from nightmares without being able to remember what they were. The room was so crammed with bad dreams there didn't seem to be space for anything but the squirm of nightmare after nightmare. The gargoyle returned and sniffed my face with fuzzy flaring nostrils; the receptionist was spying through a peephole in the flimsy plywood walls, her breath explaining the dry hiss coming from the vents; her creepy incestuous manspawn trembled with desire and called me the names of flowers as he ran the dull blade of his axe up my spine. When I ran my hand down the rough hide of the blanket, I could feel the scurry of fleas and lice dotting its synthetic fur and began to itch all over.

There was a sound at my door. Something was scratching, down low, like an animal pawing to get in. I pulled the covers around my ears and held my breath, paralyzed with terror, stinging with itches, with a pressure on my chest where the faceless gargoyle landed, and the receptionist was stepping into the room, a long knife by her side, and her hairy-chested son-husband was at the foot of the bed, licking the stump of his axe and tugging at himself in his diapers—whatever it was went away.

And then I heard dripping.

When you hear dripping in a sink and it wasn't dripping before, something has come to warn you that a bad thing is going to happen. The faucet wasn't dripping before. Now it was the only thing I could hear. I listened to the tick tock of the double drip and wondered what spirit had crept into this lonely motel to warn me.

At last the hard metal light of dawn sliced under the door.

I'd slept in my t-shirt and jeans but it didn't matter how I looked, I'd be home soon enough. I brushed my teeth and shaved with the toiletries I'd purchased for a few bucks at a gas station. I left the brush and razor on the rim of the sink for room service or the next inhabitant to dispose of. I figured I would shower when I got home. I didn't want to expose myself to the fungus in the stall, regenerating every few hours with clouds of spores that would alight on the faucet, in the cracks, around the drain, to begin its foul life cycle anew.

I checked the room and lifted the stiff cloth skirt to see if anything of mine had joined the dust motes, furballs, and torn condom wrapper under the bed. Deep underneath was a bloody finger pointing at me. Or a used tampon. Either way, I wasn't going to claim it. My wallet was in my pocket, my computer in its bag. I had nothing else to leave behind.

The front desk was abandoned and the anile woman failed to materialize when I banged the bell. I left the keycard on the counter.

The BMW was still parked next to my car. Its door was open and a man was hunched over the steering wheel in an uncomfortable position. I thought about waking him, especially since there was a group of homeless people shuffling past the aikido studio, probably heading to a local soup kitchen, but after his antics the night before, he needed the sleep.

I set out with a cool adieu to the Sweet Plains Lodge and once I got back onto the highway made good time to Columbus. There was no need to stop for lunch. Getting hungry just made me more excited for the beef sandwich waiting for me at the end of the trip. Not that beef sandwiches need anything to make them more delicious.

The air was fresh and autumnal, there was no traffic, and the road was a flat black tongue unfurling beneath my wheels with Chicago at its tip like a slightly misplaced piercing. I began to feel optimistic. Ideas for novels popped up like mushrooms in a forest after a night of rain; phrases that I loved slipped into my mind—"golden dawn's offspring" and "love's sad surplus"; characters introduced themselves and solicitously informed me that they were at my service: a lame waiter named Toby with a terrible secret; Harolde, a rich cousin with a red moustache and a terrible secret; Hammock, a Bolivian *bon vivant* with Zorbaesque *bon mots* and a terrible secret.

That's the thing about driving: it's about going forward.

You let the nightmares, the bad vibes, the sleepless nights, and the failures disappear in your rear view mirror. It doesn't matter where you're coming from, only where you're going. It's why Americans love driving. Deep down, despite everything we say, despite our parades, our Thanksgivings, our phony gratitude to the past, our solemn memorials, our jibber-jabber about forefathers, we Americans know that origins are sinister nonsense. We plummet onwards, a huge machine fueled by forgetting. Only the future matters. But it's also why there hasn't been a great American novel since the dawn of motoring. Fitzgerald, our Eurydice, wrote about a car crash and sealed our fate. Since then, every American Orpheus has looked back—and it's all over.

But that wouldn't stop me. "The future writes itself," I said aloud as I crossed from Ohio into Indiana, quoting somebody, possibly myself. "Our only duty is to make sense of what we're given to read along the way."

At this point I should mention: I had not been listening to the radio. Nor had I turned on the television before checking out of the Sweet Plains Lodge. In fact, I'd forgotten about the whole mad ape incident. I'd forgotten everything. One reason I stopped drinking was because of the blackouts, but my memory problems were not entirely related to the consumption of alcohol. Forgetting had become a habit in and of itself. Who was it who said memory throws up "twisted things"? Well, I was grateful for the smooth white pastilles of forgetfulness in my mind, the placebos that did nothing but take up space where something twisted should have been. I could forget my failures and contemplate the successes to come. And success began with my evening plans: a shower and a shave; go pick up a beef sandwich from Al's with extra peppers (hot *and* sweet); drive home while the juices and giardiniera darken the paper bag and leave a greasy smear on the passenger seat; take it upstairs, maybe stop for a chat with one of my Ukrainian neighbors, and then eat the voluptuous soggy meat sandwich while watching the White Sox, finishing up the evening with a bag of cookies and a Western.

Fate had something else in store.

The first zombie I saw was roadkill, a shaggy lump of clotted skin and disheveled clothing, like a trucker ran over a tramp. I slowed the car with a mixture of rubbernecking curiosity and annoyance. I was making good time, I didn't need the hassle, but how often do you get to see a decomposing corpse? What if it was a celebrity?

As I got closer, though, I figured it wasn't a body, just some local environmentally-callous kids had dumped trash by the side of the road. But no, there was a head-like ball of hairy skin and two hand-like claws protruding from the sticky fabric. The blurry outline over the body was not an autumn heat haze, it was a swarm of flies. Whatever it was, man or woman, it was definitely dead.

I kept the car going. I wanted to steer clear of anything to do with the police. My first major work was a detective novel, drafted as my senior thesis at the Harvard of Evanston when I figured detective novels were the way to go. *Before the Blood*— an "Austerian-Adairian postmodern head-scratcher," a "tour de force of contemporary storytelling," a "startling debut"—was a first person narrative about a private dick who hatched a plan to murder himself and was trying to catch himself before he committed the crime. I won't tell you the ending except that it surprised nobody but me.

But I had done my research—"Forbes has done his research"—and knew the following to be true: whoever finds a corpse is the prime suspect. The Indiana cops would push their hats up their brows, graze on their 'baccy, spit expertly, and ask what I was doing the night the person died. As I would hardly be able to account for myself ("Who were you with?" Alone. "Where?" In a motel down the road. "What were you doing?" Writing? Watching television? Staring into space? Or, you know?), they would spout jets of brown liquor and smile knowingly.

I didn't want to get involved with this sort of thing. Let somebody else call the cops. I sped up—but it didn't seem right. A hundred feet on, I pulled onto the verge, cursing my indecision. Not calling the police would now be a confession of guilt. No doubt surveillance cameras had filmed my car. The cops could slam pictures down in front of me: "Recognize this car, son? *Squirt.* Recognize this license plate? *Squirt.* Is it famil-i-ar to you? *Emphatic squirt.*"

I know, Indiana isn't the Deep South, but I was still in Ku Klux Klan territory.

"Ah hell."

I got out my cell-phone and dialed 911. It rang and rang. I checked the number. Nope, no mistake, I hadn't dialed incorrectly. It was still ringing.

There was movement in the rear view mirror and I looked up, expecting a car. It was not a car. It was the shaggy heap of dead person, limping fast towards me.

Its arms swung loosely, joined to its torso only by strands of muscle. The head lilted on its neck and it gazed through my back window with the gray eyes of a cooked fish. As it got closer, its mouth opened wider and wider like it was about to take a bite out of the car—but it wasn't opening its mouth. Its jaw, disconnected from its skull, was sinking, taking its lower lip and chin down to its chest, where it swung like a pendulum with a row of old-ivory yellow teeth.

I had never before comprehended the truth in the expression "I shit myself." I didn't *exactly* shit myself, but my gut spasmed with a primitive reflex, a visceral lurch of terror so bodily and expulsive that I nearly did. My foot floored the gas pedal of its own accord and I drove off, watching the awful thing get smaller and smaller in flumes of dust and exhaust.

I'd dropped my cell phone on the passenger seat.

I picked it up. "Help!"

It was still ringing: rolling metallic burrs followed by long silences. Then a click and a man answered.

"911 dispatch," a voice said. He sounded young. "If you are—"

"Hello? Hello? Help! I'm Westbound on—" I looked around for a sign.

"If you are in the South Bend area," said the man, enunciating every syllable with the controlled panic of a lower level bureaucrat trying to do his job while fully cognizant that everyone more senior had fled, "you have got to leave."

"No, you don't understand—"

"I repeat, if you are in the South Bend area, please leave immediately."

"I'm trying to leave but I just saw—"

"Sir, I'm going to hang up now. Just go!"

"Go where? Where should I go? Do you know what I just saw?"

"Sir, I repeat, just—oh no. Oh my Lord, no. Harry, close the door! Oh my Lord, no!"

We were disconnected.

It did not sound good.

IV.

I was watching a rainbow. A huge rainbow straddling the entire US-Canada border.

I had never paid much attention to rainbows before. Why should I? Who really cares about rainbows? It's like the sky is trying too hard. I tried to remember whether I'd mentioned one in my writing and was coming up with nothing until I recalled a passage in *Gargantuan Voyages*—my midcareer *magnum opus,* a "picaresque voyage into the contemporary psyche", included in one critic's "Top Ten best unread books of the year," briefly banned from several libraries in the South for its depiction of urban sex—in which I described a shirt worn by a lothario called Patchouli as "rainbow-colored." What I had in mind was one of those shirts you'd wear at a luau or a Hunter S. Thompson costume party. The colors in Patchouli's shirt were the colors of nature at its most flamboyant: the reds of apples, fresh blood, roses; the yellows of a ripe banana, a canary's feather; the blues of the sky or a child's wavy line for water.

The rainbow up ahead was not rainbow-colored; it was unnatural and artificial, pinks, yellows and pastel purples more suggestive of color than visible, describing the kind of arc that would be made by a nuclear bomb about to explode in a cotton candy-colored mushroom cloud, blasting unicorns and radioactive ponies across North America. If a child painted a rainbow using the colors in this rainbow, his teacher would scrumple it up and tell him do it again.

I watched the rainbow, I stared at it, I contemplated its colors, I even began to feel affection for it.

Anybody who received a grade higher than a C- in Intro to Psych would understand why: it was a hell of a lot easier looking at the rainbow than the world around me.

For more than an hour, I had been driving through a war zone. Ramshackle packs of the living dead searched for human flesh. Tomb-tossed rotters perched like featherless vultures on carcasses, tearing at fibrous red meat. Cars crashed, releasing billows of steam. The skies were tickled by hundreds of fingerling plumes of smoke. I was riding in a convoy of about fifteen cars racing towards Chicago. A pair of helicopters tracking alongside us crashed after one flew low over an overturned tanker and a dozen chewed-up corpses leapt onto its tracks, worming over the chopper's windscreen; it dipped and shot across the highway and—well, you know what it's like when one helicopter hits another mid-flight? No. You do not. You have no fucking clue. Imagine Edward Scissorhands and the Wolverine attacking and killing each other in the blink of an eye. It's a bit like that. Only scarier. Half the cars around me were shredded by scything helicopter blades or immolated in the explosion. The rest were picked off a few miles later when zombies dripped from an overpass, kamikaze splatter landing on windscreens like bags of guano from birds that had been eating a lot of berries. I was lucky. Mine misjudged. There was a thump and my roof buckled, then rebounded, sending the zombie rolling off the trunk and onto the asphalt. In the rearview mirror, I saw what happened to the other cars: spinning out of control with eviscerated corpses on their windscreens, they crashed blindly onto the verges where hundreds of zombie spectators, not unlike your average NASCAR crowd, plunged onto the hot wrecks to feast. Along another stretch of the shoulder, a ragged crew of zombies beat blackened sticks against the tarmac like a troupe of crazed drummers; as I passed, I realized they were beating charred bones against the road, trying to get the human marrow inside. I laughed, I cried, it was even worse than *Stomp.*

So what was I supposed to do? I kept my eyes on the pretty rainbow and pretended the wind whistling through my window was not carrying the screams of people being eaten alive.

There were a few skirmishes, the first inklings of a resistance. From a farmhouse set back from the road, someone was firing shots at a throng of zombies clamoring around the porch like starving foreigners surrounding a U.N. truck laden with sacks of rice. I could see flashes of light and puffs of smoke from the twig-like barrel of a rifle poking out the attic window. Whoever was fending off the zombies swiveled his rifle and fired a shot in my direction. I hoped his aim was better with the zombies because no bullet came near me.

My gas tank was half full, as an optimist would say, but I wasn't going to stop to top it up. At a Texaco, I saw a car at a gas pump—or to be more precise, I saw a heaving mass of zombies writhing over a car like ants swarming over a snail to get the soft flesh inside. To avoid a similar experience, I drove at the upper limits of fuel efficiency, making a calculation that put get-me-the-hell-outta-here speed into an equation with I-don't-want-to-stop-for-fuel conservation of gasoline.

And then there was nothing.

The highway emptied. No more zombies, no more crashed cars, just the wind-rippled Midwestern expanse of fields. I wondered if it was all over. Maybe it was just a local zombie uprising, maybe I had driven through a film set, or maybe this part of America—a vast dome of dust with a toupee of corn, dirty vegetable gardens, rusted cars on cinderblocks, and the plastic inflatable swimming pools where Huck Finn almost drowned—was just the asshole of the world and it needed another wipe.

But rational struggles to return to a state of psychic normalcy didn't work. The world itself had taken on a meaning I couldn't decipher. I searched out details to anchor my mental prose in the harbor of legibility: grasses as they bent in the wind like worshippers subjugated by a gust of faith; clouds like transient fists clenched in a promise of revolution, unconnected to the reactionary land below; that rainbow, with its ambiguous Oz-like promise of escape and a return home.

I checked the radio, switching it on and off just to make sure I wasn't hallucinating. Even the sports stations were talking about what was going on. Newscasters were trying to "assess the situation" and keep us "up-to-date."

I was grateful to discover that there were no experts on the topic of zombie apocalypse, although thousands of teenagers and slack-jawed horror fanatics, the zitty and knock-kneed Cassandras amongst us, were surprised to find that they had suddenly become the most respected members of their families. Politicians and diplomats were instructing us to stay calm and indoors, but they were reading from a crisis boilerplate script. On the plus side, it felt like all of humanity was in it together.

But I began to detect that this was not quite the case. All mankind did not come together. Turns out, airplanes were bombarding cities around the world, tanks were plowing down neighborhoods, and a number of wars had been re-ignited on the assumption that the attacks had been launched or, as one person interestingly put it, "funded" by neighboring countries over longstanding border disputes. There were rumors of nuclear explosions. More humans were killed by monsters than by other humans that day, but if statistics are ever tallied, I fear that the relative proportions will be embarrassing to whoever attempts to carry humanity's legacy into the future.

I also learned that if most of us were stuck on the ground fending off monsters, hundreds of millionaires and politicians were in the air, having fled to their Cessnas and diplomatic aircraft, and were circling in the sky, waiting to hear of an airport reporting safe landing. I don't know how many of these planes glided to their doom over the oceans and how many landed into the maws of hungry monsters, but there was little comfort in either thought. Still, little comfort was better than none.

I kept going. The radio went dead. Cell phone service was gone. I wanted to call my parents—not just because I was worried about their safety but because I was worried about my own. Calling my parents would have helped. I forced myself to think about something else. That rainbow again . . .

About an hour later, I saw a pack of dogs trotting along the highway. Their heads swayed from side to side and they zig-zagged like they were following a scent. They had rounded chests and mottled yellow fur bleached white in places like over-sized hyenas.

I slowed the car down to get a better look. I was curious about the animals. I've always loved nature shows about shark attacks, koalas, and birds and things. But up close, I could tell something was off, something wasn't right about these animals. They didn't move with a dog's easy glide; they scurried with the stop-and-start motion of an animal disproportionately configured for moving on all fours. And unlike hyenas with lanky front legs and short back legs, these had long back legs with shorter arms under broad shoulders—their heads swung lower than their rumps. The faces were lupine, with hairy ears peaked high on their heads, but also hideously human: blue irises and round pupils blazed with alert human savagery, the snouts were elongated human noses, and the yellowed fangs were the flat-edged teeth of the human smile.

For a moment, it didn't seem like more madness; for a fraction of a second, they made sense. I was just seeing something that prefigured humanity in the evolutionary scale by a few million years, a mossy missing link, prehistoric humanoid scavengers who slavered over the mammoth bones left behind by Neanderthals.

But no. They stopped making sense. And then I knew what I was seeing. Werewolves. Transformed from corn-eating, fair-haired Midwestern stock.

We were going the same pace in the same direction and looked at each other across the dipping grass. I sped up; they broke into a canter. I hit the gas and they began galloping. They were fast. And they could jump. Flinging themselves across the verge, they leapt towards me, one after the other, their hind legs like pistons shooting them through the air. They clattered on the windshield and scrabbled against the metal, leaving greasy streaks on the glass and claw marks in the paint; the ones that clung to the car stared in at me with ravenous human eyes, their lips raised in hungry sneers before they tumbled off with yelps and howls, wet jaws clacking and snapping. I swerved from side to side and pushed the car to 90 mph. I kept my foot to the floor. The engine screamed. Werewolf slobber and mud from their paws was smeared on the side of the car. In the rearview mirror, the galloping werewolves got smaller and smaller. Gas conservation be damned, I was now in full panic mode.

V.

I was running low on fuel. Less than a quarter tank left. I slid in a disc—a Lenny Bruce live performance I'd saved for the ride back. I found it hard to pay attention and impossible to laugh. I kept expecting him to start riffing on commie zombies and faggot werewolves. The fact that he didn't pissed me off, like it was his fault. I switched to a Brahms Hungarian Dance and forced myself to concentrate on the music, pressing my mind's ear against the notes, but it was like being cornered at a party with someone haranguing you in a foreign language. I switched it off and focused on the grind of the engine.

It was getting to be mid-afternoon. Any hopes I had of a limited monster uprising were dashed. Zombies limped beside the road and stopped to watch my car pass with empty eyes, forcing me to confront a long-held prejudice. Now that I had seen truly empty eyes, I had a new respect for the ironic spite that passed as emptiness in the eyes your average literary critic at a cocktail party.

I didn't see more werewolves. A few cars passed me on the road to Chicago, a few others passed in the opposite direction. When we were abreast of each other, we didn't wave or give each other the thumbs-up, we just made eye contact, searching for a clue. We never found the clue; the intensity of the search was the human connection we forged.

I occasionally passed people along the side of the road. They'd wave to flag me down or stand in the middle of the road. Stopping did not seem like a good idea, though it might have been charitable. I just couldn't be sure they weren't zombies or about to transform into werewolves. An assumption that they were humans with fears and loves and hopes like my own was not strong enough to make me act.

Anyway, that they might be real people wasn't reassuring either. People are treacherous at the best of times. I could see pulling over and opening the passenger door for a pleasant-looking person, at which point a vile confederate would creep up in my blind spot, rip open the door, drag me out, kick me in the head, steal the car, and leave me to get werewolf-fucked and eaten by zombies.

So I didn't stop. I learned not to check the rear view mirror. It wasn't the ones giving me the finger or shouting obscenities who upset me; it was the ones who sank to their knees.

And then I did stop.

Eventually I realized there was no way I would get to Chicago without offering a helping hand to someone. And once I decided that I was going to stop, I felt guilty whenever I didn't. I wanted to make the right choice—but what was the right choice? Would I make a crude choice, like pulling over for an attractive woman after passing one who wasn't to my taste? Or a racist one? Or, I suppose, a homophobic one? Liberal guilt, it turns out, is a sociopolitical cockroach; it can survive anything.

I felt like Noah driving a shitty miniature ark, except that when Noah picked the animals two by two, he could claim he was just getting whatever animals he could lay his hands on: he didn't pick this particular pair of lions or that particular pair of zebras. It struck me that the story was not, as I assumed, a parable for evolution, where nature demolishes whole species and preserves the fittest. No. All the animals that survived the flood were selected for because they could be captured by an 800-year-old man. No wonder humans went on to dominate the earth.

The problem of selection was solved about two hours out of South Bend. I saw four people on the side of the road. They stood casually on the edge of the tarmac. One, with a rifle, did not raise it as I approached; not one of them hailed me. Instead, we glanced at each other, making eye-to-eye contact in search of a clue. At that moment, I knew I would stop. These were humans.

Plus, they were two women, one white and one black, and two men, one white and one who was Indian or Pakistani. It's true, the women were college-age and cute. The white one was blonde, long-legged and busty in slim-fitting jeans, a red sweater, and a sleeveless puff coat. The black one was short and big-boned, almost *gordita*, in a powder-gray jacket, a menacing little gold cross around her neck, with her hair in braids so tight they looked like they were bolted into her skull. But it was reasonable to guess they were the girlfriends of the guys, so it wasn't like I was aiming to pick them up. And racially, I nailed it. Not even the most niggling, pedantic academic could accuse me of racial-profiling. If anything, I was selecting for diversity and multiculturalism.

I ground to a stop in the gravel and rolled down the window.

"Get in."

The young man with the rifle jogged over and leaned through the open window. He was handsome in a thin and sickly way, with floppy fair hair, bright green eyes, and the last traces of acne disappearing from his cheeks.

"Hi, um, how much petrol do you have?" he asked in a distinct English accent.

I expected gratitude, not an interrogation. He noticed my pause.

"I'm sorry," he said. "It's just that the last person who picked us up ran out of petrol about a mile yonder. We pulled over and he was killed by zombies. We ran for it, but—"

"Not all of you made it." I finished his sentence for him.

He shook off the memory. "Although it's kind of you to stop, we're not actually aspiring to a repeat experience."

"I've only got—" I checked the gauge. "Less than a quarter tank."

"That'll do," he said cheerily. "Come on, guys, barrel in."

He swung into the front seat and introduced himself.

"I'm Rafael. From the United Kingdom."

I shook his outstretched hand, unimpressed by the soft grip.

"This is Praj." The Indian or Pakistani kid got in. He was nerdy, skinny, and young, probably still in High School. He scooted grimly across the back seat.

"And this is Gammy and Trish."

The two young women squeezed in without taking their eyes from me, like they were accepting a ride from a registered sex offender.

I repeated their names—"Rafael, Praj, Gammy, Trish"—

and gave a silent, ambiguous laugh, as if I had sized them all up and decided with some skepticism and more than a little generosity that they'd do.

"My name is Jack."

VI.

I said very little over the next half an hour. I didn't have to. Rafael was doing all the talking. Every time he said something he thought was funny or well-put, he ran a finger across the middle of his forehead to pull back hair falling into his eyes, regardless of whether any was.

"This is not how I expected to spend my autumn," he said, drawing a finger across his forehead to accentuate an ironic understatement that really needed no accentuation. "I'm a student of fine arts at Leeds, studying the role of the church in Renaissance painting. Do you know where Leeds is? Yes, it's about three hours north of London by train, five by car, and eighteen by bike, at least the way I ride." I didn't know if this was fast or slow, but it was in some way amusing to him. His finger drew an invisible stripe across his forehead. "Our faculty has an exchange program with Notre Dame." He pronounced the name like he was talking about the cathedral in the Seine; the white girl mouthed something to the black one, who rolled her eyes. Rafael must have sensed something. "I can't bring myself to say 'Nowter Dayme', which endears me to some but not to others. In any case, I'm here in Indiana, studying the role of the church in Renaissance painting, I made lovely friends like Trish here—" The white one gave a forced perky smile. "And she's roommates with Gammy." The black girl glared at me from under her bronzed helmet of braids; I couldn't tell if she despised Rafael or Trish or me. "And—Praj, we just met, didn't we?"

Praj nodded tersely.

"We're together more by accident than design. When things went pear-shaped, we flocked to the library. You see, as students we believe scholarship is hallowed. We were drawn to the library by a primal conviction that we would be safe in the stacks, surrounded by humanity's accumulated learning, protected by the poetry of Chaucer and Donne, the works of Ovid, Thucydides and Shakespeare, the great literary fortress we've built around our naked souls.

"We could not have been more wrong. Students, faculty,

even librarians were being murdered left and right. Ghouls slaughtered anybody they came across. I saw somebody trying to bat away a monster with the essays of Montaigne. If that isn't a sign of the apocalypse, I don't know what is. One of the librarians' cousins came and we hitched a ride in his van, the one that ran out of petrol. Anyway, to get back to the story, I'm happily studying the role of the—"

"—church in Renaissance painting," I said.

"Right. Because I always wanted to be an art historian, specifically of the Renaissance, the great flourishing of humanity's genius. Or perhaps because I was destined to it by name. I like to tell people that I'm named after one of the Teenage Mutant Ninja Turtles but really I'm named after the painter."

Stroking his forehead, he paused for me to laugh, saw that I didn't, and took a breath to go on—but what he said triggered a recollection.

"Weren't the Mutant Ninja Turtles named after the artists?" I asked.

"Yes," he said, "that was the joke."

"Oh," I said.

"And my name is spelled with an 'f', not a 'ph'." It sounded like he had run out of steam, but he perked up again. "So I was happily studying the role of the church in Renaissance painting, making lovely friends, and now this."

"Uh-huh."

"None of us has the foggiest idea what's going on. I can only assume my family knows that I'm still amongst the living, but as soon as I get to a phone, I'm going to call so they know I'm safe. If there's one cliché worth repeating, it's that hope springs eternal. You must be wondering about the rest of us, what we do, who we are?"

I wasn't. I was thinking I should have just picked up one of the stone-faced farmhands I'd passed a few hours ago, who would sit glum but wordlessly in the front seat; he might try to pig-fuck me, but at least when he wasn't trying to pig-fuck me, I'd be left in peace.

"First we have Trish. Trish is a student of government,

from the great State of—? Wait, wait, don't tell me, I'll remember. You're from North Carolina, aren't you?"

Trish poked her head forward. "My mother lives in North Carolina, my father lives in California."

"I knew there was a twist," Rafael confided to me.

"I grew up in Sonoma."

"Right, so Trish is a North Carolina-California hybrid who's studying government. I believe your interest is in the role of political parties in emerging democracies?"

"That was just a term paper," she said. "I just picked government because . . . I don't know why. It sounded interesting."

"And it is," said Rafael, then he turned to me. "I'm a member of the student union back in Leeds. We're tremendously active. Last year, we raised over £400 for charities in Africa."

Trish wafted back between Gammy and Praj.

"The key is organization," continued Rafael, "Right, Trish? Government is how we organize ourselves as a polis."

"Sure," said Trish, tucked in between Gammy and Praj. "Does anybody have any gum?"

I couldn't decide if I liked Rafael or Trish less. Trish was the type of girl in High School who never looked twice at a guy like me. I might have been more handsome than the blockhead jocks in their letter jackets but I lacked social standing because I gravitated to the artists, which meant that in her vocabulary, I was a loser. On the other hand, she didn't have much to say, a quality that was becoming increasingly endearing.

"Your political system has always fascinated me," mused Rafael. "It's extraordinary to witness American politics from within. The Democrats in this country would be center-right Tories in England and the Republicans would be the corporate wing of the Tories and yet American politicians act as though the rift between the two parties is as great as that between libertarian nationalists and socialist internationalists. In the UK, we watch from an awed and somewhat frightened distance, with equal amounts of contempt and envy. You know it's a terrible insult to talk about the Americanization of British politics."

"Is it?" I sighed.

"Yes. But coming over, I've been able to see your system from the inside and it's far more complicated than we give it credit for."

"I found gum," chirped Trish.

"And Gammy," said Rafael, "What about you? What are you reading? I mean, what's your 'major'?"

"Computer science," she murmured, her two big eyes sullen.

"Oh really? *Really*? That's unexpected. So, Gammy is studying computer science—oh no, of course, I knew that: you wrote that computer game. And I do remember where Gammy is from. Gammy hails from the Republic of Texas, right?"

I saw her bob her head once in the rear view mirror, an aggressive nod.

Great, I thought. I've picked up an angry black woman, a cheerleader with minty breath, and the most boring English person in the world, a title for which I always suspected there was a tremendous amount of competition.

"Between California, Texas, and England, I think we're representing all of the great American states." Rafael laughed at his joke. Nobody else did. "I don't suppose you're from New York?"

"I lived there for fifteen years."

"Perfect, this really is the most cosmopolitan car—oh, but Praj. You're so discreet, I forgot about you. What about you? Where are you from?

"Chicago," he whispered.

"Brilliant. Are you a student at Notre Dame?"

Praj nodded.

"He looks so young," said Rafael with real affection in his voice, as though he and I were full-grown men talking about scrappy kids in the back. "What are you studying, Praj?"

"Philosophy," said Praj.

"He's a philosopher," Rafael explained.

Hence, I thought, the cerebral air of virginity.

Rafael summed it up: "We have me, a student of the fine

arts from the UK; Trish, a government major from North Carolina *and* California; Gammy, a Texan computer scientist; and Praj, a philosopher from the Land of Lincoln. I dare say that for the first time, the philosopher is the most useful amongst us." He gave Praj a wicked grin, which Praj ignored.

"For surely," he continued, unabated, "the question we're all asking is 'Why?' Why is this happening? What have we done to deserve this? How does this change our comprehension of the world? What does it mean to be human at this point in history? In years to come, my work may come in handy as we contextualize the arts of this era, and Trish may forge a new government when we beat these monsters back into the mud they've crawled out of, and if there's an electricity grid, we will need computer scientists like Gammy. But right now, we need philosophers."

Something attracted his attention.

"Oh look, zombies! Shall I shoot them?"

"Save your bullets," I growled.

The kids froze.

I had never seen my words have that kind of effect before.

I'm someone who lives in words, not places; I'm never more at peace than when I'm in the forest of language. I can spend hours wandering around a single sentence, twisting the tenses, listening to the adverbs until I find the right sound, chopping paragraphs, uprooting adjectives, pruning until I find the sweet spot where language and meaning don't just meet with a nod of recognition, they bump chests, tussle, grapple, and, while you watch in astonishment, their lips meet and they kiss with a passion that bursts from the page with all the possibilities of literature.

But this was something else. Rafael obeyed, Gammy and Trish relaxed, and Praj leaned his head against the window, allowing the last of his strength to leave. Outside the car, there may have been chaos but inside there was a clear hierarchy. I was the adult.

"Good point," said Rafael. He thought for a moment. "Have you eaten?"

I'd skipped breakfast and had been driving all day. I was ravenous. I pretended to think about it, then shrugged.

Rafael twisted in his seat. "Gammy, do we have anything for Jack?"

She rifled half-heartedly through a backpack, throwing resentful looks at me. "He can have this." She thrust a packet of Twinkies at Rafael.

"The food of the Gods," he said. "We have nothing like this in England. Go on, you can indulge yourself today."

They looked so good, I wanted to gobble the horrible tubes down, I wanted to cram the chemically-moist yellow cakes into my mouth, I wanted to suck the teeth-dissolvingly sweet puss from out of them, but instead I heard myself saying, "I need something more substantial."

Gammy rummaged through her bag and this time, after making more of an effort, produced a ham roll. I watched in the rear view mirror as she examined it, contemplating whether she should give it up—she didn't want to give it up, she wondered if it wasn't too late to slip it back into the bag—

"That'll do," I said. Our eyes met in the rear view mirror. Her eyes narrowed. I gave the smallest snort, a puff of angry air through my nostrils, and her eyes fell. She held the sandwich out.

Rafael negotiated the hand-off. Using my thighs to steer, I unwrapped it from its cellophane wrapper and gave the ball of plastic to Rafael.

"Hold onto this, we might need it."

Rafael obeyed and tucked it into his shirt pocket.

As slowly as I could, I took a bite. Instead of gulping the whole thing down, I chewed each soft salty mouthful until it was a sweet bread and meat paste.

After I was done and feeling better about some things, if not others, I leaned back and stretched against the wheel.

"So what about you, Jack?" asked Trish, with all the honey in her voice of a co-ed cooing for a sugar daddy.

"What about me?"

"Are you married?"

"No," I said. It still felt like a lie.

"What do you do?"

I kept quiet. I worried that if I said "novelist" I would disappoint them. You can always assume a writer is fundamentally a coward unless there is well-documented evidence to the contrary from multiple disinterested witnesses. Bounty hunter or plainclothes cop sounded good. But on the other hand, I hadn't been planning to reinvent myself, least of all for a pack of college kids.

"I do a bit of this and that," I said coolly, and waited a second. "I pay the rent by writing. Mostly fiction."

Nice. It sounded like I could do anything. And it was true, if "this and that" meant watch TV, clean the apartment, surf the internet, and chat in the stairway with my senile Ukrainian landlord. But it had a nice ring to it, like it might mean fix transmissions, lay pipes, defuse bombs, and take the occasional private detective job, all the while earning my keep as an intellectual. "Mostly fiction" was the *pièce de résistance*: how could you hear it and not think that in between writing tricky novels and erotic-comic short stories, I was publishing macho Mailerian reviews in the *New York Review of Books*, opinion journalism in the *Atlantic Monthly*, essays on jazz scientists in the *New Yorker*, and maybe, every few years, the odd book of verse?

"Have I read anything of yours?" asked Rafael.

"I don't know," I snapped. "Have you?"

"I'm trying to think of authors named Jack."

"Jack Lemmon?" tried Trish.

"He was an actor and comedian," I said.

She tried again. "Jack Bauer?"

"A fictional character."

"Um, okay," she said. "Jack Kerouac."

"Yes, an author—but not me. He died a while ago. And, before you say it, I'm not Jack London." Rafael giggled. "And no, my last name is not Daniels or Daripper." There was a pause, followed by the amused rearrangement of asses on car leather. Gammy peeked at me in the rear view mirror and our eyes met; she still had a sweltering look but her eyes were less inflamed with rage. There may have been the sparkle of humor in there. Trish lifted her shoulders and glowered out the window, aware we were all making fun of her even if she didn't quite know how or why.

A voice came from behind me. "Jack Forbes?"

It was Praj.

"Um, yes."

"I've read your books," he said.

Whenever this had happened before, I'd arch an eyebrow with a self-deprecating smile to let them know that I knew the truth: not untalented but too middle-brow, past his prime but maybe with one more novel in him, possibly even a great one.

I couldn't bring myself to do it. Praj's silence filled the car and threatened to crush my authority like a stale Twinkie. My breath caught in my throat. I had never been so desperate to have someone like my books. My stomach writhed. I clenched the steering wheel, unsure why I was going bananas because a pint-sized subcontinental Sartre had read my books.

And then it hit me. My fame, such as it was, was my lifeline to an existence before the unfolding catastrophe. For all I knew, the last surviving person on earth who had read my books was the boyish Indian or Pakistani kid staring out the back window. My desperation was palpable and it risked tipping the whole hierarchy.

But then I spotted something up ahead.

"What have we here?" I said, slowing the car down to a crawl.

VII.

A penitentiary, set back about half a mile from the road. Signs leaned away from the prison—"Do not stop for hitchhikers"—as if we needed telling.

We pulled past a chain-link fence and stopped about twenty feet shy of the main gates in the wind-raked bristle of no-man's land. Sunlight sparkled on coils of razor wire looping indolently along the top of prison walls untouched by graffiti, giving off a radioactive mineral glow. The gates swung open.

There was a ruckus in the flatlands to the south. Thousands of crows were alighting and flapping in a field like peppercorns shivering on a yellow piece of paper. One thing was for sure: they weren't feasting on a car-flattened rabbit.

"Why are we stopping?" asked Trish.

I had no idea.

"This is the most secure location in the Midwest," said Gammy. "Do you have a better idea?"

"That's right," I said. "Anybody have a better idea?"

Trish shook her head. Rafael stated the obvious—that the gates were open, the watchtowers unmanned, and the walls were a mile-long canvas waiting to be decorated with the splatter of our blood—but I was already stepping out of the car for the first time since that morning, when the world was a very different place.

I stretched my legs and scanned the vast empty landscape. It was like we had been transported to an abandoned prison planet with a poisoned yellow atmosphere and a labyrinthine ruin harboring alien pods. My knees creaked and I needed to use the men's room.

"Let's go."

Inside the main gates, the courtyard was submerged in a puddle of cool shadow, part recreation space, part parking lot, and not unlike an inner city playground—a single rusted basketball hoop, a wide expanse of gravel, and a wider expanse of cracked concrete. The sun came to a bright orange halt on the windows.

We took the ramp up to the main building, a block three

stories high with barred windows. Rafael ran his rifle along a guardrail, hitting each pole with a metallic ring.

"Cut it out," said Trish in a pissy voice.

"We should let people know we're here," he said. "We don't want trigger-happy guards taking pot-shots at us."

"The kid's got a point," I said. Rafael glowed with pride. Trish sniffed the air. "But cut it out; it *is* annoying."

We arrived at a pair of double-doors embedded in the brutish cinderblock. With a push of my fingers, the doors opened and a rectangular slab of light entered, a ghostly white carriage with a cargo of five shadows. We followed them in, carefully stepping in their footprints until they merged with the darkness, our double agents, our personal traitors.

We moved past a vacant control room with dead consoles and into a corridor lined with plexiglass-covered bulletin boards with instructions to be silent, obey the authorities, stop here or not stop there, and an unending relay of prohibited items rendered as silhouetted images in red circles with red slashes through them: guns, alcoholic beverages, needles for injections, cigarettes, dogs, rats, cellphones, and, for some reason, chickens.

Silence hung in the crepuscular air like a threat held in someone's mouth. There was no sign of life—or death. Just us, tracking our lost shadows. I balled up my fists, although I would have preferred to have the rifle Rafael was pointing definitively but obscurely in various directions, like a cat at night catching the sounds of ghosts nobody else could hear. The air was redolent with the institutional smell of wintergreen and bleach spiced with urine and body odors, a battle between decay and hygiene where nobody really cared who won as long as the victory didn't take place on their shift. Yellow emergency lights were gripped in metal lattices high on the wall like imprisoned fairies. Our footsteps made pathetic squeaking protests. The barred doors opened with the lightest of touches as if the building was expecting us, then closed behind us with the ting of metal against metal.

We entered a huge open space, the hollowed center of a metal hive stacked three stories high with cells, a skeletal cathedral, where in place of pews was a ping-pong table without a net and a blackboard with the first three steps of twelve written in chalk. Behind the twelve-step altar rose a metal staircase. Jailed sunlight came through slit-like windows up by the ceiling.

There was a clap of air and a burring coo—we spun and crouched, Rafael pulled the rifle to his shoulder. A pigeon settled on a railing and looked down, waiting to see what we would do next.

"Thar she is," I whispered, "the pigeon of freedom." The kids looked at me with an alien pigeon-like curiosity. I decided to keep the editorializing to a minimum until I could get my thoughts straight. "C'mon, let's go."

Crouched against danger, our ears perked, we drifted past the blackboard to the staircase.

"Shall we?" I said.

Gammy pointed to a sign on the wall, *Warden's Office, Second Floor,* with an arrow pointing up.

"Good eyes, Gammy."

We followed the sign.

"Who's there?"

The voice came from behind a wooden door with a rectangular bronze plaque inscribed with the name Warden J. John Grimes Jr., so we had a pretty good idea who was on the other side.

His secretary's office was cheap and ugly with a steel desk, cabinets, portraits of the President and Vice-President, and a calendar opened to August with a picture of prairie flowers. An American flag unfurled on top of the cabinets, trailing a drapery of stars and bars. Painted down the middle of the floor were two parallel yellow lines. A sign on the desk said, *Do not walk outside yellow lines.* I squatted on the desk, outside the yellow lines.

"I ain't intending to ask again," said the voice on the other side of the door, "Who's there?"

"The name's Jack Forbes. I'm here with friends."

"You a mutant?"

"No."

"A nightcritter."

"I don't think so."

"A werewolf?"

"I only need to shave *once* a day."

Rafael laughed. From behind the door came the scraping sound of something heavy being dragged away.

"I'm gonna open the door but if I don't like your looks, I'll shoot, ya hear?"

"Consider the welcome mutual," I said.

"What?"

"I said, 'Consider the welcome mutual.'"

"*What?*"

"Okay, okay, we understand. We're coming in."

Warden Grimes was a plump man with gray hair oiled into a pompadour like a guitarist from Nashville or an iterant preacher. We sat on punitively-hard wooden chairs in a semi-circle around his desk. He relaxed in a swiveling leather chair and told us about his day.

"Woke up this morning, thought it was gonna be a blesséd day. I always like a day after a storm. Cleans the air, makes everything shine with God's grace. I drove in, read the paper, took report. 'No incidents to report, sir.' Do you know what that's like for a warden to hear? It's like being told the Prom Queen dumped the quarterback for you. A dream come true. Do you know how many incident reports I usually get? Suicide attempts, men caught with hidden stashes of tobacco or girly mags, sodomitical assaults, stabbings—the paperwork is enough to make a grown man cry.

"Anyway, I'm feeling just grand, settling in for a calm day, and I get a call from the National Guard. They tell me an army of mutants is comin' our way. Well now, goshdarned but if that wasn't just about the last thing I thought I'd hear today. I hung up and made an executive decision. I said to my men, Get all the jailbirds out into the yard and get 'em lined up. Went out a few minutes later, took a bullhorn, and I said—now listen careful, these were my words: 'Y'all listen to me, I'll give every

48

one of you a weapon who chooses to join my deputies in fighting this unholy alliance. It's up to you. But if you decide not to participate, I will personally shoot you.' You see, I always like to give my birds a choice."

He paused for what he must have thought was dramatic effect, then went on: "About six birds decided not to participate. I can't say I wasn't pleased. The worst of the worst, bad-souled men destined for Hell. I shot 'em, one by one, with my pistol." He patted his side, realized there was no pistol there and looked around, wondering where he left it. "Anyway, from the second one on, they was changing their minds but I wanted to impress the rest of the birds with the severity of the situation, so I went down the line and sent them on their way to Satan.

"The birds got the message, oh yessir. After that, we armed 'em. They were acting like they all knew how to use weapons, they were striking poses like they were in a rap video, they were cahootin' and just lovin' it. By God, most of them had never handled a gun before. But you know, when a boy touches a gun for the first time, is surprised by how heavy it is, gets that smile on his face, that's when he becomes a man. A lot of boys became men in that yard. Huh, but truth be told, those birds were about the worst army a man could want."

"You shouldn't have killed the hardened criminals," I said. "They might have known what they were doing."

"I think I told you, those birds had bad souls, they would've joined the mutant army in a flash. So, as I was saying, my deputies led the boys out to the marsh and—well, a picture's worth a thousand words." He rolled up from his seat and waddled around his desk on a pair of chubby penguin legs. "One of our security cameras watches out over the field to the south."

He fiddled with the knobs. The screen filled with scratchy images of surveillance footage showing a line of men armed with rifles in a single row along the edge of the field. Behind them stood deputies with rifles resting on their shoulders. The image shuddered.

"Here they come," said Grimes.

The horizon blurred like a line of static was forming

along the top of the screen.

"There's the mutants."

The black line never became distinct, it just grew thicker, creeping down the screen towards the men. Some of the jailbirds got up and ran away but it looked like they tripped and fell.

"Had a sniper up here with me, took down any deserters," explained Grimes.

The black blur sped up and took a shape.

"Like a cloud of flies," said Grimes, accurately.

Beelzebub's army, I thought. And for the first time, I realized: we're all dead, we really are. The row of jailbirds lost its form. The men stood and scattered but it was too late. They were swamped. The deputies were swallowed up too. A fuzzy mass heaved over the spot where the doomed men made their pyrrhic stand.

Grimes stopped the footage. "You want to see my favorite?"

"Sure," I said, pretending I wasn't queasy.

Grimes punched buttons. A jumpy image came up, a black-and-white close-up of six men.

"Got an infrared camera over the wall," he said. "It doesn't take running footage, just a photograph every second. It focused on this boy." He tapped a kneeling figure. "I can't exactly make out which bird it is. Maybe one of the Sanchez brothers, Pablo or Paco. Eighteen, nineteen years old. Accomplices to robbery. One drove the car, one hid the loot."

The figures twitched with each frame. And then the one in the middle, the Sanchez boy, got to his knees, was crouching, was on his feet. Zombies appeared around the men, humanoid shapes frozen in full assault with arms out, jaws open. Sanchez pointed his gun in the air. Then a white plume came from the barrel. The frame after that showed another white plume around a flash of light.

"He wasn't shooting the mutants," laughed Grimes. "He was firing warning shots as they ate the men around him."

Zombies came at the boy from either side and, in the next frame, took him down in a heap. Grimes stopped the video.

"You get the picture," he said.

While he was showing us the death of the Sanchez boy, I had a strange sensation, antsy and pleasurable at once, a primitive hunger and ancient satisfaction: I could smell coffee.

"You don't have coffee, do you?"

Grimes scrutinized me, wondering what to do with yet another bargaining chip. His smile broadened. Generosity is a good place to start when you have all the chips.

"Brewed it up this morning." He pointed to a thermos on top of a boxy office refrigerator. "Help yourself."

I pushed myself up as nonchalantly as possible and strolled over to the fridge with Rafael and Gammy right behind me. They were also planning to have some of the coffee. I repressed the urge to elbow them in the neck. I picked up the thermos and could feel that it was at least half full. Rafael and Gammy never knew how narrowly they escaped death or at least a very sore throat from a half-hearted, caffeine-withdrawal assassination attempt. I twisted off the top. The brew was still warm, its aroma one of those perfect smells like new-mown grass or a peach with a single bite taken out of it.

"There's paper cups in the fridge," said Grimes hospitably, "I keep 'em there to keep things tidy."

The cups were thin, the kind you give kids lemonade in, and there was enough coffee for each of us to get a full cup. I took a sip, too little to swallow but enough to fill my mouth with the taste. My lips and tongue tingled, and a headache I didn't even know I had faded away. I took a heavy slug and felt like there was peace in the world.

Grimes watched with a wan smile. He was the type of man who gave someone a gift while calculating the value of what he expected to get back. How would we reciprocate? First, by listening to him.

"We got time before the military make it this far," he said. "Are y'all college kids?"

"Nope," I said. "I'm a writer."

Grimes frowned, embarrassed for me; I kind of knew he wasn't addressing me, but it just slipped out.

"What about the rest of you?"

Their heads bounced up and down and waited to hear what he had to say.

"I'm just your average American man," Grimes said, scratching behind his ear with humility, "and I swear, what's happening is enough to make an honest man question the Lord, but I'll tell you this: nobody but nobody can take an education away from you. 'F you study hard, you'll be given something that'll allow you to be whoever you want to be."

The kids nodded energetically—even Gammy and Praj, who should have been able to muster enough anger and skepticism between them not to fall for this guy's shtick.

"You gotta work hard," said the warden, on a roll. "Don't let the good times distract you. I know how it is for you kids with the beer and the dating and you think the world's a great big party, but it isn't. It's a test and you gotta study for it. I don't know what your religion is"—his eyes flicked to Praj—"but you are here by the grace of the Author of life. You are written into the world. His book is all around us but you got to learn in order to be able to read."

The kids were hanging on his every word. If they had pencils and paper, they would have been taking notes. I was losing my team to this clown.

"Reading is very important," I said.

Grimes bowed his head under the weight of his own thoughts, like he was trying to figure out a way to make what I said more profound, and then sighed, as if it would have been as pointless to explain to me what he was thinking as it would have been for him to try to bring God to the yeast growing in a jailbird's crotch.

"Warden," said Trish, leaning breastily towards him, "do you have any family?"

'Warden'! She called him 'warden' like he was a pope.

"My wife and I . . . " A humble smile and all-too-human nod. "We had to go our separate ways. Sometimes the book of life has twists, unexpected turns we would never have predicted. My children are with her in Florida. I've been praying all day for their souls. For all of our souls."

"You have to stay strong," said Rafael. The warden and the kids nodded at each other like marionettes with glue-huffing puppeteers.

"Have you always run prisons?" I asked him, making it sound as if I was asking if he had always been a member of the Nazi party.

"I studied criminal justice in college," he said, refusing to be baited, which made me sound petty. "It is a fascinating field. Fascinating! None of you are studying criminal justice?"

The kids shook their heads, ashamed. They were obviously considering switching to criminal justice if the colleges opened again.

"You learn a lot about man when you study Criminal Justice."

"Or Biology," I said. "You also learn what a man—or a *woman*—is."

The warden looked sadly at me. Trish scowled at my interruption.

"Anyway," he continued, "I was offered a job running a small private prison right out of college, did that for ten years. When I got tired of spending my time with criminals, I moved to Tampa and got a job in the private sector, stayed there for a few years, until I realized that the only difference between working in the private sector and working in prisons was that the boys in prison were the ones who got caught"—they laughed at his obvious little joke—"so I got back in the business of jail. About five years ago I was hired to run this supermax out here in the middle of Indiana. You see a lot when you're a warden, you see what humans are capable of becoming. But I can't say I was ever expecting a mutant army."

"So where did they go?" I asked. "Did you imprison any of them?"

The warden shook his head. "Thing about mutants is they're not smart. After they killed the birds and my deputies, they hammered at the wall for about an hour then just faded away, maybe went back to pick the bones. I sent my sharpshooter down to scout them out. He never came back. Say, you might be interested in this."

The warden had another gift for us, another bargaining chip, another way to force us to bear witness to his vulgar, theistic grandstanding. He reached down under his desk and pulled up a small oblong contraption and placed it on desk; when he swiveled it towards us, we saw a tiny screen the size of a playing card: an old-fashioned portable television.

"The television on the wall is for surveillance," he explained, "but this one . . ."

He extended a long thin metal antenna; when he was satisfied with its position, he clicked a button. A white dot appeared, blinked, and fuzz filled the screen. His fat fingers played on the dial until the fuzz resolved into four men moving in choreographed synchronicity; it took me a moment to realize that there were only two men with screen doppelgangers copying their every movement. The warden stood behind us as we huddled around the television and listened to the men with their mocking ghosts. They tried to explain what was happening, their words muffled in the static. The one in a bow-tie with the jewfro—though I couldn't be sure that he wasn't black with a real afro—had an affiliation with NASA and the other was a biologist from a California university. In the middle of a sentence, they fizzled into an electric blizzard. The warden switched it off.

"Scientists," he said. "One minute they're saying steer clear of the butter, the next they're saying we need to eat more of it."

He beamed down at Trish.

"Are we safe?" she said, with big eyes. "If they come?"

The warden patted her on the thigh, quite high up. Trish's bosom got bigger.

"We can hold them," said the warden to her boobs.

I interrupted his breast-gawping. "How many of them were there?"

He straightened up and rubbed his belly. "I guess a thousand mutants. Or a few hundred. I've learned that it's hard to tell with numbers over about a hundred."

Rafael spoke up. "Why do you call them mutants?"

"What the dickens do you think they are, son?"

54

"Zombies?"

"The living dead. I heard that on the television. Hell no. The dead are gone forever, or at least their bodies are. I believe in angels and devils, but not resurrected bodies—with one exception." He smiled humbly.

"So why mutants?" I asked, despite myself.

The warden laughed like the question was stupid. "Do you know what they spray on the crops around here? That stuff goes straight to the swingers. Our balls are wrinkled sacks of mutant sperm—I'm sorry, ladies, but times like these, a man has to speak some ugly truths." Gammy and Trish waved away his apology. He shot me a contemptuous glance, as if I was a wrinkled sack of mutant sperm, and went on, "Truth be told, I'm just surprised nobody raised a mutant army sooner."

"Do you think they'll come back?" asked Gammy. The way she looked at the warden annoyed me. Trish I could understand, but Gammy? Her eyes were moist, her lips half-parted, like she wanted to copulate with the old goat. The man was an oaf.

"They'll be back," I said. "With a vengeance."

"I'm not so sure," said the warden, warming to Gammy's gaze; I was pretty sure the tone in his voice changed when he spoke to her, but I might have been over-sensitive to his racism. "They got their fill for the day. They'll head south."

He turned to me. We sized each other up. The warden smirked like the cat that got the milk. The kids were gazing at him with reverence.

"Turn on the surveillance cameras," I ordered.

"Nope," said the warden. He paused, letting us wonder whether he had a reason or if he was just refusing because he could. "They're down. We're running on our reserve generator."

I went to the window behind his desk and paused.

"Truth is," said the warden, "we just need to wait until the—"

"Grimes," I said.

"Yes?"

"You want to come up here?"

"Why?"

"There's about a thousand creatures milling around in the courtyard and I just want to get your opinion on whether they're mutants or zombies."

VIII.

After joining me at the window and agreeing that the zombies—or mutants, as he continued to call them—had returned, the warden took us into his secretary's office and, moving aside a pail and mop, opened an unimpressive cupboard using a key and a code punched out on a number pad hidden under the calendar. The door opened. The warden smacked his lips as if he was entering a room full of cupcakes, but what was inside was much more impressive than pastries. Rows of weapons lined up like soldiers at the alert, rifles, shotguns, teargas-projectors and truncheons in hardwood racks, cubby-holes packed with orange boxes of ammunition, stacks of neatly arranged riot gear, vests folded under frog-like helmets, and on the top shelf, translucent plastic shields arranged under the ceiling like postmodern escutcheons.

The warden ran his fingers down the row of trigger guards. "I think the mutants are gonna regret messin' with us, don't you?"

He removed an armful of rifles, distributed them like a missionary giving bibles to the natives, and showed us how to load and re-load them. He shook with paternal chuckles at our ignorance, lectured us with deep paternal concern about gun safety issues, and took a profound paternal interest in how Trish held the gun.

"Let me tell you, Trish, the way you're holding that gun, it's enough to make a grown man weep. Your daddy never showed you how to use a gun? Tut, tut. Here, let me come 'round. That's right, I'll be your daddy. Hold it up here, okay, breathe in—good—nice deep breath, lift your chest like you're a puffed-up robin red breast. The heel of the butt should be right . . . here, but the secret to good shooting is lower, where the toe of the butt rests, and that should be . . . right . . . here. Oh, that's good, that's very good, your daddy'd be proud if he could see his little girl all grown up."

The warden was apparently completely satisfied with how I held my gun because I got no hands-on instruction. Gammy, a black Texan, already knew about guns and had selected a disturbingly large pistol. Rafael was surprised to discover that the rifle he had taken from the ill-fated van driver, the one he had been holding proudly all day, had no bullets in it.

The warden was right about one thing: the heaviness of the gun made me feel righteous and manly. I finally understood the primal, inchoate power that comes from being able to do go good in the world by killing things.

Gammy and I went to the second floor landing and stood at the top of the stairs. The zombies flooded into the recreation area, moaning and yawping like rejects from a Ted Hughes poem. They milled around the ping-pong table and blackboard, knocking over chairs, and were marginally less intimidating than if they had been prisoners. One or two looked up at us with a primitive senseless curiosity in their white eyeballs.

I took a few shots and winced at the bruising kick in my shoulder, not quite sure where the bullets went. The shots ripped through the air and echoed through the metal rafters with the impersonal sound of metal going crazy. My nose stung with the sulfurous cordite.

Gammy lifted her pistol, stared down the length of her arm, and fired once, twice, three times. One, two, three zombie heads split apart, spouting jets of coagulated blood. Like a herd of cows lifting their heavy skulls from the grass and trundling towards the farmer, the undead surged in our direction. They suddenly weren't so innocuous. A stumbling, clawing mess of fingernails and long yellow teeth poured towards the stairs, goaded by murder and disembowelment, possibly not in that order. I fired the rifle in their direction, Gammy executed them.

Despite the horrors of the situation, I was not oblivious to the intense young woman firing her pistol with a ravishing sneer, her arm extended, her breasts swelling until they stilled before she pulled the trigger. She clipped a zombie's head at the foot of the stairs. Inky blood spilled over its rotted features.

"Nice shot, Jackie Brown."

"Thanks," she muttered, aiming at another. Her breasts heaved, stilled, and she pulled the trigger. Another zombie head whipped back. She aimed again and repeated the deadly iambic pentameter with its devious second spondee: breast heave, pause, fire, splattered zombie forehead.

In fact, to say that I was not oblivious to Gammy is an unfortunate litotes; it was the most erotic moment in my life. She was wholly present, leaning her body into that hard metal nub, fleshily reaching out from Mother Earth with a fist of black metal, an ur-woman protecting life by dealing death. Only her braids were legible as something specific, exotic and fanciful, and they were sending a message: first, I was not her type, I was a shade too light; this was not a woman who wanted cream in her coffee (although I knew from a few minutes before that she did like cream in her literal coffee and was strangely pleased the warden had none to offer); second, the braids provided a hard, rattling, nervy frame around the softnesses of her cheeks and exuded a confidence that was not just desirable but that intimated her own desires: this was a young woman who savored sex. If the first message excluded me, the second wasn't so sure. I felt a hollowness in my chest; my eyes jumped back to watch her like she was a magnetic pole and my eyeballs were filled with iron; and I suddenly wanted her, desperately, hungrily.

If I die soon, which is looking likely, I will die fortunate, having had in middle age the type of sexual epiphany most people never had after they were juniors in High School: being surprised by the erotic. I pity the generations who grew up with the internet, able to watch anything people can do with their genitals, mouths, butts, or feet with the click of a mouse. How can you truly be surprised by a naked body when you've already seen every nook and cranny magnified, moistened, opened and jammed, before you've even stolen your first kiss? How can you be surprised to discover what bodies can do and where fingers and mouths can go, when you've encyclopedically explored the oeuvre of human sexuality as trembling twelve year old whose parents think you're doing your history project? Whole generations of kids became adults who think that race is important only because it describes the sort of couplings you like to watch, who think that weight is a matter of sexual taste, and that when women have orgasms, they shoot gallons of liquid from between their legs. Take away the surprise and you're left with addicts, people who are never surprised by the pleasure of what they need—the tragedy of addiction.

Unfortunately, I was also not oblivious to the zombies. They were making headway up the stairs despite Gammy's accurate executions and my more random successes. They tore over the corpses at their feet, climbed one another, rapidly becoming an ascending avalanche of rot. Rafael appeared and hopped from foot to foot, looking over our shoulders. It would be unfair to say that he spoiled the moment, what with hundreds of zombies clambering up the stairs to kill us, but I glared at him like he had shown up with a pair of beers while I attempted to flirt with a hot chick.

"Should I use one of these?" He had a round black grenade in his hand.

"Do you know how?" I asked, in a way that implied I did.

"Just pull and toss?" He plucked the pin out and threw it with a straight arm like he was bowling a cricket ball.

It landed in the midst of the groaning throng, and nothing happened for a few seconds. I was about to tell him what a waste it was when . . .

The explosion flattened scores of zombies in a smear of smoking entrails. We were deafened by the blast. In a daze of profound silence, I turned to see Rafael and Gammy hunched over, their mouths agape, their eyes squinting, their heads tilted—I knew I was doing the same thing. A stunned zombie made it up the stairs. It was about a foot away, hunched over, its mouth agape, its eyes squinting, its head tilted.

I pushed it down the stairs with one hard shove. (Afterwards, Gammy reminded me of that moment. She said it was one of the coolest things she had ever seen: a man comes face to face with a zombie and just pushes it down the stairs; I may have acted cool but my ersatz nonchalance was better explained by the fact that I was still discombobulated by the grenade, a truth I chose to keep to myself.)

Through the tinny silence came a distant dinging, like a

dinner bell rung in a neighbor's house to call the kids home. Maybe a third of the zombies were incapacitated by the grenade, but the rest, already stunned by death and resurrection, took less time to collect themselves than we did. They streamed up the stairs.

"Let's get outta here," I shouted.

We ran through the metal corridors to the warden's office.

Praj and Trish stood in the secretary's office with their rifles at half-mast. The plan had been for Gammy and me to stave the zombies off with Rafael backing us up; Praj, Trish and the warden would cover us from the rear, protecting the warden's office as our last refuge.

Trish and Praj had said they didn't feel ready to be on the frontline. Even after the warden's personal instruction, Trish held her rifle away from her body like it was a baton that had been touched by someone with cooties, and Praj, who had never lifted anything heavier than a pencil, struggled under the weight of the weapon. But they somberly agreed to shoot us if we came back mauled.

When we stumbled in, Trish hoisted her gun to her waist, suddenly much more at ease with the weapon.

"Were any of you bit?" she asked coldly.

I shook my head.

"How do we know?"

"Trish, I know we agreed on this," I said, "but none of us were bitten."

"You guys look weird."

"Rafael threw a grenade. We're rattled."

"I'm not sure," she said, squinting suspiciously at us. "Praj, what do you think?"

"Strip," he said.

"You gotta be kidding me," I said. "There are—"

"Strip."

Rafael held up his shirt and pointed at his slender waist.

"Okay," said Praj, unmoved. "We know you weren't bitten on the stomach. What about anywhere else?"

"Zombies are coming," I said.

"No," said Trish with a decisive shake of her blonde hair. "We can't risk all of us being infected if one of you got bitten."

"For God's sake, we were out there fending off hordes of the undead while you shivered back here like a couple of toddlers in a tent scared by snapping twigs in the forest—"

"Strip," said Praj again. This time he raised his gun effortlessly.

"Oh, you're a brave little man now," I said. "You'll point guns at us but not at the zombies?"

Trish motioned with her rifle. Was that a look of profound satisfaction in her eyes? As if all she had ever wanted was to point a gun at a man and make him strip for her? Even if I sympathized, knowing that she felt like constantly being undressed by lascivious men was her life in a nutshell, but I wasn't too happy to be the victim of her revenge fantasy.

"You're wasting time," she said.

"Right-o," Rafael said, rather too cheerfully. He pulled off his t-shirt and let his jeans drop to his ankles. "Voila," he said. He was very fit, if pallid, and had a hint of a six-pack.

Gammy unbuttoned her shirt and flashed a blue brassiere, a surprisingly hot color against her coffee skin, and unbuckled her pants. She was wearing matching blue underwear in a v at her crotch. The memory of our recent moment together and seeing her underwear had an unfortunate effect. The last unwanted erection I had was about twenty years before.

"You too, Jack," said Trish.

"For God's sake."

I plucked at my Clash t-shirt. Too many beef sandwiches, malted milks, and turtle sundaes at Margies had given me a middle-age spread I had made little effort to restrain. I'm not bad looking: when I was a student, I was a solid A/A- in the looks department. I would always say to anybody who'd listen that nobody batted an eye when I was cast as Mercutio in my High School production of *Romeo and Juliet.* And my looks weren't gone. My hair was still thick, my jawline was rock-hard. At a cocktail party for members of the artistic underclass, I was like a 1950s beefcake in a room full of kids who got sand kicked in their face—although when I was in a room full of actual beefcakes, I was like one of the kids who watched from the side when other kids got sand kicked in their face. I pulled off my t-shirt, Paul Simonon swinging his guitar at my still-undetected erection, and everybody looked away, a bit embarrassed by my gut. And then they looked down at my legs. Or really, not at my legs. If you stare in the direction of somebody's trousers, you start with the crotch.

They were staring at it.

I forced myself to think about zombie faces blown open by bullets, but my member was slow in responding.

"For Christ's sake," I said. "I wasn't bitten on the dick—"

"We can see that," muttered Trish. She had the nerve to smile. Gammy and Praj turned away politely. Rafael raised an eyebrow, rather admiringly.

I had one shot at redemption. "If killing zombies gives me a zombie-killing boner, then let her rip," I growled.

We heard a crash.

"They're coming," said Gammy. Praj and Trish let their guns drop. We pulled our clothes back on.

Trish glowered at me. "I'll be keeping an eye on you."

"I bet you will," I said.

Damn right, I thought, you made her blush.

IX.

The door to the warden's office was locked. I shook the doorknob.

"What the hell?"

Trish pushed past me and tried the knob as if I hadn't been doing it right.

"He locked it," she said.

"Wait, why wasn't Grimes out here with you?"

"He was going to keep trying to get help."

We crowded around the door and banged on the wood with our fists, calling out the warden's name. Nothing. Rafael unslung his rifle and aimed at the doorknob.

"Don't," I said. "We need to be able to lock it when we get inside."

Gammy was absently punching her fist into her hand. I assumed she was caught up in black Texan revenge fantasies, but she was the only one who was thinking. She jumped to attention with a faceful of inspiration, lacking only a cartoon light bulb over her head, clicked her tongue, then raced around the secretary's desk and started pulling out the drawers. The bottom one was locked.

A crash echoed through the corridor followed by the sound of splintering glass and something heavy falling. The zombies were getting closer.

Gammy yanked at the bottom drawer. I grabbed a hole-puncher and ran around the desk. Gammy put her hands over mine and we used the hole-puncher like a battering ram. Another crash came from the hallway accompanied by the distinct sound of shuffling feet.

"Come on, guys," pleaded Trish.

Rafael and Praj pointed their rifles at the open door, twitching with every clang or crash.

Gammy and I rammed and rammed the hole-punched into the cabinet.

"What they're doing," said Praj, "is never going to work."

It worked. The drawer buckled. I pulled it onto the floor and Gammy rummaged through it.

"Hurry, they're coming."

"They're here!" screeched Trish.

They weren't yet but Rafael and Praj fired a volley and Trish picked up a metal in-box from the desk and threw it into the hallway.

Underneath a ream of documents and empty manila files was a Jamaican flag key ring with two keys. Gammy grabbed them and ran to the warden's door. The first one opened it. The door to the hallway filled with the undead, some of them wearing orange prison jumpsuits and one of them was in a prison guard outfit.

We tumbled into the warden's office and breathlessly locked it behind us. Rafael grabbed a chair and propped it under the handle. Only a fraction of a second later we heard clawing at the door.

The room was empty. The warden was nowhere to be seen.

"Where the hell is he?"

The scratching against the door got louder and we could hear the thin moans of cold vapors coming out of zombie mouths.

We examined every inch of the room. We ran our fingertips across surfaces, lifted posters with inspirational images of bald eagles and waterfalls and poems about achievement and rectitude, checked behind lamps and under the desk. The windows were barred. The warden had no obvious route of escape. But he was not inside the room.

"Do you think he's out there? With the *zombies*?"

The scratching got louder: the door was being shaved away under sharp dry fingernails. The zombies couldn't get in for a few hours unless they found an explosive device and knew how to use it, but we were trapped.

Gammy found his escape route. The only bookcase in the room was a false one. I tapped the fake books and shook my head with contempt: the man didn't even have real books. He just hid behind the idea of books. If that wasn't a metaphor for something, then what the hell was? The false bookcase opened, revealing a metal door. I glared at the kids one by one, accusing each of them with nothing more than a stare of having almost thrown their lot in with Warden Grimes.

The metal door was locked.

"Gammy, you've got the keys."

She crouched by the door and tried the other key on the Jamaican flag key ring. It gave a satisfying click and the door yawned open.

"Yah mon," I said. "Ja-may-ca!" Gammy shot me a scornful look, holding her pupils high under her eyelids so that only the whites were showing; she was pretty unimpressed but I was more disturbed by how zombie-like she looked.

I stepped around her and shouted into the blackness, "Grimes?"

I didn't want him shooting if we cornered him in his panic room.

"Grimes?"

Nothing, not even an echo.

"Alrighty," I said to the kids, "Do we go in and risk dying with Grimes or possibly—" I glared at them, "—at his hands," I sighed with disappointment and they looked suitably abashed, "or do we stay here?"

Praj shook his head. "There's no choice. We have to see if this leads us out."

I held out my hand: "After you."

I surprised and impressed myself. A man was giving a boy a chance to prove himself after the boy had committed a public act of cowardice. What greater proof of masculinity is there than offering redemption to a boy?

Praj caught my eye. I could tell he was grateful.

"Let's go," he said, ducking into the hole.

Finding the warden was anti-climactic. He was at the bottom of a dimly lit stairway, unconscious. He must have slipped on the stairs in his hurry to escape. Praj had almost fallen down the same stairs but was able to react in time.

I have to admit that I did have a climax in mind: I had hoped we would find the warden being eaten alive on the other side of iron bars; with his last breath he would shout, "You were right, Jack Forbes. These *are* zombies. Blaaaaahhh . . ."

We inspected him, a lump in a suit huddled at the foot of the stairs, a cowboy hat beside his head and a rifle under his body.

The bulbs fixed to the wall flickered and came back to life, casting little more than gloom. They were about as effective as fireflies glued to the bricks.

"Do we take him?" Praj asked, prodding him delicately with a toe.

Rafael shook his head. "We can't leave him here."

"Yes we can," I said.

"He left us," agreed Trish.

"We're better than that," said Gammy.

"Are we?" asked Trish.

"I don't know about you."

"What do you mean by that?"

"Come on, guys," said Rafael. "What do we do?"

"No, I want to know what she means."

I stepped in. "Gammy's right, we can't leave him alive and unconscious for the zombies. Think about it. Our humanity is at stake. We may be the last representatives of the human race. Everything we say and do is a moral requiem for our species. The burden is on us to make the right decision. So let's shoot him. It'd be the kind thing."

"Yeeees," said Rafael, "I don't think we should do that."

"You're right," I said. "Why waste a bullet? Let's strangle him."

"Come on, Jack."

Rafael lifted one of the warden's arms. Grimes groaned. With a show of reluctance, I reached down for the other arm, which was surprisingly muscular under his clothing. As I pulled, something slipped off into my hands.

"He's falling apart!" I screamed, dropping whatever came off him. Praj picked it up, and then showed me the warden's watch. "I thought his arm fell off," I explained.

"Come on, Jack."

"Okay, okay, but we're not carrying him. We're going to

drag him."

Rafael, judging the heft of the arm, agreed.

We set off. Rafael and I took the lead, pulling the old bastard behind us like a sack of manure we'd found and thought might be useful. The lights flickered and then died as if a hundred fireflies were swatted at once. We were plunged into a deep darkness.

"What do we do?"

"What do you think? We keep going."

"Don't push me."

"I'm not pushing you."

"Who was it then?"

"What the hell, was it a zombie?"

"No, it was me. I bumped into you."

"Oh my God, I thought it was a zombie."

"Okay, guys, let's go."

"Which way?"

"Onwards. Hold on, the corridor turns here. Okay, let's go."

We promptly came to another set of stairs. Rafael and I slipped on the top step, letting go of the warden as we grabbed for support. We heard the warden thud down the stairs. At the bottom, he came to a rest with a muffled cough.

"Oops."

"Did you see him roll?"

"I can't see anything in here."

"I hope we haven't killed him."

"It would be the kind thing."

We picked our way down the stairs and reached the warden. In the gloom, he was a rounded gray lump like an elephant fetus in its womb.

"Is he breathing?"

I kicked him and he groaned. "Yup. Praj, you go first and warn us if we come to any stairs."

"How will I let you know?"

"Scream as you fall."

"Gggggg."

"Is that the warden?"

"Or a zombie? Not a mutant, a zombie."

"It's the warden," Rafael said. "Come on, let's go."

Trish edged up against me, shaking, said, "I had a flashlight in my backpack," and drifted into the gloom.

On the other side of me, a short ghost appeared and snorted. "Nice job, Trish."

Trish reappeared. "What have you done, Gammy, other than sulk like you got a bug up your ass."

"C'mon, guys," I said peaceably.

"I blew the heads off a hundred of those things while you peed in your panties—"

"Ladies, enough."

"Who died and made you boss?"

". . . Are you speaking to me or Gammy?"

"I'm speaking to you."

"Me?"/"Me?"

"You, Jack."

"What the—? You know who died and made me boss? You know who? Every other mature adult in the United States died and that made me your boss. Is that clear enough?"

"Jack, it's alright, let's go."

"Come on, Jack."

"Jack, please."

"Wait, what? I'm the one being calmed down? Me? What the—? Fine, I'll leave you all alone."

"Jack, no, please."

"Jack, I'm sorry, I'm sorry I said that."

"We're in this together, Jack."

"Gggggg."

"Jack?"

"Come on, Jack."

"Aah, alright." I reached down and felt along the floor for the warden, grabbed some part of him, and dragged him down the tunnel. "Praj, where are you?"

"Here."

"Are you in front?"

"Yes. I think so."

"Okay, I've got one hand on your shoulder."

"That's my shoulder."

"This is Gammy's shoulder? How is it possible your shoulder feels like Praj's shoulder? Hold on, yes, I feel Praj's head. I don't feel braids."

"Somebody *is* feeling my head."

"I have my hand on your shoulder, Gammy."

"Oh."

"Okay, Rafael, get up here behind the warden so you can take his legs. Let's make a chain. Count off. Say your name. One . . . That's you, Praj. Let's try again. One—"

"Praj."

"Two—me. Three—warden."

"Gggggg."

"Four—"

"Rafael."

"Five—"

"Gammy."

"Six—"

"Trish."

"Alright guys. Let's go."

X.

The corridor led us past a sharp fluorescent light coming around a rectangular metal panel, which emitted an electric hum. We kept going, moving through the dark at a fast walking pace. By my calculation we had gone below ground level, passed through a secret passage underneath the recreation area, and would end up emerging into one of the watchtowers at the back of the prison. We came to a door.

I laid my portion of the warden down and moved Praj aside.

"Okay, I'm going to open it on three," I said.

"Why 'on three'?" asked Trish.

She was really bugging me, and not in a good way. "I could do it on four, if you'd like. 'Three' is very much an arbitrary choice."

Gammy came up close and whispered, "I think what she means is: what are you expecting us to do on three? Shoot out the door?"

She had a point.

"We have to get on the same page," I said, "which means that you need to get back on my page. I'm a writer. So get on my page."

I know, it made no sense, but at this point, the kids were scared enough of everything that they were responding only to tone; I could have barked, and they would have jumped to attention.

"I'm going to open it on three so you have time to prepare yourselves for whatever's on the other side." As I said this, I demonstrated by pushing on the handle. I didn't expect it to be unlocked. It swung open. Turns out, we were about twenty feet away from the main door to the prison block. About a thousand zombies milling around in the courtyard turned to look at us. I pulled the door shut.

"Huh," I said. The kids looked at me. "Didn't expect that."

Gammy flung her self against the door, found a bolt, and slid it shut, then reached up for another at the top of the door, and bolted that one too. The shock wave of a thousand zombies hurling themselves at a single metal door knocked her back into us.

"Are we stuck in this tunnel?" cried Trish.

"No," I said, trying to salvage some miniscule residue of leadership, "we're *safe* in this tunnel. But we do need to consider how we will get out of it."

Gammy made a clicking sound out of the side of her mouth. "Follow me," she said, and turned back into the tunnel.

"The back of a refrigerator." Gammy brushed the rectangular metal panel with her fingers. Light came through around the edges. "I wonder what's on the other side?"

"Should we try to push it out?"

"Get your weapons ready."

I let the warden's arm flop to the floor—"gggggg"—and Gammy and I shouldered the metal, variously chilled and warm to the touch, and pushed. I was really beginning to respect her. She put herself into the mix. I kind of despised her and liked her in the same way that I found her sexy and sexless. But I didn't have time to worry on it, I had to focus on the metal against my shoulder. Rafael joined in and pushed, Praj too, even Trish, and at last we sensed a faint release as something gave way. The refrigerator began grinding over the floor, slowly at first then faster, picking up speed. Bright light flooded around us as if curtains had been flung open.

The fridge bumped to a halt. We couldn't move it any further.

There was a gap of about a foot between the wall and the fridge. Not even Praj could slip through. Holding her pistol in front of her, Gammy poked her head through.

"It's a kitchen."

"Let me see."

She stepped away and I stuck my head through. Yes, an institutional kitchen, the smell of onions and dish detergent, with long aluminum tables for food preparation, ovens with rusty edges and charcoaled grills, shelves with enormous tins of beans and stewed tomatoes, an array of hooks suspended from a rack on the ceiling for pots, pans, sieves, colanders, and woks. A row of sinks ran along the far wall. A tantalizing silver thread of water dangled from one of the faucets.

The fridge had come up against one of the food preparation tables, bolted into cracked red tiles so it couldn't be used by rioting prisoners to keep guards out of the kitchen, but in this instance guaranteeing that innocents remained trapped behind a fridge, a subtle switch in fortunes probably unforeseen by the people who fastened the tables down.

I pulled myself back into the tunnel. "So here's the plan. Praj, you and Trish go back the other way, see if we missed another tunnel." Trish glanced at Praj with frank disappointment and then tried to catch Rafael's eye. I ignored her romantic needs and went on. "Rafael, you stay with me and Gammy, we're going to figure out how to get into the kitchen."

Praj and Trish took off down the tunnel. Rafael put a hand to his chin, leaned back and inspected the refrigerator like an interior decorator not sure where to place a throw cushion.

"How do we move it? It can't go any further forward."

I suggested we pull it back. "The tunnel is wider than the passage between the fridge and the table. Once the fridge is in the tunnel, we can either slip through the front or push it to one side. Simple."

"We can't," said Gammy.

"Why not?"

"The fit is too snug between the wall and the fridge. Our fingers would be crushed as we tried to pull it through."

"Hmm," mused Rafael. "If we had suction cups . . ."

I scowled at him. "Have you ever 'had' a suction cup in your life?"

"No actually, I don't think I have."

"It's not something we should have put on our survival list, is it? Guns, can-openers, matches, suction cups? Yes, if we had suction cups we could suck the fridge out, but you might as well say we could easily move it if we had a bulldozer. Or a fridge evaporator system."

"What's a fridge evaporator system?" he asked with bright curiosity.

"Something that makes fridges evaporate."

"Oh," he said, disappointed. "I thought it was real."

"How do you know it isn't?"

"Stop it, guys," said Gammy.

"Perhaps," I went on, "we should call Praj the Philosopher back. 'Praj, oh Praj, can you disprove the existence of something you've never seen?' He could explain that zombies, werewolves, batshit apes, and fridge evaporator systems cannot be excluded from the order of things simply because we'd never seen them before."

I was stalling. I was out of ideas. And when I was done, we stood in a grim silence, staring at the back of the fridge with our hands on our hips and deeply pensive expressions on our faces. All we needed was a few cans of beer and we would have been any three Americans standing around a piece of machinery that needed fixing.

Gammy made the clicking sound out of the side of her mouth; there was something kind of contemptuous about it, not towards us, but as if the idea, once she got it, was too easy, like she couldn't figure something out without being derisive about its feeble efforts to elude her. "We tip it," she said, "That'll make an angle to crawl through."

We heard a distant call: "Hey?"

"Hey," I shouted back.

"Just checking," came Trish's faint voice.

"Okay," I called back, and then to Rafael, "Gammy's got a plan."

We reached for the top of the fridge and pushed. Our feet slipped against the floor. The fridge didn't move. We collected ourselves, wiped our palms on our trousers, and tried again. *Nada.* Not an inch.

Gammy had another idea. "Instead of tipping it forward into the kitchen, we should tip it back. We'd have gravity on our side."

"Doesn't gravity work the same either way?" I asked up.

Gammy jumped plumply up, grabbed and hung. I realized why her idea made sense. I jumped beside her. The top of the fridge was sticky with the grittiness and oiliness that accrues in the unwashed surfaces of a kitchen, but there were ridges where our fingers could find purchase. We pulled back as hard as we could, with all our weight, kicking at the walls. Rafael kneeled and pushed along the bottom. We strained and tugged with no effect—until there was a sense that something was giving. The sense became a frank movement, a lethargically slow tilt that quickly sped up into a wild swing. We fell to the side, the fridge toppled, then stopped precariously at an angle, caught on the wall above it; the plaster and crusty concrete crumbled and the fridge fell through, crashing into the tunnel and jamming into the wall on the other side. With the hideous grating of a single metal fingernail scraping a cement blackboard, it slid to the floor and came to a heavy rest in a cloud of dust, squarely on the warden's arm.

The warden's eyes popped open and he screamed. His body curled along the side of the fridge like an enormous stuffed animal trying to get back into a toy box; he hung for a second then passed out, flat on his back, with his left arm underneath the fridge.

On the other side of the fridge, Gammy clambered to her feet.

"What was the scream?"

Rafael and I contemplated the warden at our feet. There was the clatter in the hallway. Praj and Trish reappeared at Gammy's side, catching their breath.

"What happened?"

"We heard a scream."

I scratched my head and took charge. "Don't come over here. You don't want to see this. Go into the kitchen and bring me a glass of water. And keep your eye out for zombies. Rafael and I are going to get the warden out."

"Is he trapped under the fridge?"

I nodded.

"What part of him?"

I tried to think of something funny to say—the long arm of the law becoming the flat arm of the law, doing a Dick Van Dyke cockney accent to say "he'd come in 'arms way"—but failed to see the humor in the situation, so I stroked my own arm up and down to give them an idea.

"Is he dead?" asked Trish.

I considered the tubby man at my feet, pinned, pale and barely breathing, stuck against the fridge like a ridiculous magnet. "Not exactly," I said. "But he doesn't look good." I thought for a moment. "You might say he's experiencing a cold snap."

"Tell me you didn't just make that joke."

"Out of the frying pan, under the fridge." I could barely get the words out, I was giggling so hard.

"Jack."

"Come on, Jack."

Rafael put a hand on my shoulder. I pulled myself together. "Okay, guys, let's get to work."

Praj reported back a few minutes later. He handed us bananas and a cup of water, the most delicious over-ripe blackening banana and tepid water I'd ever had. When we were done, he updated us on their progress.

"We've collected tomato sauce, tinned pineapple and pears, instant coffee, and a jar of meat gravy. The kitchen has a receiving dock that leads outside, going around the courtyard. We didn't see any zombies. How are you doing?"

We didn't say anything. We didn't have to. He could tell from our faces. There was no way to get the warden out. His arm, or what was left of it, was trapped under the fridge. We'd used spit to lubricate our fingers but once our fingers were an inch or two under the fridge, there was only mush. Rafael and I were both having the same thought: who pulls the trigger? I didn't want to seem too eager.

Praj knew what we were thinking.

"We also found these," he said, holding out a pair of carving knives.

"I've never even carved a roast," said Rafael.

Gammy and Trish came up beside Praj; together, the kids looked at me without the slightest indication they were going to volunteer to save the man who, only an hour before, had them eating of the palm of his now flattened hand.

Praj held the knives out like a scrub nurse, the blades flat on his palms, the handles within easy reach.

"Okay," I said. "We don't have time to pick straws. I'll do it."

I inspected the knives with professional detachment, like I was trying to decide which to use, but I was only steeling myself to the task. Two identical long, thin knives; what the hell were they doing in a prison kitchen? I supposed the jailbirds still needed to cut meat and chop vegetables, but it hardly seemed safe. Had these knives already been used to cut human flesh? I decided to ask the warden about jail policy on sharp kitchen instruments if he survived.

After picking the nearest knife, I cut the warden's suit jacket and exposed a thin ribbon of white flesh. A musty thatch of gray underarm hair poked out. I placed the knife on top of the fridge and took the other knife from Praj, putting it over what felt like his shoulder joint. I began to apply pressure.

"Shouldn't you look where you're cutting?" asked Trish.

"Do you want to do this?" I shouted, thrusting the knife in her direction. "If you want to do this, then fine, I'll stand in the kitchen and give *you* instructions on how to remove a man's arm from his body."

"I don't want to do it," she backed off, waving her hands. "I'm sorry, I'm sorry."

With my chin on my shoulder and my eyes shut tight, I placed the edge of the knife against his flesh. I could sense their unease and uncertainty.

"We don't have surgical lamps," I said, searching for an explanation. "I want to do this by the sense of touch."

Focusing on how it felt was not a lot better than watching. As soon as I made the first slice, I felt an ooze of warmth along my other hand, pinning the warden's chest down. The bodily heat and wetness of his blood seeped over my fingers. The slice itself was palpable through the hard metal of the knife: I could feel several centimeters of flesh open into a gash. I guessed I was supposed to saw at his body. I started dragging the knife deeper into the gash. The warden shuddered. Each thrust of the blade had the same awful smoothness, the same release of tension as skin and fat and muscle parted: I realized that our bodies are held in tension, that internal pressure is a fact of being-in-a-body, that our bodies' natural state if we are not held together by a tough surface is to spurt and spew and expel. Every slice was accompanied by a silent ping of release as the tissues slackened and opened.

And then I hit something hard. I could feel the blade make a shallow ridge in the bone; I shuddered and gagged. The warden quivered under my hand. And I immediately knew the blade would never be able to cut through the bone, that it would take hours of sawing, that the blade would become blunt, and we'd be left trying to snap however much bone was uncut.

"I'm at bone," I said faintly. I didn't care what I sounded like. It had been all I could do not to bring up the water and banana.

"Find the shoulder joint," said Praj, calmly. "Cut away from the bone, and try to make it through the joint."

I took a deep breath.

"You're doing a great job," said Rafael, over my shoulder. "Gammy's boiling water."

I steadied myself for the task.

"We'll need bandages," I said huskily, and took deep breaths trying not to be sick.

Praj held something out to me. "Trish found this cheesecloth—"

As soon as he said 'cheesecloth', it was over. The word was too evocative of something fetid and bodily and ripe, of coagulated pus, of zombie flesh, of the warden's cheesy skin. I barked and vomited a slick pool of fondue with banana chunks.

Rafael was behind me and didn't have the presence of

mind to turn away; as soon as I began vomiting, he burped loudly, and vomited into the tunnel with a wet splash. Praj, unable to tear his eyes from us, gulped twice and barfed everything he'd just eaten over the top of the fridge. I heard the girls groan; one of them coughed loudly; the cough was followed by the splatter of her vomit.

"Jesus Christ," I gagged. The smell was awful, worse than zombie corpses. My mouth was gummy and I started convulsing again. I tried to smear away the vomit, which fortunately did not hit the warden, or at least not on his half-amputated arm.

"What's going on?" Gammy appeared in the kitchen beside the refrigerator; Trish stood behind her, white as a sheet, wiping her mouth with her sleeve. "Come on y'all," said Gammy. "Pull yourselves together."

"It wasn't my fault," I mumbled. "It's just that when Praj said 'cheesecloth'—"

The word had the same effect the second time: I dry heaved, and then ralphed out whatever was left in my stomach. Rafael roared out another vomit, Praj made a face like he was about to cry and sprayed the last of his food over the fridge. Trish bent over and, expertly holding her blonde hair out of the way, heaved twice. Gammy stood firm with her chin jutting out in determination. Her eyes watered. She did everything she could not to be sick. Then her cheeks ballooned, she doubled-over and puked across Praj's legs.

And then we did it again.

Everything was slippery and foul as if a leathery bag filled with sick had been slit open and swung around. I lost control of my senses. Screaming hysterically, I madly hacked, jamming the blade through the warden's shoulder joint. The warden, freed from the fridge and his arm, rolled onto my leg. Trish pushed a bundle of cheesecloth over to me. I pressed it on the oozing stump, too triumphant and elated to feel more nausea.

We managed to drag the warden over the fridge and onto a table. We cleaned ourselves at the sinks, washing our hands, wiping our clothes, and rinsing our mouths with sweet water. Trish proved herself to be a surprisingly effective nurse, a real Florence Nightingale once her stomach was empty, and we used kitchen rags and cellophane to strap a fresh mound of cheesecloth to the wound.

With lightheaded efficiency, we packed up whatever we could and set out, Rafael holding the warden's feet and me at his head, clutching his collar and trying not to look down.

We scurried through the loading dock. There were no trucks, just a pair of industrial-sized garbage bins on a cement platform with oily streaks like a robot's skid marks. Leaning against the wall were two mirrors on top of poles, like a giant dentist's instruments.

"What are those?"

"They use them to inspect the undercarriages of trucks to make sure no prisoners escape."

"Oh," I said. Gammy seemed to know a lot.

There were no zombies in sight. We jogged into the remnants of dusk, a ragtag crew escaping with our shadows, cans of beans, a jar of meat gravy, boxes of ammunition, rifles slung around our necks, pistols tucked in our waistbands, the warden slung between us like a bloated memento mori stolen from a cathedral. The sun was a red orb on the edge of the horizon, the moon bright above us. We made our way over black scrubby grass, past the chain-link fences and yellow signs with the stormtooper flash of black lightening.

Near my car, we found a zombie squatting on the grass. It was lit by the last light of sunset and sat cross-legged like it was waiting to be picked for a zombie baseball team. It didn't seem to notice us but it was awake, occasionally blinking and yawning. We crammed the warden into the back seat. Praj, Trish, and Gammy squeezed in with him.

Rafael and I took a pair of rifles. The zombie paid us no heed. It seemed to be appreciating the way the sun glowed orange on the long prison walls. We stopped about ten feet away and inspected it.

"How do you even begin to describe something like that?" I asked.

Rafael thought for a moment and then said, "It's like a 19th century marionette that's been left in a waterlogged basement, isn't it? Sodden and decayed, but recognizable as a human form, its skin frayed like an old washcloth and filigreed with rotted blood vessels. I'd rather expected a zombie to be like something out of Francis Bacon, all bulging eyeballs, toothy yowl, and twisted jaw. But instead it's like something you might find in an antique trunk in a chateau in Burgundy, untouched since the Revolution—"

"Shut up, Rafael. The question was rhetorical. Let's kill it."

"Again."

"What?"

"Let's kill it again. It's already dead."

"Oh."

The thing was gawping and stupid. I couldn't tell if it was once a man or a woman, or how old it was, or what its race was. It twisted at the waist to look up at us, gumming like a cow chewing its cud, and then turned back to watch night fall across the prison.

"I feel sorry for it," I said. Sorrow has many faces; sympathy recognizes them all.

"Should we put it out of its misery?"

"I don't feel like killing anything right now."

"I know what you mean."

"Let's go."

We trotted back to the car. I was eager to sit in the familiar seat, feel the wheel in my hands, the pedals under my foot.

Gammy slid out from the car, shouting and pulling a rifle to her cheek. Rafael and I twisted around to see the zombie bearing down on us, its arms flailing. It scrabbled through the air faster than anything I'd seen before, a flurry of death, leopard-fast, its arms windmilling, its lips bared to the nose with equine yellow teeth embedded in yellow bone. There was a loud crack and a bumble bee whizzed between us. The zombie stopped in its tracks, only meters away, a spout of black fluid spurted from its chest like oil from a punctured can.

The ferocity drained from its face, the spout slowed and the liquor oozed over its belly. It started chewing its cud again and dropped heavily to its knees. There was another crack and bumble bee. Its head split like a rotted melon.

We made haste back to the car, thanked Gammy, and had a brief discussion about not letting our guard down.

"No mercy," said Gammy. "To anyone."

XII.

Seeing the sun disappear was like saying goodbye to an old friend; nobody wanted to be the one to say that we might not meet again.

In darkness, in silence, we searched the land's unfamiliar syntax and its flat grammars, confused by the relentless punctuation of explosions and flares; the road unraveled in the headlamps like a sentence whose ending we were unprepared for, scrawled across a page of smashed blue corn papyrus.

I heard snuffling and sobs. The kids were crying. Only the warden and I were dry-eyed, but then he might have been dead. What did I have to cry about? It's hard not to ask yourself that when you're left out of a sob-fest. But what could I cry about? The distant future I promised myself, when the long-dead me would be remembered as a master? The wife I was no longer married to? The kids I didn't want and, worse, didn't have?

We were running on fumes. Two cars passed going in the other direction. One was a sedan, the other a Humvee. For the first time, I was as jealous of the Humvee as Humvee owners assume people are. Its lamps lit us up like we were in a sports stadium and it threatened to obliterate us but swerved away at the last minute, racing into the night with brake lights sneering a glad *auf Wiedersehen*.

Otherwise, we were on our own, deposited on a dark continent abandoned by the civilized colonials, left to fend for ourselves in a land inhabited only by hostile natives and deadly beasts. If it had not been for the familiar etching of the moon hanging peacefully with its bright beauty spot, the North Star, you would have thought we'd been transported to another planet in another solar system.

The kids settled down—eventually everyone settles down in a car. We had only been together for a few hours but I felt like I had known them for years. Rafael stared at the road, Gammy fell asleep, Trish was squirming against the warden, Praj was invisible. That morning, I had no idea I would meet these kids, that the world would be turned upside down, that I wouldn't be in front of the television watching John Wayne kick a pretty boy's ass into shape while I wiped beef juice from my mouth and picked hot peppers from my lap.

"Do you notice anything about the sky?" murmured Rafael, speaking quietly so as not to disturb the others.

"It's dark," I said. "It's night."

"Yes, but look. Do you see how the night comes all the way to the earth? In the Renaissance, painters gave nighttime horizons a ribbon of glowing light to show that the earth was separate from the heavens. It wasn't until hundreds of years later that the convention became real. Even when you were far off in the countryside, you could see it: the lights of a distant city, village, motorway. But tonight, nothing. Now I know why the Renaissance painters did it. Without that ribbon of light, you realize that the earth is just another lump of stone tumbling alone through space."

"Electricity must be out."

"Can you imagine? No street lamps staving off the shadows, no homely rectangles of light in the houses, nobody sitting at their desk and working until late, no television screens turning rooms blue, no nightlights protecting little children; no news, no football—or 'soccer' as you would call it—no sit-coms."

"And no gasoline. We'll be coasting soon."

"Can we get petrol?"

"A few hours ago I was worried about getting eaten at a gas station. But if there's no electricity, I don't think the pumps will work anyway. That's a different kind of problem. We'll probably get eaten out here instead of at a gas station."

"Can we get it from somebody, maybe from one of the cars we pass?"

"Yeah, easily. We'll just hail them and ask them for their gas. I'm sure they'd be happy to share."

" . . . Are you being sarcastic?"

"Not at all.

"That was sarcastic too, wasn't it?"

"Not a bit."

"Do you want me to shut up?"

"Heavens, no."

" . . . Jack, I'm having trouble telling when you're being sarcastic or not."

He finally gave up and rested his head against the seatbelt. I kept driving, watching the gas gauge more than the road. The indicator settled at empty.

I was taking them to Chicago. The signs said there was a service station forty miles ahead. We didn't have forty miles of gas. I pulled off the highway at the next exit. The road cut a straight line through fields tinted silver by the moon. Rafael fell asleep. The car was getting skittish, sucking up the last vapors of gasoline like a coke fiend with an empty bag of blow trying to sniff the last motes while cops banged at the door.

A low black bulk appeared up ahead. I mistook it for a forest rising from the corn, but as we got closer, I could make out a town. I pounded the steering wheel and relaxed as if I had known all along we'd find somewhere safe. I switched off the headlamps, which were dimming. Rafael bobbed awake and I heard stirrings in the back. Gammy sat up and Praj leaned out of the shadows.

"I turned off the headlamps," I said. "I don't want to draw any attention to us."

Nobody said a thing. We surfed in. The town was deserted and pale in the moonlight. We rolled down what must have been the main street, past grocery stores, a diner, a wooden church. The town was like an abandoned film set; if a wind came up it would blow the buildings down to reveal façades held into place by planks of wood.

It took only a few minutes to reach the straggling houses at the far end of town. The last house was decrepit, leaning steeply like it was about to fall into a crooked line of trees.

A glow of light came from a window.

I pulled up in front of the house. The car was dead.

"Are we stopping?" asked Gammy.

"There's somebody in that house," I said.

"Do you think they'll have gas?"

"I don't mind if they do, so long as they have somewhere we can shack up for the night."

Nobody said anything.

"Get your guns," I said, "And let me do the talking."

We left the warden unconscious in the back seat; his skin was waxy and he was barely breathing. Moving him did not seem like a good idea. We crept up a path, tripping over clods of grass poking through cracks in the cement, and up onto the wooden porch as stealthily as we could. The planks were blistered by summer heats and winter snows and creaked with every step. Whoever was inside the house knew we were there.

We collected around the front door.

"Hello?" I called out. "We need help. Please let us in."

My words were met with silence. The neighbor's porch swing rocked in the windless night. The blackness was going to swallow us. We needed to get inside.

I knocked gently on the door. "Is anybody home? We're not monsters, we're humans like you. We don't mean no harm."

Nothing. Even with intentionally bad grammar, I wasn't speaking their language.

"Let me try," whispered Gammy. She took a deep breath, and then in a cheerful voice called out, "Hey in there." She sounded like a new neighbor stopping by for a friendly visit. After an unhurried and amiable pause, she said with more sincerity than urgency: "We've got a sick man in the car and we could use some help."

A bolt unslid in the door.

Gammy did a shoulder dance and whisperingly sang at me: "You have to know how to talk to people."

The door burst open and a metal object flew out. It caught me on the forehead, and my head exploded with pain.

"Ouch," I cried. "For God's sake!"

The object clanged to the porch. The door slammed shut and the bolt slid back.

"He threw a frying pan at us," said Praj, holding it up.

"That hurt, that really hurt," I touched a tender spot on

my forehead, "Goddammit, Gammy, you *reached* them."

"Are you bleeding?"

"No but I'm going to have a lump."

She guiltily put out a hand to touch my forehead.

"Don't. You'll just make it hurt more."

Rafael whispered something inaudible.

"I can't hear you," I said.

"Did it hit your ear?" asked Gammy anxiously.

"I was just saying," said Rafael, "if they're throwing frying pans at us, they probably don't have guns. We could shoot our way in."

A voice hollered out from behind the door: "Jus' you try that, you Godforsaken monsters, and we'll kill the bejesus outta you!"

"Oh, do you have more frying pans?" I shouted into the door. "Or kettles? Maybe an espresso machine? We have machine guns, you farmfucks." We didn't but I was furious. "We'll mow your tax-subsidized asses down."

"The frying pan was a warnin'!" shouted the voice from behind the door. "We got artillery back here and we ain't afraid to use it."

"We're going to torch this place," I shouted back. "Praj, get the flamethrowers. Let's have us a barbeque."

The door burst open and an old man stormed out with a shotgun, which he jammed up against my chest.

"I hope you ain't a zombie," he screamed, quivering with geriatric rage, "because I want to be the first man to kill you."

The old man's name was Zachary and he lived in the house alone. He had been a farmer, owned a fair bit of land in his youth, but in the mid-1970s an agricultural conglomerate came through with the blessing of the politicians and the farm lobbyists. He held out for as long as he could, and they lowered their bid day by day until he was forced to take a pittance of a buy-out, just pennies an acre. The fields for miles around were stripped of alfalfa, cabbage, kale, wheat, pumpkins and lettuces for genetically modified soy.

"Same thing year after year," said Zachary, rocking in his

chair. The candlelight swatted at his craggy sunken features; the wrinkles in his dungarees smoothed over his round belly. "Soy, soy, soy. The soil is white with phosphates. On a windy day, it's like you're in a snowstorm. Welcome to Stratford, Indiana. Population, declining."

He showed us photographs of his boys and grandchildren.

"Everybody cuts and runs. My boys left, moved to cities, married, had kids of their own. The ones who didn't leave before drove off yesterday. I'm the only person who stayed in Stratford County." You could detect a hint of pride in his voice, not just because he stayed loyal to his county; you could first hear it when he talked about his boys leaving.

"Have there been any monsters?" Praj asked.

"I didn't see any if that's what you mean," he said, and patted a horny hand on my knee. "Sorry about the frying pan, son. Is your head still achin'?"

I was holding a bag of frozen peas against my forehead. When I shook my head, it hurt.

"You're lucky Rafael knows a thing or two about sweet-talking an old man."

He reached over to give Rafael a pat on the shoulders.

"I got a temper, always had. Drove my wife crazy. 'Why you yellin' at the minister like that, you'll get us sent straight to hell.' The minister was a fool, I couldn't help myself. He came from Kentucky. He was always in the pulpit telling us about how much more there was to the world out there." He shook his head at the memory. "I'd have thought a minister would tell the kids about a much bigger world, the world of infinite heaven, but nope, he sold them on the bright lights and the jobs. I thought it defeated the purpose until I got it figured out: he was trying to get out of here too. There came a day when he could write his bosses and say the parish was gone. They whipped him off to a soft job where the weather is nice year round and he could tell the kids how lucky they were to live there. But listen to me yammerin' on. My Lord, I'm forgetting my manners. Do you ladies want any more ham?"

He showed us how to unlatch the screen door leading out back and apologized that the bathroom was out of order. Trish and Gammy went first and did their business while we listened to Zachary explain how he grew his own heritage tomatoes. When the girls returned, Praj, Rafael and I took our turn on the back porch and peed into the void.

Zachary led us up to the attic. He built it himself when his wife passed away and the kids had gone. The room was larger than it appeared from the outside. It had a window set crookedly in the eaves and a scissored patch of quilt for a curtain. Zachary was every bit the rural hermit, content to live in a bare room separated from the elements by the skilled workmanship of his own hands.

A circular throw rug lay on the floor next to a single bed and a bedside table with a candlestick and a fading photograph in a cheap plastic frame. The picture was of a plump woman in half-profile, a smile on her face as she looked off to the side.

"That's my wife." He sat on the bed and cradled the picture. "I still get to kiss her goodnight every night."

"Have you heard from your sons?"

"Phone's dead. But my boys can handle themselves, always could. One's in insurance, the other in real estate. Making a fine living."

"Do you want to try to reach them?"

"I'm not gonna be one of those old folks nagging his kids. When they left this town, I promised I would let them be."

"All promises are broken now," I said.

Zachary chuckled soundlessly. "I never believed in such a thing as a broken promise: only promises that could use a little fixin'. But that ain't it. If they need me, they'll come for me. If they don't, they're doin' fine without an old bugger gettin' in the way. I suggest we bunk down for the night, all of us up here. It'd be safer that way. I got the door bolted and there's extra blankets under the bed. I'd offer the bed to the ladies but my back—"

Gammy and Trish insisted it was okay and he ducked his head graciously. Under the bed were two quilts, the top one stiff with dust. We shook them out and settled on the floor, folding our arms for pillows. Gammy gave me an unhappy look as I lay down between her and Rafael. It was cramped but Praj was small enough to slide under the bed and that gave us extra room.

Zachary took off his boots and slid under a sheet. "Remember now, the plumbing's out, so if you've got to do your business, you know where to go. I'm sorry about that—"

"That's alright, Zachary. You've been so kind."

He snuffed the candle.

"Goodnight y'all."

"Goodnight," we chimed.

The air was chilly but under the covers, with Gammy on one side and Rafael on the other, I soon fell asleep.

XIII.

"The warden!" Gammy sat upright, throwing my arm from around her waist. "We forgot about the warden."

New morning light was coming in around the curtain. I had been awake for half an hour but was too comfortable to move. At some point in the night my arm had fallen over Gammy's waist. Her shirt had risen, exposing a silky tummy, and my fingertips brushed against it, tracing a small path over its soft contour as it rose and fell. My head throbbed where the frying pan hit it and my mouth was pasty but I hadn't slept so well in years. I felt alive.

Zachary was hooting, snorting, and muttering dreamily in his sleep. Trish moaned and pulled the blanket over her head. Rafael was blinking and rubbing his stubble. Praj was under the bed, his mouth open, a strand of drool dangling from his lip.

Gammy wriggled up and flew down the stairs.

"He's probably already dead," I called to her back and stretched luxuriously.

Rafael got up. "I should go with her."

I closed my eyes again. Sleep had always been a problem for me. As a child I was a sleepwalker. I fell down stairs, I fell into bathtubs, if the front door wasn't locked I walked around the block, I scared my parents by suddenly appearing next to them in the middle of the night. But most of the time I just bumbled into corners and peed; in the morning, I'd be found on a sofa or curled up in the dog's bed and we'd search for the dark patch in the carpeting, my mother with a box of salt and warm wet rags. And I suffered from night terrors. Or, to tell the truth, my parents suffered from my night terrors. I could never remember them, but apparently I would jolt upright and emit a bloodcurdling scream like I was being butchered. A wise great aunt told my mother that if I was woken in the middle of a night terror, I'd have a heart attack and die instantly, so my mom sat on the end of my bed while I screamed until I rolled under my *Star Wars* duvet as if nothing had happened and she could drag herself back to bed, haunted and terrorized. Raising me must not have been much fun for her. And then after that came the melancholic, shallow philosophizing of teenage insomnia, sleep-shattering drugs and alcohol, the grunts and sharp elbows of marriage, and finally loneliness, where you realize how much better it is to be woken up by someone else's snoring than your own. A good night's sleep was a precious thing.

Zachary rolled up onto the edge of the bed with an auroral trumpeting of flatulence.

"I better go use the back porch," he said. He slipped into his boots and slouched down the stairs. Praj emerged from under the mattress and sat with his back to the bed frame, shimmying his shoulders to get the blood flowing. I asked how he slept.

"Okay, I guess," he rubbed his brown eyes. "Sleeping under an old man has its drawbacks."

"Why? Did he wet the bed?"

"No, but he had to get up a bunch of times."

"That's just being an old man," I said, cultivating the benign sympathy of someone for whom that misfortune must be a long, long way away.

I was feeling good and I wanted to talk about it: I wanted to tell Praj about how well I'd slept and I wanted to say something about Gammy, although I wasn't sure what. But just then Trish sobbed. Her hair was splayed out like a doll's, her body curled up under the blanket.

It was the first morning after the first day and none of us knew how to react. Or what to say. Touching her shoulder might be comforting or it might cause a fright or, worse, induce a complete break-down. Her animal cries were stifled by the blanket.

There was a pounding on the stairs and Gammy burst into the room. Without an explanation, she snatched the blanket I was enjoying to myself and raced back down the stairs. We could hear the front screen door clack open and shut. Praj and I looked at each other.

"Women," I mouthed.

He didn't smile. We went down after her, leaving Trish

to herself.

The warden was not dead but he was not in good shape. His skin was cold, his lips were cracked, and one of his legs was gone. It was not the bloodbath I expected after another amputation; there were just a few red drops of blood on the road. Whatever had removed his leg had done so efficiently. Rafael was trying to get him to take sips of water but the man was not really conscious.

"Do we need to bandage it?"

"There's no bleeding."

"We should cover the stump."

The warden's coif had flopped into long strands across his forehead. It gave his pudgy face an oddly feminine appearance.

Zachary came out and joined us. He was not impressed. "Y'all left one of your own out here?"

There wasn't much we could say.

"I wonder where his leg is," I mused.

Zachary winced. "You mean this man had three limbs when you left him here and now he's only got two?"

I could tell he was beginning to regret his hospitality. Zachary gritted his teeth. Then with a calloused finger, he felt for a piece of ham between his teeth and spat. Rafael and Gammy were looking at me; they expected me to explain.

"He's not *with* us," I said. "And we were the ones who rescued him from the zombies. Not mutants, zombies."

"I'd say you only sorta rescued him." Zachary said. He searched for a thought. Then he spat again. "Hell, who am I to judge?"

The warden was cocooned in the blanket like a grandmother reclining on a chaise longue.

"The leg looks like it was bitten right off," said Rafael. "Maybe by something with very large jaws. One cut."

"That's not the work of a zombie."

"Or a werewolf."

"We knew there were more out there."

Zachary surveyed the land with a sad and angry

expression. The town was even more desolate in daylight, the buildings as hollow as skeletons, the tarmac street wrinkled and creased like shed snakeskin. Windows were boarded up, paint was peeling, gutters were sagging, the lawns had yellow patches where the grass had died. Zachary was right. It did look as though it had been abandoned without regret, the type of place where the only detectable trace of life would be the occasional hint of movement in a window as the forgotten Miss Havishams waited out their last days in parlors surrounded by the decaying remnants of their youth.

"Something took his leg last night," said Zachary. He shook the thought off. "Did y'all sleep okay?"

"Like a lamb," said Rafael, emerging from the car and brushing his hands.

"What about you, Jack?"

I nodded, a bit too eagerly. Gammy blushed.

I'll admit it: I had always wondered if I'd be able to tell if an African American woman blushed, but her cheeks flushed adorably. Then I began to wonder something else. Maybe she was blushing because she was embarrassed for me—or by me. Maybe she hadn't wanted my arm over her waist, my fingers touching her belly. I felt a bit creepy and ashamed.

"Glad to hear it. The weather's good so y'all'll be needin' to head off. Say, do you need any gasoline? I got some in a can. You can have it."

"Don't you need it?"

"I only use a little for my gardening tools and I don't have a car. Haven't had to drive in years. Let's have coffee first. Afterwards, I'll get the gas for you and you can be off."

He hitched his thumbs in his dungaree straps and started up the path.

"Zachary," I called. "Come with us."

"It's a small car," he replied. His cataract-pale eyes were lively in a seasoned farmer's deep squint.

"We can make room," said Rafael.

"For an old man and his memories? Nah."

"The city's not so bad," said Praj. "And this place—" He made an apologetic gesture towards the town. An unfolded cardboard box was gliding across the tarmac, past abandoned houses and empty porch swings and plastic slides sets under a feeble blue sky, an unloving and uncaring roof to this lonely rural purgatory.

"This is my home," he said. "And I got room enough for my memories here."

Zachary looked at the plastic swing, checking to make sure it was still there; he watched the cardboard box come to a stop against a cracked curb; and then acknowledged the sky with a flinch of recognition.

It was Gammy's turn: "We can help you get to your sons."

"My life is here," he said. "My home is here. I have what I need. At least for a little while longer, until more strangers come along. And besides," he tilted his chin in the direction of the warden, "I see how you treat old folks." He gave a coughing laugh, more friendly than damning, and, wiping his mouth against his shirtsleeve, returned to his homestead. I felt better about the world. We offered the old man a way out, we gave him the chance to come with us. Good deeds reward those who offer them unconditionally.

After a few moments, we followed Zachary inside, leaving the warden ensconced in his blanket. Just the mention of the word 'coffee' made my mouth water. Inside the kitchen, we hunkered around a butane stove where Zachary boiled water. He measured out a heap of mud-brown crystals of instant coffee into tin camping mugs. Squatting by the hot ring of blue flames, he was just another weather-beaten, salt-of-the-earth farmer preparing his farmhands for the day.

I went upstairs to rouse Trish. I found her standing in the corner, a blanket wrapped over her shoulders; she was twitching like a wounded bird up against a tree trunk. When I touched her she startled.

"Trish, Trish, Trish," I said. "You're having a hard morning. Come and get some coffee. It'll warm you up."

She didn't move. Her face was pressed into the corner, strands of blonde hair pasted to her cheeks. Her shoulder spasmed under my hand.

"It's alright, Trish. Everything's going to be alright."

She took a deep breath. "I didn't want to go pee on the porch."

"I know," I said, as soothingly as possible. "It's awkward. Nobody will watch, I promise."

"I said, I didn't want to go pee on the porch."

"I heard you."

"So I went to the bathroom."

"Trish! Zachary said the plumbing's out. You didn't use the toilet, did you? Geez, I know you're having a hard time but that's not fair on Zachary. It won't flush."

She turned to me, wild-eyed and fearful.

"What's wrong?" I asked. "Oh no, Trish, you're not telling me you took a—"

"There's a human leg in the bathroom."

XIV.

I sent Trish out to the car and snuck downstairs. I could hear Zachary and the others in the kitchen. Maybe Trish made a mistake. None of us could trust our senses anymore. We'd already seen enough carnage to skew our perceptions. Maybe she saw a pair of his wife's tights hanging to dry after suffering some innocent degradations at the hands of a lonely old man, or maybe she saw his long-johns after their annual wash and even after being rinsed, sudsed and left to dry, they retained the shape of his body.

As quietly as I could, I tiptoed past the kitchen and to the bathroom. With one hand on the knob and the other on the door to steady it, I opened it and stepped inside. The bathroom smelled like soap and it was clean enough. The linoleum blistered in places but was dry, the porcelain bowl was white. A piece of cardboard was placed between white lace curtains and the window. A shower curtain was half-pulled across the tub. I decided that Trish had hallucinated but as my eyes adjusted I could discern an odd shape hanging from the shower rod just behind the shower curtain. I refused to let myself be prejudiced by Trish's panic. I held the curtain back and inspected the shape with forensic intensity. Suspended between a jerry-rigged pair of coat hangers was a pudgy human leg with five pudgy human toes on the end of a dainty foot. I measured it up in my head. The leg would fit the warden. I slipped out and wondered what to do. And then I heard Zachary.

"Can I tempt you with some ham before you go?"

I charged into the kitchen. "Do you mean *human* ham?" I shouted.

Zachary didn't blink but the others looked at me like I was crazy.

"Get out of here," I said to the kids. Zachary was bent over the gas stove with a mug of coffee in each hand. With a sad smile, he held one up to me.

"You want a cup of coffee, Jack?"

"Get out now," I hissed. Rafael, Gammy and Praj put down their mugs and skittered around me and out the front door. Zachary stood up with a squint of pain as he straightened his back. He held the two cups in his hands. I really wanted one.

"Seems like you've been poking where you oughtn't have been. That ain't polite."

"How many people have you eaten, you disgusting old bastard?"

He bit his lip and studied the ceiling. It looked like he was making a calculation in his head.

"Good God, how long has this been going on?"

He stopped calculating and held out the cup of coffee with a kind expression on his wrinkled, unshaven face.

I understood. It didn't matter what sort of world we were in now, the rules of hospitality still mattered. And besides, he couldn't make coffee out of human flesh. He thrust his white-stubbled chin at the cup. It smelled good. Maybe I'd made a mistake, maybe I'd hallucinated too.

As I reached for the cup, he flung the coffee into my face then flung the coffee from the other cup into my face. I screamed and tried to claw the hot liquid from my eyes. He grabbed a frying pan from beside the sink and clobbered me on the head. I collapsed to my knees, my face burning, disorienting throbs of pain pounding my skull.

There was a room-shuddering blast.

Trish had come back into the kitchen and shot Zachary through the chest.

In retrospect, I was harsher on Trish than I should have been. She was traumatized by her discovery of the limb, re-traumatized when she went out to find the warden lacking a limb (I hadn't warned her of that when I sent her out to the car—she put two and two together), and she did save my life.

But as we stood over the heap of Zachary in his bloodied dungarees, she began screeching. "I've never killed anybody before! Is he dead? I've never killed anybody before!" She was wailing like a princess being informed that she was an adult now and had to wipe her own ass. My head hurt and I couldn't deal with it.

"You haven't killed anybody before? You were a murder-virgin until two minutes ago? Join the gang, Trish."

"Jack, come on, she's upset."

"No, listen Rafael, listen all of you. I'm not picking on Trish. We've got to hold it together."

"It doesn't help when you explode," Praj said.

I spun to face him. "You tart little philosofuck! If there's one person here who should be shying away from platitudes, it's you. Yes, it doesn't 'help' when I explode, but it doesn't 'help' when the only person in the world who has been kind to us over the past twenty four hours also planned to eat us limb by limb and it doesn't 'help' that we're all thinking the same thing: how delicious was that 'ham' we ate last night? Nothing helps. You're the philosopher, you of all people should know that. Trish hasn't done this before? None of us have done this before. But there isn't a 'before' anymore. It's just 'now'. Time and history don't mean the same thing they once did. We used to treat history as a secret we could forget. But the secrets made us who we were and now we don't have secrets to forget any more so there is no before. There's no more being and history, there's no more being and time. There's only being. And nothingness."

Praj looked at me, unsure. "Do you mean Sartre's work?"

"What?"

"*Being and Nothingness*?"

"Maybe?"

Trish stopped flipping out. "What we need," she said levelly, "is to get gas and to get the hell out of here. You can have your conversation about being and nothingness when we get to Chicago." She looked at me sternly. "Jack. It's your car. You picked us up. Thank you. We owe you. You guys find Zachary's gasoline. Gammy and I are going to torch this place. Let's go!"

As she spoke, my anger subsided. I felt a bit proud too. The little princess was all grown up.

We found gasoline stashed in a closet with Zachary's gardening tools, which included a disturbingly large pair of shears with crusty red streaks along its unclosed blades. We didn't go out of our way to search for body parts but I couldn't help sneaking a peek into the freezer. Stuck in snowy rivets and crystalline ice were four or five hunks of meat wrapped in frosted cellophane. Probably beef, I thought to myself. But it probably wasn't.

Rafael saw me at the freezer. He asked what I found. I told him.

"Should we bury it?"

"Nah, it'll burn up with the house," I said, "And it's probably just beef, anyway."

Praj came downstairs loaded with blankets.

"Do you think we should take these?"

Rafael and I both agreed that we should not. Praj dropped them beside Zachary's body on the kitchen floor. He also brought the photograph of Zachary's wife. He placed it on the old man's back and, chewing his pinkie nail, scrutinized the still life for a minute. He bent to put the photograph beside Zachary's face, arranging one of his gnarly, arthritic hands so that it clasped the frame. His wife looked away with that happy smile on her face as his dead lips reached for her cheek.

"Do you think he ate her?"

Praj thought about it. "Probably."

Zachary had stored enough gas to fill up the tank with two canisters left over, which the kids put in the trunk. Gammy and Trish splashed some on the porch to get the fire started but the whole house was kindling: a single match on the floor would have set the place ablaze.

The car was refreshed by its hit of petrol and started right up. We had enough gas to get to Chicago. As we drove away, the funeral pyre of Zachary's house threw off a thick plume of purple smoke into the morning sky. Even Rafael could think of nothing to say.

XV.

After an hour of driving long empty highways, I put music on. Dvorak. It rattled inside the car like an insincere lament for the living. I switched it off. There was no protest.

"Let's take an inventory," I suggested.

Nobody said a word.

"By my reckoning, we have six rifles, three pistols, a dozen grenades, and a thousand rounds. Does that sound about right?"

There was a murmur of agreement.

"Praj, can you give us a rundown on the food situation?"

"We have eighteen cans of beans, five cans of stewed tomatoes, seven cans of mixed fruit—peaches and pears and pineapples—a jar of meat gravy, a bunch of bananas and enough oranges to juggle with."

"And two cans of instant coffee," said Trish.

"I'm assuming we have a can-opener?"

"We'll have to get one."

"Nobody took one from Zachary?"

Silence.

"Okay, okay, can-openers aren't rare. They're not like suction cups." I pounded the steering wheel. "Who'd have thought this car could fit four and a half people, an arsenal, enough food to last us a week, two spare cans of gas, and my box of books. We have enough to eat *and* enough to read."

Nobody said anything. Rafael shifted to face out the passenger window. They were all thinking something but I didn't know what it was.

Finally, Praj leaned forward and spoke under his breath, swallowing his words.

"Uh, Jack, are you talking about the box of books in the trunk?"

"Yes."

"I'm sorry, Jack."

"Why are you sorry?"

There was an uncomfortable silence.

"Why is there a reason you're sorry? What could you

have done that would make you sorry?"

Praj spoke quickly, "We had to leave it behind at the prison."

"What!?"

"There wasn't room in the trunk for the food and the guns and the box of books."

"So you abandoned my books? In a prison parking lot? Oh my god, oh my god, oh my god."

Praj fell back, having done his duty.

I couldn't believe it. My books. My unsold box of books. It was like they had torn my child from the pregnant womb of my car and left it in a prison parking lot, my vulnerable little baby novel, my helpless literary puppy, my darling little word-kitten. I couldn't help it: for the first time in twenty years, I began to cry.

"Jack, maybe you should pull over."

"Jack?"

"*Jack?*"

"You've stopped blubbering?"
"I wasn't blubbering, Gammy."
"You were totally blubbering."
"I was upset. Who knows, maybe those were—" I could barely bring myself to say it, "—the last ones. That was my life, my work, my sweat, I poured my soul into those books. But why am I telling you? You wouldn't understand. What have you ever created other than a general air of hostility? You don't know what it's like to have created something and then lose it."

The car became electric with tension, Rafael and Trish stiffened at what was apparently some kind of *faux pas* on my part. Gammy waited long enough to savor the shocked camaraderie of those offended on her behalf, then lurched forward so that her lips were nearly touching my cheek.

"You don't know a thing about me," she snarled. I could smell her warm, sour breath. "*War 'Sister* is gone but you don't see me blubbering."

Praj whistled. "You created *War 'Sister*?"

In the rear view mirror, I could see Gammy glaring, her face frozen with a look of constipated hatred, one I recognized from when I caught my own reflection in a café mirror as I read the *New Yorker*'s 'Briefly Noted' review of *Gargantuan Voyages*.

Trish reached across the warden and touched Gammy's shoulder in solidarity. Praj looked at her admiringly.

"What's 'War Sister'?" I asked, feeling left out. "Why haven't I heard of 'War Sister'?"

"It's an online role-playing adventure," explained Rafael somberly. "Gammy wrote it as a freshman and piloted it at Notre Dame. Trish was the first person to play it."

"It was incredible," chirped Trish in her best supporting-the-sisters voice.

"Is that so?" I asked. "It sounds like a black feminist *Tomb Raider*."

"It wasn't like that at all." Rafael spoke quickly under his breath as though I had just made a joke about Gammy's mother and, before I cracked another, had to be informed that she had been recently and unpleasantly mutilated. "Everybody was playing it. They wrote it up in the *Observer* and the *Indianapolis Star*. Gammy was going to be a millionaire."

"So what do you have to do? Is it a shooting game?"

They squirmed with discomfort.

"What?" I let an edge of defensiveness creep into my voice. "It sounds like a shooting game. 'War Sister'? Doesn't that sound like a shooting game?"

"It's more complicated than that."

"Enlighten me."

In a voice sarcastic with self-righteousness, Gammy said, "You play a character, War 'Sister. She's a war resister, that's where she gets her name. Her family's been captured by militant terrorists."

"So you kill them."

"There's no killing," Rafael whispered desperately to me. "There's no killing. That's the point."

"What point?"

"It's about avoiding violence!"

"Why would that be any fun? It sounds puritanical to me."

"It's about alternatives!" cried Rafael, frantic for me to shut up.

"Bo-ring. Kids want to kill things. At least back in my day."

"How would you know it's boring, Jack?" said Trish. "You hadn't heard of it twenty seconds ago."

"It's about peace and reconciliation," explained Praj helplessly.

"Ha. Peace is a fiction. There's never been peace, just transitory states of ignorance about wars happening someplace else."

"I hope I don't get cynical when I get old," said Trish, like a little cunt.

"Cynical? You think I'm cynical? You throw *my* books out of *my* car, ranking your survival over the future of literature, you don't have the courage to tell me, and you're calling me cynical? The fact that I haven't thrown you out of this car one by one to be eaten by zombies and werewolves proves what a freaking romantic I am, while you cynical little shits mourn an illiterate, feminist, black video game, as if that isn't affirmative action in a nutshell." There was a stunned silence. I half-pulled myself together. "Okay, fine, whatever. You've lost things too, Gammy. But when this is over," I said, "there will be copies of my book, and I'm sure there are copies of *War 'Sister* on a hard drive somewhere so people can feel good about themselves getting all peaceful on the terrorists, and I'm sure we'll find a suitable bachelor to marry Trish, and a mirror big enough for Rafael to admire himself in, and for Praj—I don't know, whatever it is Praj wants."

"Go screw yourself," screeched Trish. "I'll bet I got higher SAT scores than you did. Creep."

Rafael squinted at me. "Was that the best you could do?"

There was a moment of silence. Uneasy silence. I think you could describe it as a *very* uneasy silence. And then I felt something quit inside of me. It wasn't a bad feeling. It was like my soul was punctured, and yes, all the air was leaking out, but the tension was gone. It didn't feel good but it definitely didn't feel bad. It's like when you realize that God isn't just dead, He was never alive in the first place, or when you tap into that part of you that truly believes it really won't matter when you die, and you experience the dull existential satisfaction of relief. It was time to give up. On myself. And everything I stood for. What hadn't I ever thought of that before? It sounded really good.

"We're going to have to start over," I said, gazing at the landscape. "A new beginning."

"Yeah whatever," said Trish. But Gammy scowled at her and she shut up.

XVI.

"Why?" I asked.

Gammy was heading to Irving Park; I was going to my apartment in Ukrainian Village; Trish wanted somewhere downtown, probably thinking Bloomingdale's would be open; Rafael didn't seem to care, as long as we found a phone so he could call his parents; but Praj was insistent: Arlington Heights first.

"That's where my parents are." He tapped the map. "If we get there, we'll be safe."

Praj saw the look we shared: isn't it sweet the little boy thinks everything will be alright when he finds mommy and daddy?

"My father's a mechanical engineer," he said sharply.

"So?" I said. "He'll draw a machine?"

"He worked for the military for over two decades."

"Doing what? Making escalators?"

"He ran a weapons development team."

"Sounds like he could be useful," I said.

"We go north here, and turn off here." His delicate brown finger lay across the loop, a dirty fingernail on Arlington Heights. I folded the map and put it in the slot beside my knee in the door.

We had come to a stop along a field with prickly yellow ridges of hay. Crows coursed over the field as it dipped into a valley; according to a blue thread on the map, the valley was cut by the Birch River, a tributary of the Mississippi, churning with pesticides down to the dead waters of the Gulf of Mexico.

A flock of birds passed overhead like a swarm of bees against the honey-colored sky. The sun mellowed and day spilled into night. I got out and leaned against the car.

"What say you we eat before we move on?"

Leaving the warden mummified in the back seat, we stood around the open trunk and ate bananas and canned pears, using the can-opener on penknife we'd procured from the body of a policeman a few miles before.

Truth was, they were right: there was no way we

could've fit all the food and guns and ammunition in the trunk along with my books.

The sun was a giant red ball balanced on the far end of the fields, ready for a constellation giant to run along the horizon and boot it into another universe. None of us was ready to get back into the car. There was too much beauty and playfulness in the air. More birds, flying south purposefully, flung from Canada, running away from winter. We strolled to a wooden fence and sat, human scarecrows watching the day come to an end.

"I swiped this from Zachary."

Rafael pulled a silver flask from his pocket. He unscrewed its miniscule spout.

"To England, sir!" He took a swig. "*Kaaaaa*. I can't say much for his taste in food but the old cannibal knew a thing or two about whisky."

Before I could stop myself, I was holding the flask. The liquid sloshed inside the metal. I put the spout to my nose and sniffed the sweet oaky fumes; the skin inside my face burned, my fingers felt light and airy.

"It's good," I said, without taking a drink, and I handed it to Trish.

She took it, sipped, made a rat-like face as the whisky went down, and then passed it on. While Gammy took a shot, Trish spun to face me and said, "Truth or dare?" I could smell the whisky on her breath. I wanted to eat the air coming out of her mouth.

"Are we playing games?"

Trish repeated, "Truth or dare?"

Living was a dare enough, so I said, "Truth."

She nibbled delicately at a fingernail. "Jack. Are you an alcoholic?"

"Fuck you."

The others stirred uncomfortably.

"Come on, Trish," said Rafael.

"I'm just playing a game," she said blithely. "Isn't that what you do when you drink with friends? We don't have dice or cards."

"No, she's right," I said stonily, addressing the others. "I'm sorry I swore. We *should* play games together. And I said 'truth', so she had every right to ask me." I put a hand on her shoulder, a reminder of how I had comforted her earlier that morning. "Yes, I'm an alcoholic. I haven't had a drink in nine months. But tonight would be a good night to start again, in good company, with new friends." I paused to let my words sink in; I could feel them get tense with the frisson of witnessing a relapse, the undying delight we can take in any fall from grace. "But it's also a good night to be sober. In good company. With new friends." I took my hand from her shoulder.

"I'm sorry," she mumbled. Half the sun was under the black earth. "You can ask whatever you want."

"So you want 'truth'?"

"I guess so."

"I've got one," snapped Gammy. "Do you prefer younger men or older men?"

I was surprised by the nastiness in her voice and unsettled by how eager I was to hear the answer.

Trish snorted. "I don't see why you ask a question you know the answer to. Yes, I date men who are more mature."

She and Gammy went silent but were obviously engaging in some sort of female intrapsychic battle fought in an intense extraperceptual dimension of intuition and social sophistication beyond the scope of male comprehension, manifested in polysemous expressions and shifts in posture that came and went too fast for me to describe, much less parse. But for the first time, being older didn't seem so bad. I wanted to hear more about Trish's romances. The little princess might be quite a vixen in bed; I very much doubted that her wedding night would be her first carnal experience. In the half-light, as the pink bubble of psychic ladywar dissipated into the dusk, I glanced at Trish and noticed that Gammy was giving me an angry fish-face. Well, I thought, this is interesting—

"My turn," said Rafael, annoyingly.

"Truth or dare?" asked Praj, equally annoyingly; between them they buried any opportunity to go back to Trish's answer or Gammy's response. The sun was a rim of red burning on the horizon, a distant city on fire.

"Truth."

We sat in silence and tried to think of questions for Rafael. I got there first.

"What do you most regret about your life before?"

"I thought there was no 'before'," said Praj.

"There is and there isn't," I said. "A philosopher should know that. Rafael, answer the question."

Rafael scowled into the young night. "I wish it were harder to answer. About a year ago, I filmed myself doing something private, something *very* private. And I posted it online."

"What were you doing?" asked Trish, blurring the Trish-shaped boundary between sweet innocence and indifferent ignorance.

"C'mon," I said, "even Praj knows what he was doing, right, Praj?" I nudged him.

"I think I know," conceded Praj with a detectable thrill in his voice.

"Well," sighed Rafael. "I wasn't knitting, I wasn't reading, it wasn't footage taken during one of my more spiritual moments."

Gammy shuddered with laughter. "Are you identifiable?"

"Thank heavens, no, unless you were intimately familiar with that region of my body, and even then I don't think you'd actually be able to pick me out of a line-up."

"It must have been very humiliating," I said, quite pleased with the way this Truth or Dare was turning out.

"Yes, it was. I was going to take the video down, but then, you know, for a while I became something of a gay icon."

"What do you mean?"

"The comments underneath the video. They were actually quite flattering in a crude, salacious way."

"Like what?" asked Trish.

I said we didn't need to know, but Rafael was all too willing to expose his shame.

"Oh, you know, there were a lot of 'Hey Big Boy'

comments and stuff like that, and some people were more inventive. I was nicknamed 'Big Ben'—"

"How did they know you were English?" asked Gammy.

"My tag was British Borgia. Some comments were initially perplexing. I thought someone was comparing me to a dog until I looked up Old Faithful."

"So in other words, " I said, "the thing you most regret in life is posting an anonymous video of yourself jacking off, for which you got a lot of positive feedback?"

"I suppose so, yes."

Trish shivered next to me, possibly with the cold. It was hard for me to disguise my resentment.

"What about Praj?" said Rafael, leaning over. "Truth or dare?"

Praj glanced down from the fence, kicking his heels. He was struggling with what to choose, although I couldn't imagine what a frail skinny nerd would have to worry about.

"It better be truth," he said. "I'm too frightened for a dare." He gave a self-deprecating laugh.

"Are you a virgin?" asked Trish sourly.

"Yes," he answered immediately, and with evident relief.

There was not much to say to that. Praj had a tendency to be a buzz-kill, but it seemed churlish to point out that maybe that was why he was still a virgin.

"It's your turn next, Gammy," I said.

She stiffened. "What's that?"

A rustling. Something was in the stubble in the field. A shadow of a shape, scuttling.

"There!"

In the moonlight, we caught glimpses of a long back breaching the rows of uncollected hay like a shark coming up to the surface—but instead of a fin, there were scaly protrusions.

"Oh Lord," said Gammy. "Let's go!"

We raced to the car with the beast hissing on our heels. I fumbled with the keys, the car started, and we roared off, sending a blast of gravel at whatever skidded onto the road behind us.

XVII.

By midnight, whatever had been in the field was long gone and we relaxed. Exhaustion hit. I grimaced to stay awake and even played the game of I'll-close-my-eyes-for-just-two-seconds, two seconds that uncoiled as flickers of dreams played across the conscious resolve to rouse myself and the duvet of sleep wrapped me in its soft embrace, which I had to heave off as the two seconds blurred into the chasm of dreamless sleep. Two times, three times, I nearly drove us off the road. I was too tired to go on. I pulled over onto the shoulder. Rafael asked if he should take the wheel, but the consensus was that we should rest; there was no point ending up in a ditch or wrapped around a tree.

Sleep came uncomfortably but immediately.

I woke with dawn, sticky-mouthed in the front seat, and wiped a patch in the fogged window—a wet blur of farmland. The kids and the warden were breathing heavily around me. I stepped out into the chilly daybreak, cramped and bored by a new world with nothing to say. And then it hit me. An unexpected realization: I didn't have to be a writer anymore. The farmland offered me nothing else, there was nothing to imagine or desire in the American landscape of flavorless corn, but—ay, here's the rub—I didn't care.

I felt free. It was like the dull, moral, healthy liberation of sobriety.

In the car, the kids stretched, rolling their shoulders, mumbling good mornings. I suddenly felt sorry for them. They were so young. They'd barely even started. They hadn't lived yet. Such a waste.

But then, I thought, maybe I was wrong. Maybe I shouldn't feel sorry for their immaturity, their unformed selves; maybe they were lucky never to get to middle age. They would never see their dreams crash and burn, they would never be blindsided by the dull humiliation of discovering their lack of competence and talent; they would never despair. They would never know that their inability to direct a ball across a diamond to a bemused father truly meant they would never become a major league pitcher. They were forever tripping over the infinite perfections of youth without seeing how those cheerful, celebrated perfections led directly and irrevocably to the stumbles and broken-hipped imperfections of age.

No, that wasn't it. They'd already faced disappointments, they'd already seen dreams die. They just hadn't reached the age where they would face the extinction of another dream and—the real loss—not care. That is the benign, mild, bland, humdrum tragedy of getting old: it's not the missed opportunities; it's not caring anymore about the missed opportunities.

And when you stop caring, you reach the point where you are your real self and you can take all the blame for what has happened to your life. In whatever time they had left, they could blame everything on the monster uprising, they were just exuberant with unjust tragedies. They would never get old the way the rest of us did: waking up in the morning, steadying ourselves on the sink in front of the mirror, and saying, "You're where you are because that's where you got yourself."

Nah, I thought to myself, they had it all. They were lucky, they were missing out on nothing.

One by one, they joined me, blinking away the puffiness, their young faces absorbing their sleepiness; it would take me an hour before it would look like I hadn't just woken up. Our breath condensed in the cool air. We sipped milk and had pineapple as a treat. We took turns making steaming dark patches on the gravel behind the car—Trish asked if I wanted to go first as if I was an old man with a bladder problem—while the others sat on the hood and pretended to examine the cornfields. We set off with the windows open to freshen the air in the car.

"Does the radio work?"
"We can give it a try."

After running through the static on the FM and AM dials, Rafael found a fuzzy transmission on an NPR station. We listened. A nervous, rushed-sounding woman was reporting on a religious summit; we perked up when she said something, I can't remember what, that suggested she was transmitting from Chicago. Her voice kept disappearing as if she was forgetting she was supposed to be speaking into a microphone.

"I love NPR," I said, somewhat sarcastically.

Gammy shushed me.

"Do you think they'll be doing a pledge drive?" I asked.

"Shhh."

"Maybe we can get a Garrison Keillor mug."

"Quiet, Jack."

"I wonder if the monsters in Minnesota are above average."

"What are you talking about?"

I shut up; I didn't want them thinking I spent Saturday evenings listening to *The Prairie Home Companion*. I was a bit disappointed in myself that I knew it was on Saturday evenings. But I did like it.

The woman's voice became quieter, she faded out and came back in, until she drowned in a lake of white noise.

A little after noon, plummeting north but somehow not getting any nearer to anything familiar, we discovered that we had taken a wrong turn. I pulled the map out; the sun was overhead and so singularly unhelpful. We argued about which way to go, gesturing across the flat fields and speculating about whether a flock of geese would be directing their v north or south.

I made a decision, Gammy backed me up, and, in the late afternoon, we rolled onto a highway and found signs that made sense. We had been going in the wrong direction—far, far in the wrong direction, cruising right up into Michigan. We settled down into a steady thrumming pace, with the sun sinking on the correct side of the car. In the distance was the chimney of a nuclear power station; from its mouth came a thin, not very reassuring filament of yellow gas.

We were low on gasoline again so I made an illegal U-turn across the matted grass on the center strip and pulled off the highway, following signs to a gas station with three unsheltered pumps and an office with a padlocked door, the windows starred from an act of violence. I pulled up to the pumps, driving past one, then the next, coming to a stop at the last.

"Would you look at that?" I hit the wheel excitedly. Black numbers blinked on the console.

I jumped out, found my wallet in my back pocket, and slid a credit card into the slot. The machine thought about it, came to a decision, and the numbers whirred to zeroes. Accepted! I gave the card a kiss before returning it to my wallet. With smiles all around, I filled up the tank, topping it up until a sweet-smelling squirt of gasoline shot out onto my fingers. We stretched, relieved ourselves behind the office, and snacked on the last of the pineapple carelessly and relieved and proud. With a full tank of gas, we were going to make it. Maybe not the warden, but the rest of us.

The sun went under as we pulled out of the gas station. Something scuttled from the road, just out the range of the headlight's sweep.

"What was that?"

It was too fast and low for a zombie, too coarse and long for a werewolf; it might have been a gigantic scorpion or frog or whatever had chased us in the field the night before: its movements were ancient and ungainly, the mechanical, soulless scurry of something primitive.

"Let's get outta here."

It was a great idea, except whatever was out there had another idea: something hard crashed against the side of the car, low enough that nobody could see it. Everybody screamed.

"Sayonara, monster," I said and hit the gas.

The car lurched forward, we sank back in our seats, and the motor roared, 20mph, 30 mph, 40 mph.

"This car has life in her yet!"

I spoke too soon. With a horrible screech like a key scraping across metal, the monster grabbed the side of the car; I put my foot to the floor, and again, we felt the satisfying lurch of a car powering up, the tumbling of scales and claws—but it hit us again and this time, the back wheels skidded, maybe on an oil patch, or maybe the car just freaked out, but we started fishtailing. I managed to straighten us out, but when I did we weren't facing down the road: we shot over the verge with a gut-heaving second of free-fall before bouncing onto dirt; I spun the wheel and we skidded and spun and rattled to a stop, the headlamps shining through clouds of yellow dust like flashlights held by spooked children in a forest.

"What *was* that?"

We crowded into the center of my vibrating, stunned car, which felt like it was made of plastic and cellophane.

"Do you think it's out there?" whimpered Trish.

"Over there," whispered Gammy. She pointed to a black cube at the far reach of the headlamps, maybe thirty or forty feet away—a cabin. "We can spend the night, leave in the morning."

"Okay, good idea," said Rafael cheerily. "We're not going to forget the warden this time, right?"

"Let's stay here," I said.

Gammy muttered, "This car is a deathtrap. Let's go."

We counted to three then scrambled out of the car, lightweight kernels popped out of a dinky old pot. Gammy, Trish and Praj sprinted to the cabin. Rafael and I saw to the warden: he took the shoulders, I took the leg, and we set off as quietly as we could.

There was a scuffle behind us, the dry scratch of hard claws on dusty ground. The others disappeared into the cabin. I gave up any pretense of being furtive: "Go! Go!"

We ran as fast as we could, not daring to look back; whatever was chasing us let out a wet hiss like a pipe snapped and shot out a jet of steam. My foot caught on a clod of earth and I fell onto my knees. Rafael and the warden came down on top of me.

"Come on," screamed Gammy from the cabin door. She raised her gun but dared not shoot in the dark.

A shape skittered behind us. I grabbed what I thought was the warden's shirt. It was Rafael's collar. There was a pulse of scaly skin, a blast of foul hot air as if a carcass belched on us, and the pitchy lump of scales falanged into something with teeth, a hideous *vagina dentata* at the end of a snake, it lunged: the warden woke and screamed.

Blinded by the sticky hot air, we grabbed the warden's clothing and pulled him to the cabin; even in a panicked state, as we levitated across the last twenty yards in a single terrified bound and threw ourselves into the shack, I could tell the warden was lighter—whatever it was had bitten off his other leg.

XVIII.

We could hear the slithering and snapping of whatever was outside, the sounds of a predator stalking a hiding space, inspecting brittle wood walls fossilized by the seasons and the chemicals in the air, and wondering how to get in; the thing slid against the cabin with the sandpapery sound of calloused hands rubbing together, and we tumbled across to the other side of the cabin, huddling on a metal cot with a thin mattress and a ratty blanket. After a minute, we knew it wasn't going to come in right away. We lay the warden on the bed, covered him with the blanket. The bleeding from the Warden's thigh stump was staunched. Though he was now effectively limbless, he seemed medically stable. A doctor might have disagreed with my diagnosis, but for all we knew, all the doctors were dead.

We waited, focusing on the sounds outside: the rustles, another long hiss, and, just one more time, the sound of a body scraping up against the wall, testing it, possessing it, enjoying it.

Time passed; there were longer and longer periods when we could hear nothing other than our own breathing. Then maybe an hour passed without hearing anything. And then another hour. It's gone, I thought. Gone for good.

I had been sitting tensely on my haunches; I eased onto my butt and wrapped my arms around my legs. I was hungry but we'd left everything in the car except for Gammy's rifle. There was nothing to do but think. Our third night together. Just our third night. My eyes adjusted to the murk and I looked at them. Gammy was beside me, her arm lifting and falling against mine with the steady movement of her breathing. She began to lean into me and I knew she was falling asleep. My own eyelids were heavy and I leaned into her. It felt good. It felt right. The room sank into darkness so deep it absorbed all sound.

There may have a noise, an unusual moan, a snore, but something made me snap awake. The others were awake too, slouched, cross-legged in a circle around a nonexistent campfire, mulling imaginary flames, pondering the heartbeat glow of absent embers—except for Gammy who rocked against me. Was Gammy the lucky one, sound asleep and dead to the world, or was she having a dream that would become a nightmare as soon as she woke and realized that the dream, maybe of family or a boyfriend, was only a dream? And the others? Were they thinking or were they dulled with terror into the absence of being?

And under the thatch of these thoughts, a feeling began to flicker, a match dropped on a barnyard floor; with a shudder, I stamped it out. Nothing, but silence and the gelatinous dark, my soul suspended in lidocaine jelly, my body chilled in a lost cabin. But it came again, differently, more subtly; through the anaesthetized coils of my mind came the prick of a needle, prodding the back of my brain, then probing deeper, stinging, a tang of pain inside me. I couldn't recognize what it was pushing through but I knew it was mine; I examined the prick like I was tonguing a dead-to-the-world gum after the dentist was done, touching something inside me that was familiar but insensate, sore but numbed, knowing that within the thick swathes of numbed flesh was real and fresh pain.

"Is it too soon?" whispered Trish, her voice cracking.

I knew what she was asking. We all did. Three nights, three days, and we had said so little—well, most of us had said so little. She was asking if it was too soon to start naming what we had lost.

"No," said Rafael. "It's not too soon."

We waited to see who would go first. It fell to Trish, who had been the one to speak of it.

"My family," she whispered. "My labradoodle, Samson. My cat, Lady Miao-Miao."

There was a solemn hush. Trish strained in the silence against tears, tensing herself to hold herself together. She was tough, I thought, tougher than I thought. She was showing us how it could be done. When she settled down, Rafael whispered: "My parents. My sisters. Mr. Fitzpatrick. Ms. Donahoe."

Again, a hush.

"My brother," whispered Praj, his voice high-pitched with the effort not to cry. "My parents. My uncle."

Gammy was awake. She righted herself, moving from my shoulder, but she said nothing. We gave her the chance to speak but she didn't. She was the most private of us. We accepted that.

It was my turn.

"Ricobene's."

"Who's that?" asked Trish so softly I could barely hear her.

"Hmm? Oh, Ricobene's," I said, as though she had roused me from a reverie, "they sell the best breaded-steak sandwiches in the world, with mozzarella and tomato sauce in a white bread roll, and you can get sweet *and* hot peppers."

There was an unsure silence. I felt Gammy's smirk. So did the others.

"Shut up, Gammy," hissed Rafael.

"We all have the right to mourn what we mourn," said Praj.

Jesus Christ, I was kidding around! I was just trying to introduce some levity. It was supposed to be funny. The kids lament their families and I go for a steak sandwich. But they believed, they *really* believed, that the one thing I had lost was a steak sandwich. It's true I am a great eater of beef but these little shits thought that I was so old and lonely that the only thing left in my life was a trip to a fast food joint under the El on the South Side. For fuck's sake. Yes, it was the first thing that came to mind but I had other things too. There was Al's Beef. The saganaki in Greektown. Hecky's, but only in Evanston. La Pasadita's burritos. And other things I'd lost. Lots of other things. And people. Lots of people too.

I wanted to say something but the timing was shot. If I said I was only kidding, they wouldn't see the humor, they'd think I was pretending it was a joke to hide that it wasn't. But then how could I say nothing and let them think that the one thing I had lost was a lousy breaded-steak sandwich?

The silence built up, and their sense of my tragic loneliness built up along with it. These kids were working themselves into sympathy for an old fart had lost so little—and yet so much.

The little assholes!

Trish spoke up. "Your parents have already passed?"

"How old do you think I am? No, they haven't 'passed'. They're retired, they moved to Gurnee. Yes, I miss them. I hope they're okay."

Trish was hurt by my outburst. She was trying to be nice. She was trying to get me to say that I had lost people too and that I could share their sorrow. And maybe she wanted to hear that you could survive such a thing, that life could go on.

I should have just said 'my parents' and not cracked a joke about Ricobene's. This was a disaster.

"You know," Praj said, "Jack is right."

"I am?" I said. I thought he would be a vegetarian.

"It *is* too soon. There's too much to mourn. Maybe later, we'll be able to see what was valuable. It's hard to say," he went on in his mature but sing-songy way, "but maybe the true loss won't be our lives or the lives of people we've loved, but the loss of the unique things we created as humans like Ricko's bunny sandwiches."

"Ricobene's," I said. "Ricobene's steak sandwiches."

I wasn't sure I intended what Praj suggested, but once he said it, I was pretty sure it was what I was trying to capture.

"You may be onto something," concurred Rafael. "But there's a twist. When you think about it, so much of our humanity will actually survive us. Architecture, Michelangelo, Da Vinci. Buildings will crack, museums will fall into disrepair, libraries will crumble, but there will be archeologists and art historians in the future to restore them and treasure them.

"But cuisine, that's another matter. It's not just that cookbooks are generally rubbish; they also don't actually capture what food *means*: not just what we ate, but how we ate as families and friends; not just what we did to bake bread, but how we broke bread together. I agree with Jack and Praj: it could be that the greatest tragedy is the loss of Ricky Benny's."

"Ricobene's," I said. "R-I-C-O-B-E-N-E-S."

"Ricobene's it is," said Rafael. He removed the flask and

held it out. "To Ricobene's." He drank and handed the flask to Trish.

"To Ricobene's," she said, taking a drink. She passed it to Praj.

He weighed it in his hand, sniffed the top, and with a forceful "To Ricobene's" took a healthy swig.

Gammy took the flask and said quietly, "To Ricobene's."

She handed the flask to me then put her hand to her mouth, aghast at her own mistake. I held it, too choked up to say anything. I tilted it towards them in a dry toast and put the stopper back on.

There was a long silence.

All of us, at the same time, realized that we had not heard anything outside the cabin for hours.

"Do you think . . .?"

We listened, trying to pick up the clack of teeth, hissing, the crunch of leaves or the snap of a twig. Minutes passed. More minutes passed. An owl hooted and then the silence filled with the cottony fuzz of deepest night. Nothing. A wave of relief swept over us. Rafael began chuckling. It was contagious and we all joined in. The chuckling became louder. Gammy shuddered happily next to me and when I leaned so that my arm was along hers, she did not move away.

"Bloody hell," said Rafael. "Now I'm hungry. Thanks, Jack."

The chuckles bloomed into laughter. I reached around Gammy's shoulders to hold her and she clapped my thigh. Rafael and Praj and Trish tried giving each other high fives and missed, and laughed louder and flailed. The laughter settled happy grunts, echoed laughs, then into smiles and we caught our breaths.

"I'm a vegetarian," confirmed Praj, ". . . but all I want to eat right now is a steak sandwich."

There was a beat and then we roared. It was the funniest thing I had ever heard. We were like drunks at a fraternity reunion howling over a private joke only we would ever get. The warden groaned and this made us laugh harder. Rafael rolled over, his legs kicking in the air like a dog wanting to get its belly rubbed. Gammy and I put our heads together and laughed.

The thing outside shrieked. Laughter was throttled in our throats. It shrieked again like it was trying to join in, a hideous sound like a loser who didn't get the joke and laughed too loudly and too late and made everybody uncomfortable—but on a horrific scale. The creature thumped against the cabin wall, a hollow sound like a car reversing into a garage door.

It wasn't over. Nothing was over. We held our breaths. I understood what happened: the thing was not trying to join our laughter; it was reminding us it was there.

I shook my head. "I guess the only thing on the menu tonight is us."

In retrospect, I think it was the best joke of the evening. But nobody so much as cracked a smile. We waited in withering silence. Nobody talked. The bond had been broken by the thing outside; its cruel interruption shattered the moment when friendship was about to blossom out of the random accident of a journey together. We shifted into our own spaces with nothing but the power of our minds to will the beast and our fears away. I forced myself to think of beef sandwiches, old Westerns, anything, but could only listen intently, with the awful suspicion that I was listening for the creature to attack so I would not die surprised.

The quiet and silence could no longer be trusted; the creature was waiting. And listening for us.

Yet after a few hours, with time measured in missed moments when we fell into short bouts of sleep, a sort of optimism crept up on us like a cat we'd thrown out the back door but who had found its way home and was sneaking up onto the bed, first just a recognizable weight by our feet, then settling on our legs, until coming up onto our chest, purring, kneading its claws into the duvet. Optimism in the face of imminent disembowelment is a thin and frayed lifeline to hope. It would be better to let go, to steady ourselves for what was in store. But the optimism came anyway. Perhaps it had been quiet for long enough this time. Perhaps the thing had become hungry and gone to find other prey. It occurred to me that the prey would be other humans—people with their own fears and optimism. But I hoped, with all the optimism I could muster, that my optimism was more justified than theirs.

The thoughts passed. Between quick dreams and long heavy minutes awake, we fell into solitudes that had no depth, no lifelines of hope, just blank exhaustion.

It was getting towards the morning when one of us dared speak. A trembling slug of light was inching under the door and for the first time we could see a skylight, a gray rectangle in the pitched roof. We were haggard, exhausted, with sour tastes in our mouths, cold, hungry and thirsty, but alive.

"Hey," whispered Rafael. "Hey."

"What?"

"I've got to go to the loo."

I was relieved to hear this. My bladder was beginning to throb and I didn't want them thinking I had prostate problems.

"I thought it was going to be one of the girls who had to go first."

My comment did not go down well. Trish scowled at me and Gammy stared straight ahead, refusing to dignify my remark with a rolling of her tired puffy eyes.

Rafael rasped, "Look, guys, come on, I've got to go."

Praj snapped his fingers, "Got it." He rolled over the floor to a wicker basket in the corner, reached in and pulled out an empty soda bottle; he rolled back and handed it to Rafael. "Use this."

Rafael looked at the bottle and then at Praj.

"I'm not going to poo in a bottle."

This did not go down well.

"What?" he said. "I've got to do a poo. It's not my fault."

"You didn't have to say that word," said Trish, shivering wretchedly. "You could have just said 'it's not number one' or something."

"Just hold it in," I said.

"I've been holding it in for two days. I can't hold it much

longer. It's going to come out."

"If you don't hold it in," I said, "the only way it's going to come out is when you leave this cabin and that monster rips you open and the shit comes pouring out the front of your stomach like you've given birth to a chocolate rabbit—"

Gammy wrenched away from me with disgust.

"You definitely didn't have to say that," moaned Trish. "That's even worse than what Rafael said."

"He can't do it here—" I began, and then stopped myself. "No, fine, you know what? I don't care. It's not a problem for me. I've seen worse things in my life. I'm sure I've smelled worse things. I was trying to protect you," I waved through the cave-like light to Gammy and Trish, "from having a man defecate in front of you."

"We can decide for ourselves, thank you very much," snapped Trish. "You don't need to speak on our behalf. We already have fathers."

Thank God I didn't say "not any more," which I was about to, but Trish went on: "Rafael, if you have to go, you can. Over there." She pointed to the far corner. "Right, Gammy?"

Gammy shrugged hopelessly.

"Whatever," I said. "I don't care. Rafael, go grow a tail into that diet soda bottle, I don't care."

Rafael inspected the bottle in his hands. "I don't think I have to go now," he said. "It went back up."

The warden let out a short rasping screech. His eyes blinked open. We rushed over to him. His mouth gaped like he was about to scream again. With his round head frizzed with gray hair, a big round torso and a single hand held up in a twisted limb, he looked like an old spider whose legs save one had been ripped out by kids. He let out another dry arachnid screech. I bundled up the blanket and put it over his head.

"You'll smother him," hissed Trish.

"It would be the kind thing," I said. "Do you have a better idea?"

She pulled the blanket from his face and knelt beside him.

"There, there," she said and reached around him,

avoiding what was damp and sticky, trying to find dry areas to place her hands. "Hush," she said. "It's alright."

The warden watched her with beatific wonder, his eyes wide, his mouth flapping. "It's . . . alright?"

There was a scurry outside, the creature was back, and a reverberating crash as it rammed itself into the cabin. The walls shuddered. Dust fell from the ceiling as if the cabin was giving up its powdery ghost. A butane cooker over by the wall tipped over and rolled in an arc. There was another crash, a desiccated plank cracked in the middle, and a sliver of light split the cabin in two. The creature emitted an ear-piercing scream. We screamed too.

"It's . . . alright?" said the Warden.

The thing let out another hiss and smashed into the wall again. Planks of wood splintered. A foamy, dusty pillar of light collapsed across the floor; the light evaporated as a serpentine snout as big as a pig rooted through the shards, a forked tongue shot like a snake from the lipless mouth. The snout was wrenched back, and the column of light collapsed across the floor again.

"That's it." I was gripped by a sudden, incontinent madness. "That's it!" I said, and grabbed Gammy's rifle and stood ramrod straight by the door.

"Don't open it," cried Praj.

"My name is Jack Forbes, you foul-breathed snake," I shouted. "Hear but my name, and tremble!"

As soon as it let out its hissing scream, I flung open the door and darted outside. For the first time, I could see what we were up against. A massive reptile with a body as big as a tank, phalanxed with scales, and a stout neck with a rippling neck frill; it rammed its dinosauric head against the side of the cabin, breaking through another plank. I watched through the open door as it extended its neck to within inches of Rafael, who somersaulted away. The gap was too small for its body, which is what I counted on. It backed out for a final blow before feasting on the wriggly fleshy things inside their hard wooden shell.

When its head came out. I lifted the rifle and aimed. I

expected it to be surprised; I thought I would have a moment to stare it down before pulling the trigger. But its reptilian brain did not register anything except attack and it scuttled towards me as soon as it pulled its head out, its frills flapping like a winged beast, its jaws open, the black forked tongue arched in its mouth. It came so fast I didn't have time to react. The gun went off in my hands—the bullet tore through its jaw. It stumbled back, shaking its head with confusion and primordial pain, its speckled sail collapsing against its neck; quick as a flash, it came again. I pumped on the trigger as fast as I could, falling backwards on my heels. I got off three shots before I hit the dirt and curled up instinctively, as if that would protect me, and waited for the fangs.

A second passed.

Long enough. I looked up. The lizard-monster was on the ground, its dick-long fangs mere inches from my ankles. Its tongue stroked the soil, picking up clods of dirt and leaves. Blood oozed from broken scales beside its eyes and its ribcage was stuttering under the dying shivers of the neck frill.

The slit of black in the yellow eye looked at me, dilated, and went dull.

I brushed myself off and went back inside.

Everybody—even the warden—was clustered on the bed, their eyes huge with fear and reverence, their faces pale.

"Rafael," I said, slinging the gun over my shoulder, soaking in their admiration. "You can safely poo outside now."

XIX.

I wish I hadn't said that to Rafael. It's not that it might have been a bit too humiliating for him, though it must not have been pleasant; it's that it was too humiliating for me. It involved uttering the word "poo." What a nasty rounded word, onomatopoeic in its popping and emptying, released from a puckered mouth with a tart, bodily scent.

My next thought, which came with typical *espirit de l'escalier*, was that if I was going to humiliate him, I might as well have gone the whole hog and said something like, "Rafael, it's safe to poo now . . . if you haven't already." That would have been worse for him, and almost as bad for me, but it would have been a better line.

A few minutes later, as we laid the corpse of the warden (dead now, heart attack) next to the corpse of the lizard monster, I said, "Anybody want a Godzilla steak?"

That's what I should have said when I came in the door.

Rafael, rest in peace, did not need a second-rate action hero epitaph for his eulogy; and I, at that moment, was not a second-rate action hero.

Part II: Regression to the Mean

I.

These are the facts I know.

As of about a year ago, the number of people alive equaled the total number of people who had ever lived. The explanation for the monster uprising that most people subscribed to was that it was cosmic retribution for overpopulation. There were just too damned many of us. A cull was in order.

The intellectuals and pundits who had promoted theories about overpopulation and subsequent catastrophic population collapse made one mistake: they thought the cull would happen to other people. Or at least they said they thought it would; really, they were *hoping* it would. I wondered if they had mixed feelings when the monsters smashed through their front windows; nobody wants their last words to be "At least I was half right!" but then there are worse last words when you are ripped open from mouth to asshole by the undead.

The environmentalists could also find some comfort in having been somewhat right while they were being savagely eviscerated by zombies or werewolves. The toxins we spewed into the air, the radioactive goop we injected under the earth's skin, the havoc we created in weather systems and ocean currents, and the weight of so much human flesh reached a tipping point and the world didn't implode or become a barren rock hurtling through the infinite void, it just unleashed itself on us with our own relegated, denied, and feared excess.

What looked like civilization was just humanity's crusty growth on the surface of the earth, the work of industrious termites using metal and cement in place of ant-spittle and dirt to coat the earth with a prickly carapace. A poet once called the earth the "excrement of the sky." The most pessimistic of us thought he was right and that we were all eyeless maggots living in the filth; turns out, we were the scutterbugs and microscopic crabs, food for the eyeless maggots to hoover up when they finally bust their eggs incubating in the filth.

There were other theories—political ones, economic ones, mansplaining ones, whitesplaining ones; everybody had a turn if they wanted, before they were killed.

Rafael had an art historical perspective. He said the monsters had been with us all along, mostly keeping to themselves until they got fed up with us. The cue, he said, was when art finally became too boring and textual: aesthetically, we'd crawled up our own posteriors and, there embedded, found ourselves defenseless or, as he memorably put it, ostriched up our own arse. In a way, I understood. But I thought the provenance was literary rather than what was happening in Chelsea and the Biennials. And if it was literary, you had to look to Shakespeare. Specifically, Jacques. All the world was a stage and we were the performers on't. But we weren't as impressive treading the boards as we thought. No, we were vain prima donnas, lousy line readers, vamping to our own amusement; the curtain fell and we took a bow, expecting applause from each other and a standing ovation from the pits. We didn't expect the critics to explode from behind the stage lights and tear us to pieces. First, we screamed like babies, crap-pantied and jaws a-quiver; then, with eyes as wide as the moon, we belligerently trudged off to hide in the zombie-blasted theatre, dragging our kits and old costumes in our wake; in the wings and in trap rooms, hot-breathed, we discovered new identities and began to fall in love with our new selves, with whispers that became louder until, brave, unshaven, we crawled out and beat our chests and fought back; those of us who made it, grizzled but overfed on leftover candy bars and the director's hidden stashes of liquor, rubbed our bellies, scrambled up into the rafters, and pontificated as if the theater still belonged to us, until, starving and scared, wizened and weak, we cooed and reminisced stupidly; at last, babbling, crap-pantied and jaws a-quiver, we dropped like stunned pigeons onto the stage where the sharp-jawed critics were patiently, loathsomely waiting.

Praj took a different view, disappointingly reliant upon science rather than philosophy or, as I had secretly hoped, mystical Eastern visions of a Hindu, Muslim, or Buddhist eschatology (although I would have been particularly surprised to learn that a Buddhist eschatology involved the mass murder of the human race at the hands of monsters, banshees, and demons). He postulated that the earth hit a black hole. Apparently, according to him, all matter gets sucked into a black hole and disappears forever, but the *information* in the matter survives on the event horizon. We had already been materially annihilated but had survived as thought on the event horizon. The monsters were a form of celestial holograph, or, as I translated for Trish, intergalactic cyber-ghosts.

Trish, *que sorpresa*, preferred tabloidy explanations ripped from the supermarket shelves and glommed onto the lowbrow staples of alien invasions, celebrity transfiguration, or mass psychosis, which was pretty funny when you think about it, or sad, depending on your views of madness. In her more serious moments, she offered that the U.S. government created the monsters in petri dishes and kept them in a bunker in a Wyoming mountain until an unlucky tech forgot to lock the door on his way out. Basically, hers was a reality-based perspective, proving once and for all that reality could include whatever you wanted it to.

Gammy listened and kept her mouth shut but we all knew what she was thinking: God.

She wasn't the only one. The bishops, rabbis, clerics, imams, and priests—the religologists—came together at a hastily arranged meeting in, where else, the Vatican and announced that the monster uprising was a divine act, a sign of End Times, and, if you looked closely at their collected texts, was obviously predicted in them, give or take a little poetic license. They only disagreed about the cause—the rise of unbelievers, gay marriage, gay divorce, sexual license, worshipping false idols (a bone of contention, no doubt, in their discussions). But one of the curious things was that all the religious leaders thought that it was their own God doing it. Nobody looked at the havoc and the mayhem and the murder and said, "That's somebody else's God going apeshit."

The group that was supposed to have something

meaningful to say was the science community. But no matter how hard they tried to sound calm and professional, the fact that they were not only stumped but entirely unequipped to explain *how* they were stumped and what they would do to unstump themselves made them sound like religious leaders put in the role of talking heads: out of place and making promises they had no intention of keeping. "We're going to study this phenomenon" had the same hollow ring as "we love the sinner but not the sin." Still, they had access to humanistic truisms that were as encouraging to me as religious platitudes must have been to the faithful. One scientist said, "We've always been living on the edge of the unknown. We were just surprised to find ourselves pushed so far over."

Where the monsters came from, how they were "activated," whether or not they were a "radicalized" form of life itself—these were just more questions to ask of the cosmos. The underlying scientific faith was that it was only a matter of time before we would come up with the tools to answer those questions. If that conjured up images of werewolves with tracking collars, lizard monsters on a dissecting slab, zombies answering psychological questionnaires, and water creatures running on treadmills with wires monitoring their heart rates, then those images were more reassuring than other images that sprang to mind every time a frizzy-haired scientist in a bow-tie tried to explain what was happening: the image of that scientist being devoured alive, screaming, his clipboard splattered with blood.

But I wasn't convinced. I had my own theory, and why shouldn't I? The terror had become personal. I shared my theory with Gammy, maybe with Praj. I was interested in what they would say but I don't remember if they agreed or not.

It went like this. Maybe it wasn't our fungal spread over the earth's surface or our mutant swingers; maybe it wasn't radioactive waste and the carbon dioxide; maybe it wasn't blasphemy against God or art or nature; it was just the cumulated blasphemies against the moral universe that finally amounted to something that could not be washed away with another heartfelt whining apology. We had always been the unclean spirits. In one screeching convulsion, we were separated from our demons, our twins, and they turned on us.

To be more precise, my own theory was a synthesis of two ideas. One came from a great film from my childhood and the other came from my intellectual hero as I turned the corner on adolescence: *Ghostbusters* and Jung, respectively. My theory was that we conjured these creatures out of our collective unconscious; when there were enough of us, when we reached a critical mass, we were able to turn humanity's common dream into reality.

The thing is, our common dream was a nightmare. We were all to blame. Not the gays or the bigots or the polluters or the procreators or the heretics. All of us.

Worst of all, we weren't getting what we deserved; we were getting what we wanted.

II.

Regarding matters of hygiene, things were getting itchy and aromatic. Even with the windows down, the car reeked. Trish pulled at her shirt, complaining that she smelled like her brother when he came home from football camp. Touching her stringy hair and feeling the bumps on her cheeks, she said she looked like a meth addict and began to cry. I found it hard to be sympathetic watching her enthusiasm for life dampened in this way; I would have preferred to see her enthusiasm for life dampened by the realization that there were no more children on earth.

But she was right, we were the worse for the wear and we did look like meth addicts. Hollowed eyes, runny noses, scratching at mites and itches and scabs on our skin. Rafael was carrying about him a gym-like odor and I suspected I did too, though I was aware that a gym-like odor in a college-aged male contains a lot of musky pheromones, whereas a gym-like odor in an older male is not quite as repulsive as a skunk's but is a lot more frightening, because it's what young people think death must smell like. Gammy had a spicy tang whenever I got close enough to smell her but she was looking good; her braids had come out into a thick round afro like she was auditioning for a role in a 1970s blaxploitation picture. Praj had a permanent bed-head, although I was surprised to notice that he did not smell at all.

We were driving along at a steady 55 mph when Trish broke down.

"We either need new clothes or we need to wash the ones we've got."

"What we need," I said, "are blue jeans."

"Why?"

"Blue jeans are like human hair," I explained. "After a while, they start cleaning themselves."

"Is that true?" Praj asked.

Trish said it wasn't.

"It is," I said. "After a week or two of not being washed, jeans get gummy and smell cheesy, but just when you think they can walk off by themselves, they become a shade lighter, the smell goes away, and they're clean again. They stay that way for months. Just soft and clean."

Trish tore at her hair with her fingers, unconvinced. "How do you know somebody doesn't just take your stinky jeans and wash them?"

"Because they don't smell like laundry detergent. They don't even have a smell, except if you sniff hard, if you stick your nose deep into the crotch, you get a faint smell of something familiar."

"I don't want to know how you know that."

"It's the same with human hair. Sure, for a few days it gets oily, but then presto, it starts to clean itself."

Trish wrinkled her nose like she smelled someone else's fart. "That's disgusting."

"Actually, it's very credible," said Rafael. "Do you think that we should get a whole blue jean wardrobe?"

"That's right," I said.

"We're too far north to find shirts made out of jeans," said Gammy, sensibly. "And we definitely won't find underwear made of jeans."

"Great thought, Gammy. We can *make* shirts and underwear out of jeans. That would solve a lot of our problems."

"We'll look like a 1980s rock band," Rafael said with a smirk.

I almost pulled over. "Would that be such a bad thing?"

"Sorry, but it's not a good thing."

"You'd rather we found eyeliner and went emo?"

His brow knitted with amusement at what was probably an outdated reference. "If we have to model ourselves after one era's fashion," he said, "I can think of many I'd prefer than 1980s pop bands."

We argued for a while about the 1980s but I did not give in. The 1980s were not, I insisted, a cultural anomaly, they were not a deviation from artistic autonomy into superficiality, they were not an unfortunate and awkward epochal blip between the earlier commitment of punk, the freedom of funk, the jouissance of disco, and the later intellectual rigor, political activism, and existential alienation of grunge, hip hop, and "alternative" music.

The kids were astonished. None of them had been alive in the 1980s. They thought they were blessed to have avoided the 1980s. They had never heard someone speak of the decade without the smirking contempt those of us growing up in the 1980s once had for the 1970s. It was like I was telling them that Idi Amin and Robert Mugabe had their finer points, and perhaps they hadn't given Saddam Hussein or Muammar Qaddafi a fair shake. Although they probably wouldn't have known who they were.

"If the eighties were so great, then why was there never an eighties revival?" asked Rafael.

"Yeah," said Trish. "How come?"

"Ha! Every day of the past decade has been an eighties revival. You're just too young to know it."

I eventually satisfied them with my reasoning and a few well-sung snippets of Wham! and Bon Jovi. Or they decided to humor me. Either way, the solution to our problem appeared on the horizon.

We had been driving through a suburb in the southwest of Chicago. Houses were set back from streets with colonnades of trees; green lawns which had once been well-tended had already become shaggy with crabgrass and fallen leaves; on the driveways, cars jealously pointed at freestanding garages. But it was peaceful. If it had not been for the occasional flambéed house with sides like burnt toast, black triangular smears under the eaves, and crumbled sooty roofs, it might have been a hushed Sunday morning before everybody woke up, made pancakes, and got into their neckties and pearls for church. We took a feeder road out onto a highway and were veering between abandoned cars, vans, and long-haul trucks when we saw the cement flatland of a parking lot around a mall.

I could hear Trish panting.

"Settle down," I said, pulling off the highway.

We drove into the parking lot, up to the commercial village of white stucco boxes, and eased into a handicapped parking spot near one of the entrances.

"Hooray," said Trish, home at last.

"Keep your weapons handy," I said. "Shoot anything that moves."

"What about other people?"

"They're just as bad as the monsters," I said. "You know places like this killed America? This is the death of Main Street right here. The people who shopped here murdered this country."

"I'm afraid those worries are over," said Rafael, getting out and stretching.

The mall was as wind-swept and bare as Moloch's own sepulcher, a depressing synthesis of functionality and fun that was supposed to lull you into a mood of consumerist oblivion and to think—to the extent that you could still think—that spending money was a rewarding and communal experience in and of itself

We walked around dry fountains and phony-cute statues of frogs and princesses; past quasi-fancy high-end versions of fast food restaurants offering faux-cuisine steaks and pseudo-Mexican food and sticky Caesar salads; past chain retailers whose names were associated with high prices and middle-brow fashion; past shoe stores, banks, ATMs and a multi-screen cinema. Gammy stopped at a computer game store and looked through the shattered windows at the shelves of games like a penniless bohemian outside a restaurant, ogling diners inside feast on roast beef.

I tapped her shoulder to keep her going, and we took point, leading our disheveled platoon deeper into the heartland's last jungle. The mall was fast falling into disrepair. Trash and leaves collected alongside the fountains. The speakers in the corners of the walkway were dead. No Beatles, no Tom Petty, no Bruce Hornsby. Windows were cracked and broken, mannequins were knocked over, window dressings were strewn with pebbled glass. The sole bookstore was the only shop that hadn't been smashed open, which struck me as sad, though nobody else, not even Praj, noticed.

"It's spooky," shivered Trish, who was, in fairness,

awake in her own nightmare.

Rafael shrugged. "It looks like people have already come for essentials."

Gammy stopped and spun to face him.

"What did you say?"

"I said it looks like people have already been through here."

She scowled. "If this was in a black neighborhood, you'd have said this place was already looted."

Rafael was taken aback. "I would not have."

"Gammy, come on," I said, putting an arm around her shoulder and enjoying a whiff of her spicy tang. "We're in a post-racial world now."

Trish and Rafael nodded but Gammy threw my arm off. "I don't need another old white man telling me we're in a post-racial world. Why do white people always think they can get away with telling people of color it's time to be 'post-racial'?"

I gasped angrily. "What do you mean 'old'?"

"I mean just what I said."

I looked at them. "How 'old' do you think I am?" None of them said a word. "No, I want to get this out in the open. How 'old' do you think I am?"

"Gammy didn't mean anything."

"Come on, Jack."

"No, apparently all of you think I'm some sort of geriatric ready to join AARP and settle down in Florida to live out my last days on a patio where I can play backgammon and blame my farts on the geezer in the chair next to me. How 'old' do you think I am?"

"I think you're 42," said Trish.

She was right. "Yes. I'm 42."

Trish looked at the others with triumph in her eyes.

"What?" I said. And then I realized. "Did you make bets about how old I am?"

"It wasn't a bet," said Praj. "We don't have any money."

"It was just a friendly wager with no stakes," added Rafael, swiping invisible hair from his brow.

"So what did the rest of you say?"

"Jack—"

"I want to know. What did you say?"

"I would have said 42," said Gammy, "if Trish didn't say it."

"So you said?"

"44."

"You didn't go younger? Jesus. I don't look 44. What did you say Rafael?"

He paused. "45."

"Oh come on!" I spun around. "Praj, you're the genius—why are you walking away? Where are you going!? Praj, what did you say?"

Praj had sauntered over to a garbage can and was examining the contents as though he couldn't hear me.

"He said 50," said Trish.

"50? *50*? That's basically a decade older than I am."

"I knew he was wrong," said Trish, generously.

"People usually think I'm in my late thirties."

"To people our age—"

"I wasn't your age that long ago, Rafael. When I was your age, I didn't confuse a man who looked like he was in his late thirties for a man nearing retirement age."

"It was just a game, Jack."

"We didn't mean to insult you."

"And besides, you're not in your late thirties."

"Alright, fine. You go your way and I'll go mine." I slung my rifle over my shoulder. "I don't want to be a burden. I'm sure you'd be having a grand time if old man Jack Forbes weren't here, slowing you down with his old man shuffle, boring you with rheumy-eyed reminiscences of the old days way back in the late twentieth century. You'd be having orgies and getting drunk and enjoying yourself if 'Pops' here wasn't in the picture."

"Jack, you're not *old* old," Trish said.

"You're just mature," said Rafael.

"Like a cheese?"

Praj slipped back, his eyes cast down, with such sincere authority that we quieted. When he had our attention, he took a deep breath.

"Jack," he said, barely above a whisper. We leaned in to hear him. "When I was nine, I heard Dvorak's Violin Concerto in A Minor. I hadn't thought of it in a long time, not until I was reminded of it when you put the Dvorak on—

"My father was driving me home from a French tutorial. We were listening to a performance from Ravinia. The first movement grabbed my attention. The violin was everywhere. One moment, it sounded like the score to a cartoon, the next it was the soundtrack to every immigrant's arrival in a foreign country, then it was playful, then it was romantic, it was dizzying, a roller coaster, I almost fell off. I felt like my soul was racing after it. But then the second movement, *Adagio ma non troppo*, began. Suddenly, I couldn't breathe, it was the most beautiful thing I had ever heard. The first movement felt like the prologue to a whole life. I came alive in the front seat of my father's Lexus—

"I'd always wanted to be a doctor like my mother. A heart surgeon or brain surgeon. But hearing the concerto made wanting to be a doctor seem as silly as when I put on a cape and pretended I was a superhero or dancer. I knew what I wanted to do: I would play first violin in the Chicago Symphony. Everything in my nine-year-old life fell into place. At night as I lay in bed, I would appear in a tuxedo to the side of Pierre Boulez; he taps his baton on the stand and looks at me to begin, I take a breath, and—

"My father is the most perceptive man I've ever known. He saw what happened. The next week, on the way home, he told me we were going on a detour. To a music store. It was closing time, the door was locked, but the owner was a kind man and he let us in. My father told him why we were there. The owner took us to the violins. They had their own room—

"Ruby red, amber, brown, black. Straight strings, wooden curves. He sized me up and picked one. It was lighter than I expected but sturdier. I tucked it under my chin and let my fingers tap the strings, taut and sharp—

"It made no sense and it made complete sense: the bodies of the instruments took their shape from the curls of sea shells, the whorls of wood; the strings were straight, wiry and technical. The art of the violin was in taking another device, a bow, linear and curved, to make the straight strings sing against the curved body—

"The owner handed me the bow. I made terrible sounds, like they say: torturing a cat. But by adjusting the pressure of my fingers on the bridge and smoothing the arc of my arm, I made a note. And I said, 'I'm going to be first violin for the Chicago Symphony.' My father and the owner laughed—

"My father laughed with pride, but the owner's laugh was different. 'It's too late,' he said, 'you're too old, the bones in your hand are too stiff. You have to start when you're three, like the Chinese do.'"

Praj stopped.

"I'm sorry," I said. "That wasn't right. You're not too old at nine."

"Or at 42," he said, pointedly.

I didn't know what to say. There was a difficult silence.

"Did you get the violin?" asked Trish, obliviously or perceptively.

"Yes." He paused; we waited for him to go on. "I can't remember what the storeowner looked like when he told me it was too late. What I remember is the look on my father's face. When he saw my reaction—I'd never seen so much sadness in someone's face."

"So why did he buy the violin from this dick?"

"When I thought about it later, I decided it was because he had too much dignity to react to another slight. Other people thought he was arrogant, just because he wouldn't react to their insults. But I think it wasn't about him. It was because he wouldn't let a man ruin his son's dream. He never asked me about the violin again—

"I have one regret. If there was one thing I could do, it would be to thank my father for caring that much. I always thought he wouldn't understand my dreams, my reality, who I am. But now I know. I'm sorry I couldn't thank him for that. And all the other things he would have accepted with his love."

From off in the distance came a roll of faint booms.

140

Maybe explosions, maybe thunder.

"Alright, guys," I said. "Let's go find jeans. And Praj?"

"Yes, Jack?"

"You never had to thank him. He knew."

The next hour was as much fun as I'd had in years.

We picked a department store, charged in, and ran riot. Not everything had been looted. Far from it. We raced through row upon row of shadowy racks, we rummaged through shirts and trousers on hangers, jackets, sweaters, jeans, scarves, knitwear, vacuum-wrapped packs of socks and underwear in pyramids on tables. Clothes flew in the air and landed in puddles of wool, nylon and cotton. We filled our arms and, in discreet spots behind cash registers, we dumped our booty, pulled off thin sticky clothing that stank of sweat, blood, vomit, pineapple and the warden, and put on new clothes, stretching to feel the slip of clean fabric against our skin, throwing things that didn't fit into piles at our feet.

And once we had satisfied the hunger for something soft and clean and suppressed the craving to take more just because we could, we met up by the front window to admire each other in our new weeds, asking with coy solemnity for second opinions.

"What about this shirt? Is it too pre-apocalyptic?"

"I've never had the courage to wear orange but I love the cut."

"Does this make me look fat?"

"Does this make me look old?"

We made decisions and changed into the clothes we would wear, taking turns modeling our outfits on a platform where mannequins had once displayed Ralph Lauren's and Calvin Klein's finest.

Praj went first. He had chosen a black turtleneck, straight-legged black trousers, a charcoal gray pea coat and black Converse sneakers, looking every bit the denizen of the Left Bank. He cracked us up by modeling with a trilby he found beside a decapitated mannequin. He struck fierce poses with the trilby pulled low over his eyes, removed the hat, rolled it over his shoulder, along his arm and into an outstretched palm, then lifted the torso of the mannequin and did a graceful dance along the platform, leading the mannequin in a foxtrot, a cha-

cha-cha, and ending with a waltz and a dip.

He hopped down to our applause and shyly explained, "A few years ago, I went through a Fred Astaire and Ginger Rogers phase."

Gammy took the platform in a white shirt and a red neckerchief, a gray hoodie, blue jeans and leather boots. It was unsettling at first: she looked like she'd raided a middle-aged white woman's wardrobe. But I was alone in hesitating in applause as she bounced along our impromptu catwalk, flashing sassy looks; she ended with a callipygian freeze, a pout and a single raised eyebrow. It wasn't middle-aged or white at all. It was flattering. Even dangerous.

I complimented her as I held out a hand to help her step down. "Very ghetto."

"I'll let that pass," she said, and then stopped herself, looking at her hand in mine. "No, this time I won't. It was very Texan. They're not the same thing."

I leaned forward, still holding her hand and said quietly in her ear, "I'm sorry about what I said earlier about a post-racial world. I didn't want to hurt your feelings."

Something disturbed her and she looked away abruptly, snatching her hand from mine. "Good intentions aren't enough," she said in a hushed voice.

"Nah, you're wrong this time," I said. "They were all we ever had."

She looked me up and down and marched to join the others. The creases of her underwear ran diagonally from her upper thighs to the inner crotch of her jeans, insurgent trails across two round hills into the valley below.

Nobody was paying attention to us because it was Trish's turn. It was the moment she had been waiting for since the monster uprising. She rose to the platform like a forgotten stepdaughter in a new ball gown ascending to the prince on his throne while her ugly stepsisters watched jealously with the servants and crones. She had expertly picked out a silky forest green shirt and left it untucked around tight slacks, completing the ensemble with a long black raincoat and Jimmy Choo suede ankle boots with double leather straps and a thick metal heel.

Taking high steps, swaying in our applause, and spinning with the coat tails splaying around her knees, she could have been plucked from a scene where she kisses Roger Moore on lips and then pulls back to say, "But James, what about the diamonds?"

After extended applause, Rafael took to the platform with cool nonchalance; he had managed to find designer clothing that made him look as amiably deadly as a hitman in a Tarantino movie. Suits always made me look stiff and uncomfortable but Rafael knew how to move in good clothes. As he strutted along the catwalk, it suddenly made sense why crooks always dress well in the movies. I had thought it was a fashionable affectation, just another way that cinema takes life and lavishes it with luxuries to make dull reality more beautiful; but watching Rafael, I realized that with the right body and the right moves, nothing was more practical for killing than a well-fitted suit. He stalked the catwalk, pushing an imaginary strand of hair from his eyes. It occurred to me that my problem was vanity: Rafael chose suits that were just slightly too big, which gave him room to move and allowed him to fill the suit, whereas in my self-conscious desire to find clothes I'd like to fit into, I chose ones that were slightly too small, which meant that I was stuffed into them like a sausage in its casing.

He stepped down with a self-deprecating grin. "Your turn."

I took a step up. My *London Calling* t-shirt was replaced with a Calvin Klein pink V-neck sweater over a light blue oxford shirt; I flicked up the collar on my navy blazer, pulling the sleeves over my elbows. The jeans were skinny distressed denim, but a few days without eating had tightened my belly and they fit nicely. I'd found thick leather-soled shoes that added another inch to my height. I stomped down the catwalk and struck a pose, my hands in my pockets, my head cocked jauntily.

"You look like you should be in a John Hughes movie," said Rafael, and the others laughed.

It was exactly what I was hoping he would say.

"Wrong!" I went down into a Kung Fu stance, pulled out a pair of aviator shades from my breast pocket and jammed them onto my face. "*Miami Vice.*"

I did a karate kick, stood as tall as I could and moonwalked down the platform, leaping off at the end and heading to the exit.

At the door I stopped and said, "Our job here is done."

In the open-air courtyard, with our rifles between our knees, we sat on cement benches where the mall "guests" had once eaten fried mozzarella sticks, cheese-fried potatoes and stuffed pretzels with vat-sized polystyrene cups of "fruit" juice sold from a stall in the center of the courtyard. It was closed, its sign—*Juicy Juice!*—hanging by a single bent nail over the boarded-up window where just a few days before vapid teens dispensed frozen fruit pulp laced with plastic spoonfuls of all the nutrients being sapped from their customers' bowels by mozzarella sticks, cheese-fried potatoes, and stuffed pretzels.

We drank a bottle of water and shared one of the oranges we'd found in the ruins of the food court, enjoying our new clothes and the feeling that we'd gotten away with it all: the pleasure of consumerism without being obedient consumers.

"I didn't know you could moonwalk."

"There's a lot of things you don't know about me, Rafael. I can crump too."

"Really?"

"When the mood strikes."

Praj asked if I would teach him the moonwalk.

"You're too young," I said. "You have to have lived to do the moonwalk."

They laughed and we passed another orange, breaking the fruit into sweet segments. I began to wonder if I had become too defensive about my age. Maybe they were picking up on something else in their deference and distance: not that I was their elder but that I was a writer. It's easy to confuse the way people react to the two. Both demand respect and derision. And getting old and being a writer have a tendency to lower expectations. That's not without its advantages. The great thing about being a writer is that nobody honestly expects you to be able to do anything else. If you can cook an omelet, if you know the horse on a chessboard is called a knight, if you can fill your own gas-tank or moonwalk, they're impressed. Lance said it's even better for poets: if you do something basic like dress yourself, people applaud like you've solved a quadratic equation.

"What are we going to do in Chicago?" asked Trish. "Other than eat at Ricco's Bunny Steakhouse." With her new clothes, her confidence was coming back. "What about you, Gammy, anything special?" The question made Gammy flinch. There was a weird silence.

"It's Ricobene's," I said, choosing not to let any tension linger. "It's probably not open. I'll bet even La Pasadita on Ashland is closed. It was probably the last place to close. They'd be chopping steaks and barbacoa with atom bombs raining down around them. You know, when the original La Pasadita, just south of Division, shut down, I went across the street to the other branch for the first time—"

"Jack, you're not making sense."

"Then let me explain. You guys won't understand where we're going unless you understand Mexican food. Chicago is two things: architecture and Mexican food. Now, I know a lot of Poles and Romanians would go nuts if they heard me say that, and, Praj, you know how great Devon is, and I'm not dissing the South Side, Gammy, but—"

"But what's the plan?"

"Yeah, Jack, you can tell us about Chicago later. Right now we need a plan."

"We have a plan," I said. "The plan is we go to Chicago and meet up with whoever's left in the safety of a military compound, surrounded by men—and *women*—with artillery, air support, and vaccines."

Praj studied me. "That's not a plan, Jack. That's an idea of how things should be."

I thought for a moment and realized he was right. A cold wind blew through the air. A harbinger of winter. Suddenly, we were just a crew of survivors stuck in a mall with the abandoned air of ancient ruins but with none of the glamour of ruins; the air was unenlivened by rumors of heroes' deaths, there were no fabled myths to make the plaster and cinderblock come alive. It was amazing how fast this place became lifeless again, perhaps because it never had much life to begin with. Our rebellion began to feel like a final complicity.

"Praj is right," said Trish. "It's not really a plan."

"Well does anybody else have a 'plan'?" I waited and let their silence incriminate them. "Then I guess we'll just have to make do with an idea of how things should be." They looked glum. I took the rind of the orange and sniffed it. It smelled like summers in Florida, like my grandmother's kitchen, like a gift from the earth. I broke the rind and inhaled the miniature jets of sweet juice that squirted out.

Praj sighed. "It doesn't look good, does it?"

"Nope," I said. "But at least we'll look good." I surveyed the kids. "And not unlike an '80s rock band."

IV.

We left the mall and its acres of blustery parking lots and headed north past deserted fast food restaurants, down-market electronic stores and car dealerships sprawling out like a dissolute and disorganized camp of prostitutes, unwanted family members, and entrepreneurial lackeys around an army base.

The urban development ended abruptly in a forest preserve. One minute we were surrounded by gray cement, signage, and parking lots; the next, the sun came out and we were driving through lagoons fringed by bent trees, their leaves turning orange.

The forest preserve had already returned to nature. Tangled dried grasses rustled in the breeze, humming with insects. Woodpeckers dipped in the air and starlings darted from the branches; a hawk was gliding in slow circles above the lagoons, feigning boredom and dignity. White herons stepped out from the reeds and posed with crooked legs and long sharp beaks on the look out for frogs and newts. Trout and bass jumped and slapped the water. A family of raccoons tumbled for cover. Deer looked up with glassy black eyes and watched us, chewing pensively. You could tell what they were thinking. *At last we're done with them, at last we can cross roads without being buckled into fenders.* Or maybe the bored contempt in their eyes was a profound fatalism: they felt sorry for us the way we felt sorry for the last tigers or Orangutans.

We came to a crossroads. Yellow signs instructed us to give way to cyclists. There were no cyclists. Kitty corner to us, an ice cream truck was stationed on the verge, with white and gold wrappers strewn around it like fall foliage.

"I don't suppose the freezer still works."

"It's worth checking."

"I'd love some ice cream."

I parked and we got out to take a look. As we approached the truck, Trish moaned delicately. "Last night, I was dreaming of popsicles—and before you say anything, Jack, my dad owns a popsicle factory in Sonoma."

148

"I wasn't going to say anything, but now I am. You were dreaming about your father's popsicles? I wasn't a Freudian until about five seconds ago."

She decided to ignore me, although it wasn't fair because she basically invited me to comment. Anyway, she went on.

"I was standing beside a corn field, but instead of ears of corn, the stalks had popsicles. Red ones, yellow ones, blue ones, raspberry, lemon, and blueberry. I plucked the popsicles from the stalks and sold them to children for a nickel a popsicle. Children lined up as far as I could see to buy them. And then the dream was over, but it felt like a whole lifetime, like I was seeing my future. I was seeing what I could be."

"A popsicle farmer?" I asked.

Gammy elbowed me in the ribs.

"Somebody who does something, somebody who makes something of herself, somebody who makes people happy," said Trish. "You wouldn't understand, Jack."

We reached the ice cream truck and Rafael rubbed his hands together. "Let's not fight now, shall we? Let's see if there's any ice cream."

There wasn't. It had melted into multicolored goo at the bottom of the freezer. Tempting though it was to stick my finger through the crust for a taste, I resisted the urge.

"Jack, look!"

Gammy was in the driver's seat, peering out the windscreen like a child watching a house burn across the street. We crowded around her.

The truck was pointed towards a muddy creek thick with bulrushes, separating us from a wide glade limned by the skewed white masts of birch trees, hazy with midafternoon heat, and dotted by the fluttering confetti of white butterflies. Off to the left, near the trees, were three people: a man and two women in black leather, sand-colored where it had been worn in. The women crouched; in each hand they held a dagger. The man had a terrifyingly long samurai sword, which he held above his head, a scabbard hanging from his back. At their feet were three or four corpses with bloody throats.

On the other side of the glade, across the grasses and the tumbling popcorn butterflies, was a pack of bristling werewolves. Fifteen of them. They crept forward, their jaws snapping as they made impatient huffing sounds.

The man and the women were posed for a fight but didn't look worried. We were too far away to see their faces in detail but they seemed to have serene expressions. I had a feeling that the werewolves were in more trouble than they were.

One werewolf launched itself from the head of the pack and another broke away, looping around to come at them from the side. The man took long, steady strides towards the wolf charging head-on. The women bent and scurried towards the wolf coming from the side. It was over in an instant. The werewolf attacking from the front leapt and was disemboweled midair with one silver streak of the samurai sword; the werewolf coming from the side flung itself at the women and was immediately confused as they separated, and it found itself stuck between them, pincushioned by a whir of daggers along its flanks. It didn't know which way to twist, and haplessly bit to the left and to the right as dagger-thrust after dagger-thrust pierced its pelt in a flurry of metal and blood.

The man, holding his sword high above his head, took long, steady strides backwards; the women raced behind him, their hands besmirched with werewolf blood. The two werewolves shuddered, became still, and then they began to twist and coil like pieces of plastic burning in a fire. They took on human form. Both were young men, dead and naked and bloody.

The remaining werewolves were not sentimental. As one, the pack feinted and tensed, collecting for the attack.

"Let's help them!" Rafael rushed to the car for our weapons.

The air between the wolves and people became quiet, the butterflies dispersed like civilians fleeing a battlefield. Rafael returned and handed me a rifle. He offered Gammy a rifle or a pistol. She took the pistol, I took the rifle. We hustled to the bank and crept down amongst the rushes. The werewolves arched their backs and dug in their heels.

Rafael unslung his rifle and held it up to his shoulder, Gammy aimed her pistol. The slime sucked at our feet, frogs plopped under water leaving plump bubbles where their eyes had been.

The werewolf at the front of the pack bayed, a long human howl, almost a word. As soon as the sound died out, they charged, galloping across the grass.

"We shoot on three," I said. "Three!"

I opened fire. I meant to count up to three but was too excited. Gammy and Rafael joined in. The werewolves jolted and bounced in the barrage of hot metal nubbins. The staccato cracks were deafening; flocks of birds burst from the trees, beating through the air in terror. Eight or nine werewolves crashed into the grasses and bucked in agony.

Another bolted towards us, zigzagging with its teeth bared. Rafael and I blasted at it, sending smoky clods of turf into the air. It was fast, racing low, hitching to the left, then the right, racing fast enough that it would have killed Rafael or me. But not fast enough for Gammy. It reached the bank of the creek and compacted itself to pounce. Gammy aimed, her breasts stilled, she shot it in the head. Its body went slack and it rolled into the water.

Three werewolves made a run for the tree line. Gammy took a step forward and fired. Two of them somersaulted into oblivion. One, only wounded, tried to scratch its way to the birches, its back paws limp and twisted. Gammy aimed, fired, a puff on its neck—a fine spray of hair, skin, blood—and the thing collapsed.

The air was smoky, my hands tingled, my ears were ringing. We lowered our weapons. In the middle of the field, a mass of dying werewolves pawed at the ground and nipped at the sharp pains in their bellies.

The strangers looked curiously at us. With a word from the man, the women sprinted across the glade. Crouching beside each wolf, they slit their throats, a ruthless *coup de grace.*

The wolves shuddered into human shapes, their paws

extending into arms and legs harshly angled with rigor mortis, their snouts and brows softening into faces; men and women, naked and streaked with mud, with bullet holes in their skin, cut throats, blades of grass in their hair.

The three strangers met up again. After conferring with occasional glances at us, they strolled across the glade in our direction. They did not put their blades away.

We faced each other across the creek.

"I guess we should thank you?" said the man, with the wry smile of a schoolyard jock saved from bullies by the fat kids.

He was slight but he was perfectly proportioned, like an almost-life-size Greek statue with steel-blue eyes and longish black hair, which he kept off his face with flicks of his head. A silver loop through his eyebrow looked like someone had drunkenly tried to pierce his ear and missed, but the effect was impressive. He wasn't big but he was perfectly proportioned, like an almost-life-size Greek statue. He contemplated the distance, allowing us to linger with his features.

He must have been in his early thirties, although my gang would say he looked about 45.

The women were petite, coiled and taut like terriers on a hunt. One was scornfully Asian, with jet black hair and eyebrows styled into daggers rising above her eyes, giving her the pissed-off look of the permanently affronted. The other was white with sparkling green eyes and a pornographic sneer. Her blonde hair was short and spiky with two long strands like payot curled in front of her ears.

The Asian had multiple piercings: a row of silver studs ran up both of her ears, and two silver bolts jutted out of her lower lip. Her nipples were budding through a black tank top; one supported the outline of a hoop, the button of her nipple tailing a fallen silver halo.

"You're welcome," I said. "Who are you? Where are you from?"

"I'm Jerome," said the man. "Ophelia—" The metallic Asian smirked thirstily at Rafael. "Starshine—" There was no smile from Starshine; she looked at Gammy hungrily, chewing one of her blonde curls.

"We've come from Minneapolis," he said.

That explained a lot. I'd heard about the industrial-folk-punk scene in Minneapolis.

"My name is Jack Forbes," I said. "From Chicago. And New York. Mostly Chicago. This is Rafael and Gammy, from England and Texas respectively, and over in the ice cream truck, we have Trish and Praj."

"Charmed," said Jerome. He bowed his head in the friendly if superior manner of an aristocrat from somewhere distant and formal—Old Europe, perhaps. Vienna or Berlin. Very Minnesotan. "In which direction are you heading?"

"Chicago."

"Us too." He pointed to three motorcycles parked by the trees. "Did you say your name is Jack Forbes?"

"Yes?"

Jerome nodded thoughtfully. "I enjoyed *Gargantuan Travels.*"

"*Voyages,*" I said, as quietly pleased as any man has ever been in all of history. "*Gargantuan Voyages.*"

"That's right," said Jerome, with a searching look. "That's the title. Bravo." His eyes wrinkled kindly.

V.

When we stopped for a break, Rafael took me aside. Awkwardly avoiding anything that might raise suspicions, he coaxed me over to a wooden picnic table, into which generations of passing yokels had carved their names: Earl and Betty were tucked inside a heart, Bob carved his name on his own behalf and on behalf of the millions of others who once shared it, somebody called Frazzle left a more unique signature accompanied by a cross, and I spotted a Gloria who was, according to the black ink under her name, a "slut."

My stomach was hurting. Before we left the ice-cream truck, I'd surreptitiously slipped in and dipped a finger into the congealed ice cream, just for a taste. Once I broke through the crusty rind, the paste below was a sour strawberry and chocolate yoghurt, not good enough to eat but sufficiently potent to give me a nasty stomach ache.

Rafael examined the picnic table, running his finger over the etched names.

"Jack," he said, kicking wistfully at a crushed beer can in the wheatgrass, "Do you trust them?"

I stifled some regurgitation and sighed. "No, I don't. But I like them."

"Is that because Jerome liked your book?"

"I can't say that made me feel antagonistic towards him. But no, I like them because although they're weirdoes, they're fierce, and right now, we could use ferocious weirdoes on our side. What about you, do you trust them?"

"I don't actually. I barely trust you. Ha, ha. It's just that Ophelia seems to like me. And I quite like her too." Rafael had demonstrated enough trust that he agreed to ride bitch on her bike.

"Yeah, I noticed."

"I'm quite partial to rough trade," he said, picking at the table. "And she smells like cinnamon."

"Interesting."

He sighed and traced names carved in the wood. "My first girlfriend was Asian."

154

"So you have a thing for Asians."

"Oh no, not at all, this just seems to be a happy coincidence."

"That's what all fetishists say the second time they get a kick out of their fetish. I guess we won't know for sure until the one after Ophelia."

"That's a strange way of looking at it, but I appreciate the sentiment. I just thought I'd see how you were feeling about them."

"I dunno," I said. "I've never had an Asian girlfriend. Or one with so many piercings. The metal must get in the way."

"It doesn't," said Rafael enigmatically.

"We should get back—hey, Rafael, we look okay, don't we?"

Rafael seemed unsure what I was asking and then he got it and nodded ruefully. We all wished that the clothes we'd obtained made us look as badass as our new friends. They looked like they had been cast in *The Matrix*, we looked like we had just come from a 1980s Renaissance Faire.

We rejoined the others. After a brief conversation, we gave a collective shrug and were back on the road, a neat convoy of three motorbikes around my bruised but loyal beater, a Beethovian symphony of black leather and silver metal around the Mozartian operetta of my Chevy. They rode beside the car, overtook it, drifted in tow, a swarm making patterns in space as we made our way to the Windy City.

When they came alongside the car, Rafael and Ophelia were the picture of glamour. Young and beautiful, their mouths pursed shut against the wind; her hair flapped, he crouched along her back, his chin on her shoulder. If he slipped, he could grab one of the pieces of metal in her face or her nipple ring. It was a surprisingly erotic thought and I felt a reassuring and pleasantly dissatisfying tension in my jeans. I'd always said that piercings and tattoos weren't my thing but I began to wonder if maybe I was just repressing something.

"Gammy, do you have any piercings?"

She was in the front seat next to me. She gazed through the window at the wild grasses, pylons, overpasses.

"Hmm?"

"I asked if you had any piercings."

She mumbled something; I thought she said, "I've got a clit-ring", and I gasped. "You what?"

She turned to look at me. "That's not my kinda thing," she repeated, more clearly.

"Oh, I thought you said . . . never mind."

An hour later, we arrived at the trim low hillocks and sandy ulcers of a golf course, dotted with tangled copses as if nature were improvising with petulant messiness inside the regulated landscape. Jerome came alongside the car and signaled for us to pull over.

I rolled down the window. Jerome leaned down.

"There must be a club-house. We should stay here tonight."

"Don't you think we should get to Chicago?" I asked, holding down more regurgitation. My stomach was spasming.

Trish poked her head forward and caught Jerome's eye. He held her gaze.

"You can try," he said, talking to me but looking at her, "if you want." He then looked pointedly at me. "But we're going to rest here tonight."

He glanced over the car at Starshine and Ophelia for confirmation. They nodded. Rafael, his cheeks flushed, adjusted his position behind Ophelia, his thin hips slipping tight against hers. She was audibly purring.

It was pretty clear that if we split up, Rafael and Trish would seriously consider staying with the Minneapolis punksters. Part of me wanted to make them choose.

In fact, I was already seething with jealousy. Given a choice of three men, Ophelia hadn't given me a second look. She went straight to the floppy-haired, green-eyed boy with the British accent. I had been ranked deep down in the basement of masculinity with the Prajs of the world, once a crowded basement jostling with geeks dressed like their favorite Star Trek characters and overweight asthmatics who could recite every line of Monty Python, a subterranean peanut-free world lorded over by the pencil-headed math nerds and pasty, overconfident debaters who knew that one day power would be theirs, and they awaited what lay ahead, wheezily biding their time until they could launch careers in politics, banking and business, gearing up to return the favor with the cosmic, nihilistic, sour "fuck you" of the once-bullied. I hated it when I was ranked with the Prajs of the world.

"We're heading to Chicago," I insisted. Rafael and Ophelia were practically copulating at the hip.

"Tonight?" Trish said between parted lips, in a tone of voice that made it clear that she was in no hurry to leave. Jerome flicked his hair and scanned the distance, giving us a clear shot of his profile, as feline as it was classical. He contemplated the distance, allowing us to linger with his features.

"We're going to Chicago," I said.

"Tonight?" sighed Trish.

"Yes."

On the other side of the car, Rafael made a pouty Anglican moue; Ophelia leaned back into him, staring at me with bored confidence. She and I both knew he would stay with her.

Starshine revved her bike and bounced closer. She looked first across the car at Jerome and then set her sparkling green eyes straight into the car at Gammy. Her pointy pink tongue came out, grabbed a strand of her blonde hair and tucked it into the corner of her mouth, and she chewed it, twitching with that perfect erotic tension between self-amused interest and hot, desperate desire. Gammy adjusted herself uncomfortably, although I wasn't sure what the nature of the discomfort was.

Okay, I thought, how much worse could this get? It was clear that if we stayed, there was going to be sex, a huge amount of rampant humping, none of it involving me. A number of scenarios played out in my mind: me clumsily attempting to join one of the couples forming in front of my eyes; me, watching them with hot misery from the side; me, being forced to sit in a clubhouse lounge with Praj, discussing philosophy and Dungeons and Dragons and pretending not to hear the thumps coming from where Jerome and Trish, Ophelia and Rafael, and Starshine and Gammy consummated ancient passions with ferocity and passion, clawing each other, mouth to mouth, breast to breast—

"What are you thinking, Jack?"

"Uh, I'm trying to figure out whether it would be safer to go or stay here, how much gas we have, and"—I fumbled for something to say—"whether we can trust you."

"Here's the thing," smiled Jerome. He scanned the horizon again, collecting his thoughts and gracing us with his perfect Greco-Roman profile. I wondered if he called his motorcycle Bucephalus. "The way I see it, I'd rather ride into Chicago at dawn so we can scope the city out during the day. It's going to be dark." He paused. "As the poet wrote, 'By day we are here once / but we are twice doomed at night.'"

I didn't recognize the line but Praj leaned forwards and said, "Eboule."

"You know Eboule?" asked Jerome with open surprise. I snorted. Did he think Praj wouldn't know some stupid poet because he was Indian or Pakistani or whatever he was?

Praj nodded. Quiet smiles of recognition passed between them.

What the fuck, I thought. "Who's Eboule?"

"He was a Jazz man," Praj said. "He played the trumpet and published just one book of poetry, *The Good Nocturnes*, before dying of a heroin overdose. It was dedicated to his partner, a drummer with Bing Chasman's Trio. I think the lines are: 'By day we are here once / though we're twice doomed at night / Solitary in waking hours, / split at the star's delight.'"

Jerome reached across me to give Praj a delicate but ever-so-slightly prolonged fist bump; as he did so, he winked at Trish, who shuddered with delight. And it dawned on me. If we stayed I would in fact be left alone, all by myself, while the rest of them had a massive orgy—Praj included. One by one they'd excuse themselves and leave me with diminishing company until the last one would mumble something about forgetting something somewhere and stumble out of the room, not trying too hard to hide his or her impatience. For them, the night ahead promised multiple sweaty orgasms and crap poetry; for me, *nada.*

"Bang Eboule in the ass," I said. "I'm going to Chicago." As I spoke, my guts pinched; a green wave of nausea washed over me like my body was internally puking on me. I wasn't going to make it to Chicago. I had little time, maybe only minutes, before I needed a toilet.

I affected an ambiguous laugh. "On the other hand," I said, trying to come up with a reason to stay, "Why not? I've always wanted to stay in a country club."

There was a gulp of embarrassed silence. The punksters made no effort to hide their disdain.

Nice, Jack, nice. Could I have come up with a worse excuse? I'd contrived to confess that I was a white man without the money or status to get into a country club but whose entire goal in life was to sit in overstuffed chairs with pompous blowhards in Lacoste shirts and white pants, nursing Shirley Temples, and talking about how the help isn't what it used to be while lifting our thighs to pass gas at the bustling Mexicans with averted eyes.

"Because I loathe them," I mumbled. "Bastions of privilege. Racist institutions." I faded away. "I've just been curious . . ."

"This way," said Jerome turning his front wheel towards a road leading through the golf course.

VI.

An oxbow driveway curved around a lawn kowtowing to a stately white mansion, a white gothic monstrosity with a columned portico and skeptically welcoming green doors under a fanlight.

We parked our fleet in the raked gravel beside a solitary Silver Willow, shimmering in the breeze like a submarine life form on a coral reef. Jerome dismounted, removed his sword with a vibrating *piiing*, and led us up the flagstone path next to Gammy with her rifle slung low.

Jerome pushed them open with the silver-pointed tip of his boot and then lifted his sword high in both hands, ready to slice in half anything that burst out. Gammy pulled the rifle to her shoulder and hunched.

Nothing came out, not even the whisper of the servants' ghosts, finally freed.

We swept into the entrance hall, spinning under a wine-colored wood ceiling two stories above us. At the top of a grand staircase with elaborately carved bannisters of Revolutionary-era soldiers was a balcony, empty of spectators. The floors were polished cherry decorated with a frilled carpet bleached where it had been stamped into its original tan. Standing in the center of the rug was a marble-topped table with a blue and white porcelain vase decorated with Chinese people carrying each other around on litters; the vase was filled with a bush of dried flowers. The reception desk was guarded by two mute sentinels: a rough-hewn brass statue of a golfer in mid-swing and a grandfather clock that needed winding. Time had stopped here long before the monster uprising.

Being careful not to touch anything, we fanned out. Jerome gestured for us to follow him into a lounge flooded with the red light of the late afternoon sun coming through French windows framed by stout curtains ribboned into curves by gold ropes. A magnificent stone fireplace with a sooty gray flagstone hearth and a black iron grate dominated one wall; the legs of the grate were carved lion's paws and a heraldic lion roared silently from the marble header. We spread out, listening and sniffing the air. Placed in front of the fireplace with calculated sociability were plump chairs and sofas around low wooden tables each one with something to amuse old people: stacks of glossy magazines, backgammon sets, coffee table books. I was glad to see that Rafael could not help opening a hardcover book about English country estates and flicking through the pages with a hazy expression of sentimental longing.

We met by the fireplace and decided to make the lounge our base. Although the windows made us vulnerable to attack, the room overlooked a patio, brick-paved in a herringbone pattern with scattered lawn seats around a pool, and out across the golf course: as long as one of us was keeping a look out—me, I guessed, while the rest of them rutted—we'd be able to see an attack coming a mile away.

Jerome, Rafael and I went to reconnoiter while the others brought in our food. Jerome and Rafael took the staircase up to the second floor, probably to scout out a good room for sex. I skulked past the reception desk and into the corridor on the other side of the entrance hall, which led to a gloomy dining room and bar. Other than the broad-windowed lounge, the clubhouse had the type of murkiness that old people felt was cozy; the rooms were lit with trapped sunlight, held in place for decades, the air as stale and musty as old breath. But it was calm. It felt untouched by what was happening in the world outside, harboring the unsettling insouciance of its elite members, treating the monster uprising with the same otherworldly resignation the members had towards the exigencies of living in a high tax bracket or in a country not wholly run by the Republican party, with an air of privileged carelessness, like a millionaire who had forgotten his wallet, or a priest about to die; what would fluster the rest of us just didn't seem to matter that much.

The corridor led to the locker rooms. The men's room was indicated by the silhouette of a male golfer in a jaunty pose, one hand on his hip, the other resting on a golf club beside his crossed legs. Inside, there were wooden-slat benches under padlocked or empty lockers, a pair of sneakers, scattered tees.

It smelled like Old Spice and mildew. I examined the pictures on the wall: sepia-toned photographs of long-forgotten club heroes, lantern-jawed men teeing up or with an iron held at the end of a perfect swing as they eyed a ball shot far out of the frame. My gut heaved.

Across the corridor, the women's locker room was indicated by a silhouette of a slapper with a putter. The room was just as disappointing and shallow as the men's room, with pink wallpaper and framed reproductions of nineteenth-century still-lifes with plump peaches, pineapples and pears in wicker baskets, the odd butterfly or dead fish.

I kept exploring this functional wing of the aristocracy's playground, wincing with the contortions of my bowels. Beyond the locker rooms was a club store with wire baskets filled with marked-up golf balls, tubes of tennis balls, rolling garment racks with appalling clothing only the very rich would be brave enough to wear, and, behind a cash register, rows of irons. Off to the side was a worktable for whatever needed repairing in the country-clubbing world. Pristine golf bags were lined up under a window with a view of the putting green. I picked one, fire engine red leather, and gulped at the price tag but then remembered that I didn't have to pay for it. In a state of digestive panic, I filled it with heavy woods, a length of rope from under the worktable, and spiked shoes.

My stomach cramped up and I knew I had only seconds before I soiled myself. As I lugged the golf bag out, I noticed a black door with chipped paint, a rackety bronzed door knob and a charmless *Private* sign. It opened into a glum employees' changing room, decorated only with a two-year-old calendar from a local auto dealership. The ugliness and functionality of the room, and the casual irony of the sign, was a way of telling the club members that whatever was "private" was something they had no interest in. The ultimate snub.

The help had a dusty but clean bathroom with a single cubicle. The plumbing was out but nobody would come back here.

I squatted with relief.

The sun was setting, sending a flare of hot light into the lounge. I'd returned after what was unfortunately but indubitably the most satisfying physical experience I'd had in days; I knew that it served as a sort of anticipatory explosive prelude to the more elegant and attractive carnal explosions the others would soon be enjoying. They'd settled down in the lounge and were checking their weapons and inventorying our findings. In addition to the shoes, rope and golf clubs, which Ophelia and Starshine twirled like deadly batons, Jerome and Rafael had procured an armful of sheets from the rooms upstairs and, from the kitchen, a can-opener, knives, and several bottles of bourbon and rye.

They were all giving each other knowing looks that probably conveyed the exact time they would make their excuses and slink out to a suitable location for an orgy.

It was too much. I needed to be by myself. The dangers were obvious but since dangers were quite literally everywhere, I decided to steal a moment of solitude of my own choosing. If a werewolf or lizard monster or zombie killed me, I might as well scream in privacy. At the very least, if I got killed, they'd feel a moment of guilt in the middle of their orgy. Plus, who wants to be the fool? I'd give them the chance to make their arrangements without doing it right under my nose.

I slipped from the lounge, slinging a rifle over my shoulder. Just behind the reception desk, I discovered an unobtrusive, unmarked door, the wood paneling of which matched the wall around it; I opened it and passed through a storage room crammed with unpromising torn cardboard boxes, club photographs, and a wheel for a golf buggy, and exited out the back into a hedge-lined dirt walkway, with a trio of garbage cans rested like sedentary workers, their metal lids at rakish angles, and a green hose coiled like a snake in the dirt, its serpentine brass head poking up, alert and ready to strike.

I peeled away from the clubhouse and emerged from around the hedges. Off to my left were the rolling, cropped dunes of the fairways, leading all the way to the big houses whose backyards were separated from the country club by a fringe of trees and a road. I set off to the right, following a wood-chip path around the putting green into a shaggier, wilder area, a crooked sliver of nature between the parking lot and the golf course. A cardinal landed on the path, cocked its red-crested head in my direction, and fluttered away.

After tramping in a funk of unsatisfying me-time, I came across a pond ringed with stiff reeds and milkweed, crouched down low, a black frog of water keeping still in the foliage.

All of a sudden, the sun broke on the horizon, spilling gold across the golf course; the leaves in the trees lit like emeralds, the surface of the pond creased and glistened; a million silvery motes—bugs and seeds and fairies—were illuminated above the pond. My rifle dropped to my side. It was so beautiful.

I had never seen anything like it, a muggy bog transformed into a jewel box. "Oh sweet God," I muttered.

I cursed my inability to say anything other than appeal to the sweetness of a God who didn't exist; but at that moment, in a state of wordlessness, smacked with an inability to speak, I realized something was left for me. There was a place for me in the world, not just as a man but as a writer. In silence, it was revealed. I was to write of the world as it had become.

I was the one to do it. I was old enough, I had lived enough, I had written enough, I may have been finished but I was fresh, I'd been to the bottom but I'd crawled back up. I was the one who would record the precious moments in the horrors, I would speak of epiphanies after the monster uprising.

And then even my thoughts disappeared. Words fell from my mind like keys falling from someone's hand in front of an open door.

Coins of light blinked between the leaves. A breeze came up from the earth as the soil exhaled its day-dying breath. From out of the reeds, a blue heron jumped into the columns of sunlight. It caught an invisible slipstream with its outstretched wings, beat heavily once, twice, gripping an air current out of the woods. I whispered the words I should have said first, the words that my soul was searching for when I lost all words, the words that now came to me, graced as I was: "Thank you," I said, "thank you, heron; thank you, pond." I sighed my thanks like a lover, like a parent finding a lost child, like a man dying with a smile on his lips, like the proudest revolutionary bound to a post as the sergeant says, "Ready aim—" and I listed the beauties I beheld: sunlight, birds, leaves, the breeze, the opportunity for gratitude and, almost, God.

From deep within the reeds, a shadow unfurled and rose; I blinked, confused, still humming with gratitude as the tall malformed shadow stepped out of the reeds; a shimmer of light fell across it, casting it into relief, and I could see it was not a shadow but a shape, bulbous with green-black gelatinous skin. Another jelly-like glob rose and unfolded beside it, swaying and dripping. Pond weed slipped from its shoulders into the pond with defecatory plops. And then another and another and another: five sleek brackish figures stood across the pond, like a composition of a basketball team dipped in pond goo painted by Vermeer.

The sun plunged behind the hills and the rich luminosity was replaced by a damper light in which the creatures appeared and disappeared. I was fixed into place with sickening terror, my gratitude for the beautiful scene expelled from me like a plug of sweet phlegm coughed from my lungs. The beings seemed not to have noticed me. I inspected them in frozen terror. They did sort of look like a drunken basketball team that had been hiding in the reeds. They stood wobbling in the air, with rubbery muscles on elongated arms leading to spade-like hands; their faces were fish-like with goggly green eyes, they had no nose and, in place of mouths, they had clacking, crab-like beaks and fibrous snappers; above their forehead rubbery protrusions in place of hair swayed like fat eels poking from their skulls. Gills fluttered and steamed along their necks. The horrible dry clicking of their beaks sounded like the burrowing noises of an insect caught in wood.

Words came back in a torrent. *Run, Jack, run, oh please, just start running.* But I stood my ground. "Run," I rasped aloud.

They heard and turned to me with globular, gelatinous eyes. All at once, they dove into the water and in a flash appeared at the bank by my feet. I ran.

If they had been as fast on land as they were in the water, I would have been fish food. Fortunately, they had webbed feet and waddled on land like humans wearing flippers, taking big floppy steps, their fin-like hands flapping at the air in front of them like they were trying to do the doggy-paddle. In a blind panic, I raced along the wood-chip path, down the hedge-lined dirt path and made it into the clubhouse, slamming the doors behind me.

"Guys," I said, when I arrived panting in the lounge. "Monsters are coming after me."

"Where were you?"

"How many?"

"Zombies?"

"Werewolves?"

They shot the questions at me.

"No," I said, trying to catch my breath. "These ones are new."

"Did you lead them here?" shouted Gammy, her voice rising with hysterical disappointment.

"Where the hell was I supposed to lead them?" I gasped back. Jerome removed his sword from his sheath with a whooshing sound followed by the high-pitched ring of vibrating metal. Ophelia and Starshine took their attack positions behind him, daggers in hand.

"I've got an idea," said Gammy. She tapped Rafael on the shoulder to follow her and they raced out of the lounge with their rifles. We could hear them clambering up the central staircase, their footsteps becoming quieter on the second floor.

While I had been gone, Jerome had started a fire in the stone fireplace. Behind black mesh to keep sparks from floating onto the carpeting, the heat-snapped veins of sap popped and released pine-perfumed smoke.

Nobody said a word but they shot annoyed glances at me like I was a teenager who had come home after crashing the family car. Yes, I had survived, but . . .

"It wasn't really my fault," I said weakly. Jerome sheathed his sword, Ophelia elaborately smirked, Starshine looked at me like I had wet the bed again. Trish and Praj fingered their weapons with downcast eyes. I let the side down.

There was a crackle of gunfire, like fireworks going off at a Fourth of July party to which I wasn't invited, and we tensed. And another, then silence.

A few moments later, we heard Gammy and Rafael trotting down the stairs. They appeared in the doorway with inscrutable expressions.

We evidently did not give them the reception they wanted, so they entered and leaned sulkily by the fire, absorbing its heat with haunted looks on their faces like a pair of Arctic explorers after a disastrous expedition during which they had to kill their sled dogs and Inuit guide for food.

We waited for them to speak. After a few long seconds, Rafael gave us a surprised, interrupted look as if to say, "Oh, you're here. I was lost in thought about . . . the terrible things . . . you wouldn't understand . . . how could you?" His eyes were drawn back into the warm hearth, searching for the awful truth in its crackling core, knowing that man's great expedition to the heart of darkness only ever ends with studying firelight in terrible solitude.

Jerome broke the silence: "What kind of monsters were they?"

Rafael spun around. "There were five of them," he said brightly. "I've never seen anything like them! Jack has discovered a new monster altogether. How can I describe them? They were human salamanders, swampy but vicious, like something Goya might have sketched—no, not Goya; El Greco. The Greek," he caught Ophelia's eye in the firelight and then peered up to the shadows pulsing across the ceiling, as he delicately ran a finger along his eyebrow. "They were elongated, not with Modigliani's exotic eroticism but with the cursed, wrought elongation of an El Greco saint, stretched by the rack of life. If I had to describe them, I would describe them as El Grecoesque fishpeople. Anyway," he brought himself back to the moment, "they followed Jack but didn't know what to do when they got to the door. They were walking in circles like this—" He waddled in a small circle. "—and we just shot them from above. It was like shooting fish—"

"—in a barrel," concluded Gammy.

The fire blazed. Jerome pulled the mesh back to allow the fire its glory, casting its living light across the room, playing tag with the shadows, slapping the walls with hot yellow palms like a bully smacking nerd foreheads. For the first time in days, we ate warm food, passing tins and jars from one to the other without a word.

I was depressed. When I was a kid, my fantasy was that adulthood would be like camp without the counselors: you could do whatever you wanted and at the end of the day you cozied up around a fire and ate as much as you like, followed by lots of sex. This was the closest I had come to living that fantasy and it was not panning out like I had hoped. There were no more rules, no more people telling us what to do, and here I was with a pack of grown-ups (more or less), free and sitting around a fire, spooning hot beans and pasta sauce into my mouth without worrying about table manners. But fundamentally nothing had changed: I was horny, aroused, alone, and wondering how on earth everybody was having sex except for me.

Rafael sat cross-legged in front of the fire, staring into the flames. He could tell I was hungry and let me finish off his portion of the pasta sauce, and then he began making blowing sounds, five little drumbeats with his lips, *poh poh poh poh poh*, a pause, then five more, *poh poh poh poh poh*. A cryptic smile crossed his face and in the flickering light transformed into a frown.

"Sorry, I was trying to remember," he said in a hushed tone, "and I couldn't. I was chasing down an image. Or actually, it was chasing me. I had to stop to clear my mind and the image caught up." He waited until we were paying attention and then caught Ophelia's eye. "There's a painting by Piero di Cosimo in the Ashmolean called *The Forest Fire*. It's from the early 1500s, a truly great era for painting. In the middle of the painting is a black, snarled forest with fields to either side," he held out his hands and pointed to either side of the fire, "and then more forest to the left and right. The central forest is on fire. You don't see flames, which are implied in the knotted blackness of the forest, charcoal silhouetted against the glow of combustion. Animals and birds flee. But the birds fly away gracefully like spirits abandoning the world; the animals are awkward, slow and confused. A lioness strolls to the side as if nothing is happening, a bear family ambles up a hill, a bull sticks out its tongue. There are monsters, too. *Lusus naturae*. Animals with human faces.

"I love this painting because its story is so simple—animals and birds run away from a forest fire.

"The painting is usually understood as di Cosimo's depiction of an ancient world, but it's a parable: it depicts two ways of being when the world is burning. There are those who seek flight by charting a course, sailing, gliding away with everything that's precious, and those who lumber along the ground, jumbled and ugly."

He fell silent.

Well, I thought, if those aren't the words of someone looking to get laid, I don't know what are. I snorted quietly, wondering if Rafael's monologue was the cue. Gray-charcoaled logs crashed with a fizz of orange sparks, then settled into a dark hot glow. Jerome and the rest of them stretched out on the carpeting and sofas, their eyes open, watching the fire, waiting for me to fall asleep. I wondered if I should excuse myself and let them get on with it. Jerome eased himself up and came over to me.

"Jack, let's take first watch."

"Do you want me to do it alone? If you guys want to—I don't know. If you want to—you know."

"Let them sleep."

He motioned for me to follow. I couldn't believe it. I scrambled up, trying to hide my delight. It was like being picked first for the camp baseball team. The rest were staring into the embers, somewhere private and lonely.

I followed Jerome through the doors and into the night. The air was cool, a relief after the stifling heat of the fire. We took a pair of chairs on the patio and pulled them to the edge of the swimming pool. During the day, the water had been a bright chemical blue freckled with leaves, but it was pitch black now, a murky rectangular portal into Hades. The broken vertebrae of the moon danced down its back. Above us, stars sparkled.

We said nothing for a long time. I listened for cracking twigs or a scuffle in the grass. From way off in the distance came the creaking of crickets and the occasional low hollow pop of a bullfrog calling for its dumpy mates. Maybe an hour passed. When I looked up, the moon had crossed the zenith.

Eventually Jerome spoke. "What do you want from life?"

The question lingered, then settled like a drop of dew, a crystalline tear suspended on my psyche, weighing it down like a blade of prairie grass. The longer it hung, a clear pearl of a question, the more my mind bent. With a force of will, I shook it off: "Life is something that happens when you're off killing zombies."

Jerome reached into his jacket pocket. He pulled out a fabric pouch and a thin cardboard packet with cigarette papers.

"Do you mind if I smoke a joint?"

"Do you think that's a good idea?"

He pondered my question, tapping the cigarette papers against the pouch.

"Yes," he said, "it's a very good idea."

With nimble fingers he pinched weed into a rectangle of paper and rolled it up into a perfect tube. He lit it under a cupped hand. His cheeks puffed out, his face glowed orange. He exhaled a cloud of silver smoke. After luxuriating in another drag, he handed it to me, careful to keep the ember shielded in his palm. I held the spliff and contemplated it, wondering if I should.

Jerome settled in his chair, unconcerned. I took six or seven quick puffs and held the smoke in my lungs. I hadn't smoked weed in twenty years. My throat burned. My lungs felt like they were going to burst—I coughed, scouring my mouth and nostrils with the sweet herbal smoke. I held the joint out, too busy restoring my capacity to breathe to shield the lit end. Jerome took it with a bemused look.

"That's wild, man," I gasped. I used to say that in college when we passed my roommate's Grateful Dead hash pipe.

My head began to feel light. Jerome took another drag, his small perfect face spotlit by the fragrant ember. A feeling had not felt in days, weeks, months, even years ran through me. There was a word for it. Relaxation. My mind was freed from my body, smeared across the firmament, given a massage, and was lying pleasantly anaesthetized on the night's sparkling table with a dumb smile on its face.

I struggled to connect with the other person right beside me, that lovely amusing problem for the stoned. "What the, what is it, what do you *do*, Jerome?"

He flashed a mysterious smile, one that may have been a prelude to a confession or a warning that what was about to follow was being made up on the spot, and then unspooled his story: he was a poet and a singer for as long as he could remember, a composer of folk ditties and murder ballads—he mentioned Nick Cave and Johnny Cash—earning his keep in a tattoo parlor where he inked students and college professors with Celtic knots, tigers, skulls, and lovers' names. At night, he sang for a house band in a college bar. Ophelia played bass and Starshine played the electric organ.

He told me how they'd met at an independent café with only three tables surrounded by hemp sacks of coffee beans purchased from a single Guatemalan farmer, which would be individually selected and hand-ground with a ceramic grinder for each cup. Jerome was putting up a poster on the tack board by the door; Ophelia was immersed in a novel; Starshine was the barista. They got to talking about who they were, where they came from. They'd left home in their teens, they came from small towns far, far away, a long time passed— "lifetimes"—and ended up in Milwaukee.

I nodded as he spoke, recognizing something in the story. What was it? The art? A way of being in the world? They were living the bohemian life I'd lived in my twenties, in love with art, proudly despairing that they alone understood the world, hitting the psychic sweet spot where solipsism and narcissism meet; the success they strove for came to me and yet as he spoke I realized that I missed out on something wistful and romantic that no Gibsons or smooth-necked reviewers could make up for. A glamor. A sensuality. An eroticism. Or maybe something more profound: the realization that success never comes, even when it does.

"Life isn't over, Jack."

"Yes, it is. We're doomed."

"We were always doomed. But life will go on. If every book of poetry is burned, if every novel goes up in flames, there will still be a trace of what was said. The world's an abandoned garden given over to nature: it'll soon be untamed, but for centuries, the paths will remain under the brambles, the remnants of walls will be found behind the ferns, the deer will drink from the mossy fountain, squirrels will sit on the bench around the old oak tree. Byron is drowned, Shelley and Keats are but names carved in headstones dissolving back into the earth. But their words changed the air and will still be felt in the winds."

"So did Hitler's. Maybe that's what's in the air."

"Evil is extinction. The good won't go away."

The joint, however, was gone. We looked into the night. What sweeter state is there than the melancholic optimism of stoned memories? A view of the stars from the gutter, love in a time of monsters, a fleeting conversation on the train from Vienna to Paris with a gorgeous woman you'll never see again. The disjointed unity of reality and hope.

Perhaps I was going to have the last laugh. The critics of my books were now dead, their families horribly and pedantically devoured, their essays and parodies and pastiches of my hard work all gone, wiped from a world without an internet; yes, they were gone, but, yes, my box of books remained, a solitary cairn of novel in an empty parking lot in Indiana, an isolated Donald Judd library, a portable block of literature, a crate of word, my Stonehenge of sentences, my square brick pyramid, the nine-inch high Colossus of Forbes: *The Forgotten Swansong of Malcolm Bones*.

I flicked my eyes to the right and watched the nocturnal world catch up, the stars lazily shifting across the sky; and then

I looked to the left, and the stars sighed and duly trudged to the left.

After a while Jerome interrupted my game of star tennis. "Are you in love with Gammy?"

The question was like a glass of cold water in my face. "What're you talking about?"

He leaned back in his chair, his small hands tucked behind his head. A smile decorated his features. I was pretty sure he was looking to the right, waiting for the stars to catch up, and then looking to the left.

"No, really: what are you talking about?"

"I've seen the way you look at her." He squinted sideways at me. "And the way she looks at you."

"Judging by her reaction to Starshine, I'm not what's she looking for."

I hoped he would dispel any disturbing notions I'd developed about Gammy's sexual orientation.

"Starshine?" He giggled childishly, and I remembered that he was much younger than me. "Starshine could seduce anybody. She could show up for a Good Friday service and have the Pope eating her out on the altar before the end of Mass."

"Christ, that's vulgar."

"That's how it is."

I suffered for a moment and then blurted out, "So you think she *could* seduce Gammy?"

"Do you care?"

"No."

"You really don't?"

"Not a bit. Not even a little bit."

"Then yes, she could seduce Gammy."

The effects of the weed dissipated and a glum misery set in.

"But if you did care," he said, "which you don't, I'd say not to worry."

"Well, I don't. And I'm not worried."

"Because she likes you."

"Starshine can have her," I simpered.

"The truth about Starshine is that she never satisfies anybody. That's why she's so good at seducing them. She's like a gift."

"I assume you're speaking from experience."

"I only speak from experience."

I snorted half-heartedly.

"Look at me, Jack." I did, although he still gazed at the stars. "Life is experience."

"No it's not," I said. He didn't turn; he was still chasing the stars with a dreamy look on his face. I couldn't tell if he was listening, but I went on anyway: "Life is value. Experience is just a way of learning what you should value and when you should value it."

He seemed impressed but then shook his head, his thoughts catching up.

"If there's one thing you should have learned, it's this: sometimes the right thing to do is the wrong thing to do, and sometimes the wrong thing to do is the right thing to do. The moral universe has a black hole at its center and the best you can do is enjoy the ride into outer space before you're sucked in. Values are just a way of judging your experiences. They can be wrong. Your experiences aren't."

I tried to disagree but the buzz came back. Imagining Gammy in the arms of Starshine was not entirely unpleasant and I felt the burn of desire return.

Jerome levitated from his chair, came around, and squatted beside me, folding his arms on top of mine. He had a funny smile on his face. His arms were light. I was not sure what was happening.

"Kiss me, Jack."

"What?"

"I don't have to repeat myself."

"Yes. You do."

He darted up until his mouth was an inch from mine and stopped. I didn't pull back. I could smell the grass on his breath. His lips were parted, his eyes barely open. Without knowing what I was doing, I leaned towards him until my lips grazed his. Neither one of us pressed forward. Our mouths touched, the dry but sticky friction of lips; his breath was hot. He pushed forward, his lips hard against mine, the tip of his tongue pushed through my lips. A moist mouth, a willful tongue, the unfamiliar graze of stubble.

His hand reached around my head and we kissed harder in thick gulps; I shivered, warm and cool in the night air, my legs trembled wildly. I ran my arm under his jacket, under the steely length of the scabbard, around his thin, cool waist, and pulled him closer. Without taking his mouth from mine, he slid across the chair, straddling me, the hot diagonal solidities in our crotches meeting with hard aches. He paused for a fraction of a second then kissed harder again, our faces pressing together; with a tender gasp, he pulled back, leaving his forehead against mine. He breathed fast, his features in a passionate scowl. With one hand holding my neck, he kissed my cheek, beside my nose, my upper lip, each kiss accompanied by a delicious tickle that caught the breath in my throat; I found my hand running down the pebbles of his spine into the smooth small of his back, then pressing under his belt to the hot crack of his slim, buttocks. He kissed my ear, tickling it with soft pecks and sucking in my ear lobe; my face tingled; he kissed my neck, harder and harder, sucking on my neck, licking it, sucking again. My groin burned, rubbing against his as we pushed against each other in erratic thrusts, out of rhythm with his kisses; arcing delights of pain from my neck ran straight down to the pit of my stomach; we pushed crotch against crotch with pulses of fervor, I felt myself getting nearer and nearer to coming, I shook with an uncontrollable burning as we fell into a grinding rhythm; my groin and my thighs quivered and ebbed in searing flows, his crotch jamming against mine, his bar-like cock against the underside of my own; the sucking against my neck gave way to a sharp pinching as I started to come, the pin-prick stabbing in my neck making my coming peak into prolonged shuddering and one, two, three hot flows

I half-screamed and, twitching uncontrollably, pushed him off; he fell onto his knees, and I doubled up in the chair, panting, my prick still jerking wetly and burningly in my jeans with the last gushes.

"What the *hell*?" I reached for my crotch and my neck. Both were damp, but my hand came away from my neck dark. I stood up and almost keeled over.

I looked down. Jerome was kneeling in front of me, his mouth bloody, his eyes shut tight; he licked his smeared lips, ran his fingers over his glossy-black chin and sucked my dribbling blood from his fingertips.

"Jerome, are you a—? You're a—?"

With his other hand, the one he wasn't licking, he fumbled for his sword. Shakily, I picked up my rifle and waved it at him; my throbbing prick gave off a last few squeezing twitches.

"You're a *vampire*?"

He bowed over, feebly grabbing for the sword on his back.

"Oh my God!" I let the rifle droop and stared up at the sky. "Am I now a vampire? Did you just make me a vampire too?"

"No," he said, drawing in deep breaths, "You have to drink the blood . . . to become a vampire . . . you have to drink vampire blood . . . it's a choice."

Deep down, a miniscule, enormous part of me was disappointed. Then another thought struck me. "The others!"

VII.

We tied Jerome, Ophelia, and Starshine with the rope I'd found in the shop, looping it around their limp waists, wrists and ankles. The first time we did it, we hogtied them, which felt mean and spiteful, especially because they looked so small: it was like hog-tying elves or Japanese people. We released them and kept them at gunpoint but their strength was returning, their eyes glinted, and we got the jitters, so we coiled them like three bugs in an impromptu spider's web of rope, lashed between the grating, a wooden table, a chair, and the sofa.

When we were done, we stood sheepishly by the fireplace. Nobody knew what to say. Gammy, Rafael and I had bruises around the oozing holes in our necks. I looked at the ash, the charcoaled log, the warm light of the embers. I was feeling better about some things and confused about others. I caught Gammy's eye and knew she felt the same way.

We waited in an astringent silence that was hesitant and awkward at first; as the conversation we wanted to have failed to take place, the silence became a recrimination, until it was too late to have the conversation at all, at which point the silence became mushy and oppressive.

Finally, Rafael spoke in a low voice. "The issue, as I see it, is whether we need to kill them or not." He rubbed his neck and added, musingly, "But can they even be killed?"

"A stake through their hearts?" suggested Praj with a fierce sneer. Trish was not the only one casting bitter glances at Jerome. Praj was glaring at him. That suddenly explained a lot. I felt quite proud, nipping Praj and Trish to his fancy. In fact, they were probably in here discussing Dungeons and Dragons just a few minutes before.

"Let's end them," hissed Trish.

"It's too morbid and personal," said Rafael. "Killing zombies, werewolves, and lizard monsters is one thing—"

"What about Zachary?" I asked.

"Yes, the same thing as zombies and werewolves. I didn't make love with Zachary."

"You made love with Ophelia?"

"Of course. Didn't you make love with Jerome?"

I wasn't sure how to answer. Gammy looked away. Trish was rigid with fury.

Praj took a deep breath and intervened. "If we don't kill them," he said, "they might kill us. But I agree that killing people after . . ." he paused, swallowed, and went on, "making love with them could have its own consequences."

"That's right," I said, looking across the room at Jerome, who was pretending not to listen. "Values!"

A while later, when the fire was dead, and the only light in the room was coming from the first gray hint of dawn, I went over to them. The room was quiet and the air hung heavy with fire smoke. They sat like spurned lovers, gloomy and mum, although perhaps their moody silence was a variant on contempt; I'm not quite sure what we were like: busybodies in the late night, occupying ourselves to avoid thinking about what had happened; ignorant fools who had no idea what had happened; or perhaps we were the spurned lovers?

Starshine and Ophelia contemplated the inklings of dawn. Jerome looked up with the casual hatred of a student hauled to the front of class by the most loathed teacher.

"We saw you in daylight," I said.

He shrugged insolently.

"Are you real vampires, or are you hip vampires manqués?"

"What the hell is a hip vampire monkey?"

I tried to explain what I meant. "Are you real vampires or did you just read a few too many books aimed at teenage girls?"

"Is there a difference?" he sneered.

"Yes."

He rolled his eyes; the teacher-student relationship was becoming trying, especially after what we had been through. I kicked him quite hard in the thigh, harder than I meant to. He grunted and slouched into the ropes around him.

"You're a real vampire?"

He nodded.

"How old are you?"

"You have no idea," he scoffed.

"That's why I'm asking."

"I was born seven hundred years ago."

"You look good for your age."

"So do you."

"Can you eat garlic?"

"Yes."

"So why do they say vampires can't eat garlic?"

"I didn't think you were this stupid, Jack."

"What am I missing? Other than about a pint of blood?"

"Why don't vampires eat garlic?" he said, mimicking me, and then: "We seduce people. If we had garlic breath, do you think people would want us kissing their mouths?" He looked narrowly at me. "Or their ears? Their cheeks? Their necks?"

"Well then," I said, blushing despite my blood loss, "what about daylight? Doesn't the sun turn you to dust?"

"It doesn't kill us but if you're going to live for a thousand years, you might want to avoid sun damage."

"Does holy water burn your skin?"

"Everybody cringes when they're doused with water."

I scratched my head and sighed. "For all your poetry, Jerome, you're quite an empiricist. All the lore and myths around vampires for hundreds of years have practical explanations?"

This time, his smirk wasn't affected.

"I've learned over time," he said, "to give you humans answers that you can understand. If someone asked me about garlic or sunlight fifty years ago, I wouldn't have said the same thing. Nor did I give the same answers a hundred years ago or two hundred years ago. Further back, it gets murky."

He smiled sadly and opened his mouth, but I was worried about what he would say. And one other question was niggling me, so I interrupted.

"When we first met you, you were surrounded by bodies. Were they killed by you or by the werewolves?"

He closed his mouth. I guess I knew the answer. I left him alone.

In the dewy light of the morning, we took their sword and daggers and stuck them into the moist turf by the silver willow and we pushed over their motorcycles: not very elaborate means of delaying their escape, more schoolchildish than anything else, but it would add a minute or two to our head start.

Trish and Praj sat in the back seat of my car. I kicked away three cans of beans left lying beside the road and got in. I had to stop myself from rubbing my sore neck. We were waiting for Rafael and Gammy, who were balancing a smoldering log against the rope: when it burned through, there would be enough slack for them to uncoil, shuffle together, untie each other's hands. Rafael had cleverly let air out of their tires, not enough to make the bikes unridable, but enough to make the wheels boggy and dampen their movement. By my estimation, these tricks gave us a twenty-minute head start, but at the same time we would not leave them vulnerable to other monsters. It was a satisfactory compromise, which is to say, unsatisfactory.

As soon as Gammy and Rafael bundled in, I hit the ignition, the car spluttered to life, and we headed away from the country club. The car felt unusually sluggish. When we got to the main road at the end of the drive, the car shuddered, whined, and coughed; the engine froze, the steering wheel locked into place. I turned the ignition off and tried to start it up again. The engine did not turn over. Click, click, click.

I got out, flushed with fear and confusion. The sun was up and the morning was crystal clear. Running like a moat between the road and the edge of the club's grounds was a trickling stream. A dragonfly buzzed out of the reeds and hovered over the water.

The others got out, glaring at me like the breakdown was my fault. I walked around the car looking for a clue as to why it had died. A trail of sticky brown fluid dribbled down from the gas tank. I touched my finger to the goo and brought it to my nose.

"Little bastards!"

"What?"

"Those miniscule freaks put beans in my gas tank."

A few minutes later, the vampires came down the road from the clubhouse, stiff with anger, wobbling on motorcycles with deflated tires. Jerome held his sword out like a cavalry lieutenant on his mount; Ophelia and Starshine gripped their handlebars, daggers between their teeth. They pulled to a stop twenty feet away and revved their bikes. Our guns were out but we pointed them to the ground.

We glowered across the stretch of gravel for a minute, two minutes, three minutes, each one of us taking in the other's faces, except for Ophelia and Rafael who looked only at each other. The three pale, snarling moon faces peered at us, but under their anger was fatigue and defeat. If they charged, we could shoot them down.

"Jerome," I shouted.

"Yes, Jack?"

"No bloodshed today?"

He glanced down, then at me, and nodded pertly. "Okay, Jack." He lowered his sword so that the tip trailed in the grit, revved his bike, and trundled down the corridor between the high trees; their eyes were set on the road behind us. They biked towards us, Jerome bringing his sword up over his head and slipping it into its sheath along his spine.

We glared at them but they ignored us. The anger and defeat was gone from their faces. They were now placid and uninterested, if evidently conscious of being watched—less a forced obliviousness than a charade of carelessness, as if we were tourists from the boonies gawking at the local wild kids.

But we might as well have vanished. We were forgotten. I felt a pang of hurt, like I had ended a relationship only to discover that the person I dumped had already met someone else. I muttered a slur as Jerome passed and immediately felt ashamed, hoping that nobody heard. I was not brave enough to say it loudly, but I did say it, and so my cowardice was itself audible.

Jerome did not flinch, his expression did not change; I

will never know if that was because he didn't hear or didn't care.

They wobbled out onto the main road and went left, heading back the way we had come.

VIII.

On the Seventh Day, God rested. The monsters didn't. For them, this was a midsummer picnic that wouldn't end. And we were their cold cuts, their hot dogs and their burgers, except they ate us raw; we were their cider and their brewskis, served at body temperature; we lit up the sky with fireworks, flares and big explosions, we amused them with our screams and our death-dances. Not once did I see a grinning werewolf, a laid-back zombie, or a monster lizard lying on its back, chewing a blade of grass and watching the clouds pass overhead, but I swear they were enjoying themselves. There was a vivid elation in their attacks. I suppose that being able to kill without fearing death was a state of ecstasy, and when their own death came, it was only extinction. For us, whatever pleasure there was in killing them became as routine and unrewarding as their deaths: if the first battles burst with the evil joys of a toddler stamping on ants, the later ones were as exhilarating as using scissors to remove weeds with the unhappy realization that the scissors were getting blunt and you'd only cleared a small patch in a never-ending garden.

I drained the engine, refilled it with the last of our spare petrol, and managed to get the car started, although it was not happy. We resumed our drive to Chicago, the car acting out with occasional threats that it wanted to give up.

A slow hour later, we passed through another suburb of fancy deserted houses and came to a grass park as big as a city block; in one corner was a playground: a slide, a swing set, and monkey bars over a mat of woodchips.

We pulled over just past a flatbed truck with Kentucky plates, its body lacy with rust, its windows opaque with caramel-colored dust.

What made us think that someone in a wealthy suburban neighborhood, where houses sold for millions of dollars and the few cars left in the driveways were the latest model, had abandoned an ancient flatbed next to their pristine park and playground? It lounged amongst the elms and sycamores like a pervert in a trench coat.

But the world had changed. We were losing touch with the sense of reality that had comforted us before the monster uprising, the cotton sheets of explanation and the narrative duvets we inherited, generations-old and threadbare but sufficient to keep us encased in their gauzy skeins of inherited wisdom, sheltering us from the inexplicable phosphorescence of night. Stripped of these, we trudged through the lit darkness, covering our nakedness with our hands, our faces bent down, and accepted whatever we saw at our feet as true for what it was, no matter how often these truths turned out to be lies.

The sun was shining and we wanted to sit in the fresh air for lunch. Without giving the truck a second look, we got out. Rafael scouted out a patch of grass. Trish and Gammy joined him with food and a sheet, which they flapped open. They lay down around the sheet and opened up jars of pasta sauce and sliced a loaf of bread that was almost not stale. In the sunbeams and the quiet, with squirrels rustling in branches far overhead, there was a crushingly pleasant sense of normality being restored.

I stood with Praj beside the car. I wanted to ask him a question but didn't know if I should. Nobody would have thought to ask him because of the dominating impression that he was just another nerdy, philosophizing East Asian, which somehow precluded any other identities, especially sexualized ones. Maybe he wanted it that way. But I was the grown-up, the adult, and I needed him to know that if he wanted to talk about it, I was there for him.

"Praj, as the leader of our gang—"

"Are you the leader?" he asked, quite seriously.

"Yes, of course," I said. "Who else would it be?"

Praj gave me a frown like it was obvious. "Gammy."

"Gammy?" I said, loud enough that she, Trish and Rafael looked over at us. "Gammy?" I hissed. "What do you mean, 'Gammy'?"

"She's always the one figuring everything out. And shooting things before they kill us."

"But I'm the leader," I said, staggered.

"Okay, Jack," said Praj, quite campily. "If that's the way

you want it."

He gave a friendly shrug like the conversation was over and went over to join the picnic. Stunned, I walked to the swings and sat. The kids spoke, casting glances at me, until Gammy got up, came across the grass and took the swing next to me. We pushed off. Without thinking about it, I remembered how to pump. It was like being a child again. We kicked higher and higher, rushing forwards and backwards; back and forth, we whirred up towards a cloudless sky then backwards to the other apogee, to look straight down into the scatter of woodchips laid out to soften a fall. At each apex, we turned to each other from behind taut chains and something unspoken was being said, something was being shared, and I knew that I was falling in love, and we kept going—until we heard Rafael cry out for us, a desperate shout, my name, her name. In that order. We ground to a halt, dragging ruts in the woodchips, and tumbled from the swings.

Rafael, Trish and Praj were sitting bolt upright like rabbits who spotted a fox on the other side of the field. The bread in their hands dripped pasta sauce. Out of nowhere had come three men. They stood between us and our car.

The one in the middle was a barrel-chested guy in dungarees. Strands of hair hung over his ears and he had a bald pate shining pink like he had been scalped *in utero*. The other two were wiry, one of them tall, the other short, both of them with greasy hair sprouting out from under truckers' baseball caps. All three men held shotguns at their hips.

I looked over our picnic spread, at the pasta sauce, the bread, the cloth—yes, we had left our guns in the car. The awful silence was interrupted; the passenger window in the flatbed creaked down. A woman leaned out and directed a very long pistol towards us. She squinted down the site, using both hands to hold the gun steady.

We raised our hands. This pleased them.

"Y'all monsters?" the bald burly man barked.

"No," I yelled back. "You?"

"Nah," he said. "You seen any golems?"

"What do you mean 'golems'?" I called back.

"Y'ain't seen 'em yet?" He smirked like we were freshman at our first kegger. One of his buddies kicked the ground with a dismissive grunt.

"Do you mean zombies?" I shouted.

"Hell no, not zombies. Zombies look like zombies. The golem look like they made of clay."

"No, we haven't seen golems," I said.

The one in the middle shook his head derisively; he tucked his shotgun in the crook of his arm and rearranged his junk in his dungarees. I was pretty sure he mouthed "virgins" to his friends, who laughed and shook their heads.

The need to one-up them was irresistible.

"Is 'golems' the plural of golem?" I shouted. "Or is golem its own plural? It sounds like it should be 'goli' or 'golickides.'"

The burly man pretended to think and gave his junk another tug. "Nah, we jes' call 'em golems. 'N then we kill 'em."

"Have you perchance seen werewolves?" said Rafael, also aggravated. These yokels were emasculating us. We'd battled demons spewing out of the mouth of hell, we'd taken on monsters that had destroyed entire cities; we weren't in the mood to die at the hands of a bunch of inbred rednecks with jock itch. Rafael sensed vulnerability. "What about our lupine foe?" he shouted again.

"Ah killed over a hunerd," the one in the middle said. One of his henchmen punctuated the statement with a jet of tobacco spit.

"That's our ballpark," said Praj, joining in. A glob of red sauce dripped from the bread in his hand onto his shoulder. "What about godzillas?"

"The lizards?"

"Yes," said Praj.

"We seen 'em."

"We killed one," I said. "*I* killed one. Bare-handed."

"Jes' a one? Hmm," the leader looked up at the sky, calculating. "Four. Yessirday. Tha's not countin' the ones we got in—where was it, Mitch, was it Carbondale?"

"Yuzzuh," said Mitch. He squeezed out another arc of tobacco, this time towards us.

186

"Wow," I said. I let my arms fall. As the only one in our group who had killed a lizard-monster, I was in a position to admire their accomplishment. I knew how hard they were to kill. "That's impressive."

"Come o'er here, nice 'n' slow," said the one in the middle. "You kin bring down your arms. This ain't a hold-up. Jes' don' do nuttin' stupid."

We took a few cautious steps forward. "

"What about water creatures?" Praj tried.

"Too many to count, more'n twenty. Mitch here e'en tried to eat one. Thought it might taste like crawfish."

The men frowned at the memory like redneck epicures wondering if the roast squirrel hadn't needed a touch more truffle oil.

"And?" I asked, "Was it good?"

"They flesh jes' shriveled up on the barbeque," said Mitch with a pout, "and I doan wanna to eat no goddammed Black Lagoon sushi."

We stopped about ten feet away from them and faced off, at an impasse.

They had no intention of killing us, or at least no desire to do so; a shared misery overcame us. We wanted to be allies. But we couldn't. Maybe it was literacy, maybe it was education, maybe it was our cosmopolitanism and their rural genetic homogeneity, maybe it was just old-fashioned class, but something unbridgeably deep and wide fissured the ten paces of Illinois soil between us.

The one in the middle brightened. "'N we killed three vampires," he said. "Picked 'em off their motorbikes one by one, jes' a few hours ago."

He went to his flatbed truck and pulled out a sword.

It was Jerome's.

IX.

I can't put into words what I felt at that moment. Sorrow? Relief? Despair? Maybe there's not a single word for it, a feeling so essentially human and yet personal; maybe it is what we are always alluding to when we speak of heartbreak as something more than just the pang of being rejected. Agonies of loss under the surface of my being, swarming like a colony of ants in an underground nest, poured from my pores in wriggling black threads that widened into gushing streams, every zigzagging skittering ant another memory, another piece of me fleeing forever. For my entire life I'd guarded that surface, parrying any sharp object that could pierce the baked mud coating my soul, but I wasn't prepared for Jerome's sword, and it cut through the clay, into the nest below, and the ants came flooding out.

"Jack?"

A hand stroked my forehead. Blurry light overhead. Shadows swaying like dancers' arms in a bright yellow beam. They resolved into branches waving in the wind.

"You fainted."

It was Gammy's voice.

"Are you okay?"

I struggled to get up but didn't have the strength. My head was sore. I closed my eyes.

"Stay still." With the back of her fingers, she combed the hair from my forehead. "When you fell, you hit your head." She paused. "They've gone. They left us the car and a jar of sauce and two rifles and two pistols. They took the rest—the food, the guns, the ammunition, grenades, your laptop. We couldn't do anything."

I could have rushed them. If I hadn't fainted. I groaned.

"Did they get the jar of meat gravy?"

She nodded blurrily.

"I was saving that," I said.

"Hush, we're still alive. Do you get that, Jack? We're alive."

"I'm such—I'm such—"

"You're not. Whatever you're going to say you are, you're not."

"A loser."

"No," she laughed lightly. "You're a person. A real person. You just never let us see it."

I got up onto my elbows. She was kneeling beside me.

"So until I fainted you thought I was a loser?"

She put her hand on my chest. Rafael, Praj and Trish were sitting in the car with the doors open.

"No. You just weren't real. You were a half-baked idea."

I was still coming to my senses but her words hit me hard.

A half-baked idea.

It was true.

"That's the worst thing anybody's ever said to me."

"That was Rafael's phrase."

"He's such a dick." I rubbed my eyes. "What do you think?"

"I just thought you were sad. But Rafael put it better. He always does."

"So you all think I'm a 'half-baked idea'?" I snorted; it made my head hurt. Nothing hurts like the truth.

"No, you're not." She paused delicately. "Did you love him?"

"Rafael?"

"No. Jerome."

I looked at her like she was crazy. "I barely knew him. And I'm not . . ." I trailed off.

She shifted onto her haunches, taking her hand from my chest.

I gazed up at the branches. The leaves were turning. It was autumn. Again? Nothing made sense. Maybe it never made sense before and I just hadn't paid attention; but now I was paying attention and it definitely didn't make sense.

Gammy sang a short refrain then cut her song short. Not because she had something to say but because she was about to cry. She made unhappy expressions to hold back the tears.

When she was in control again, she spoke.

"What happened with Starshine and Jerome and Ophelia—it wasn't the same as with the other monsters. When they rode away, I thought I saw the future. For the first time, I had hope. We'd come out of the valley. It wouldn't be peace but it wouldn't be war either, it wouldn't be about death and killing, it would be about how we see each other. Do you understand?"

I said I did but I wasn't sure. She continued. "The game I wrote, *War 'Sister*—you couldn't win. There was nothing to win. It was about going forward." Her hand brushed against my forehead and stroked my cheek. "Nobody believed someone like me could write a game like that."

"Because you're black? People are idiots that way."

"No," she said, and shook her head, annoyed. "Because I was the most competitive kid in my class. If I didn't get the top score, I left school like I was chased by bees, I went home and studied harder. I *had* to be chosen to sing solo in my church choir. If I didn't make the basketball team, I practiced until I couldn't lift the ball anymore. Everything was about winning. I wasn't competing with other kids or what others expected of me, I was competing with something inside me. That's why I never won, even if I did. And I left things behind. Like who I was or why I wanted to win in the first place. I didn't want to come to Notre Dame. It was my safety school. It was as if the other schools saw me for who I was and passed on me. It just made me madder. When I got to Notre Dame, I kept doing it. Competing, fighting to win, I was so unhappy. Until one day I woke up and thought, I want there to be a place where you don't have to win, I want to make a place where the best way to be is to try to make peace."

"That doesn't sound like you."

"But it is. Until I wrote that game, I was just a half-baked idea too. And then the monsters came. It felt personal. I cracked the code with *War 'Sister* but instead of a world of peace, the monsters came, and I'm fighting for my life again and it just feels like everything I won has been lost again. Like it's all over this time."

"Jerome said that life isn't over."

She kissed me on the forehead and then whispered in my ear, "Was that before or after you fucked him?"

We laughed.

"It's strange," I said. "I miss him."

"I know what you mean."

"Vampire sex is good, isn't it?"

"Yes."

We looked at each other.

"So," I said.

"Yes," she said.

She helped me to my feet. Arm-in-arm we hobbled to the car.

Rafael was staring towards the trees, a smile on his lips from something somebody had said, held there by sadness. I gripped his shoulder. I didn't have to say anything. Nor did he.

X.

And after a millennia-long courtship the wedding ceremony was conducted and savagely consummated, but there was no honeymoon, only a quick descent into the bored horrors of everyday married life, while the spawn of the union took over.

The war between the fallen and the falling was waged, and whichever we were, we were losing.

Everything changed.

Our concept of space changed. What we thought was our rightful inheritance—the land beneath our feet, the sky above, the oceans, the rivers—was ripped from our expectant hands and we grabbed at nothing; at a loss, empty-handed, we were wretched in our unexpected poverty and pathetic in our resentment. This land was no longer our land. The world was no longer our world. Maps, compasses, directions, road signs: these were old jokes, out-of-date punchlines, things that only made sense in a context that was gone. They didn't so much hide as advertise that even though the earth was smashed with our footprint, it was no longer stamped with our ownership. We were lost.

Our concept of time changed. No matter how fast we moved, time was sucked into the void; hours passed and we were still driving through the same cornfield, or a whole afternoon was gone, every conversation we'd had whisked out of existence like we'd been hypnotized then were snapped awake, unsure if we'd been barking like dogs for the amusement of whatever deities, sprites, pucks, or faeries were watching the bloody entertainment from behind clouds, ears of corn, or tucked into the sky's cheeks. What of natural time? Long before the monster uprising, most of us forgot that spring brought fruit, summer lettuce and tomatoes, autumn garlic and apples, and winter the root vegetables; but the ancient cycle still revolved inside us; now there was estrangement from natural time, based as it was on the unnatural nature of our agriculture, our feasts, our religions, an idea of time wrapped up like a present, and for all its promises of mortality and decay, always promising bounty and return. Gone. Gone. Gone. What is time without time? The weather. It was warm or cold, windy or not, the earth was sooty and the sky was gray, or it was cold and unforgivingly clear; there was no sense of what was supposed to come next. We were out of time. But unlike space, we had never owned time; we had just bypassed it with a different kind of contempt.

Our contempt for space was vicious and violent. Our contempt for time was patronizing. Without our contempt, metaphors popped like bubbles. The wheel of life was shattered. The clock stopped, though the cuckoo didn't. When space and time fall, so does meaning. And so our concept of humanity changed. Culture and human bonds, poetry and speech? When we were not fending off monstrous armies marching in committed chaos, we were spectators at the flowering of unthought.

The worst loss was music. It was gone, as surely as the film you saw when you were thirteen and thought was amazing turns out to be crap when you watch it again in your twenties. All the symphonies and concertos were nothing more than an orchestra tuning up, whining and bleating around an A, before the cacophonous opera; the music of Bach, Mozart, Brahms, Mahler, Wagner, Sondheim, the Beatles and chanting Indians were scribbly tunes and throat-clearings; Bernstein and Toscanini were morons preening in the pit, before the arrival of a monster maestro with a sharp baton to conduct a chorus of screams.

And the least loss? I wasn't being humble in thinking it might be me. I began to think that it was possible, entirely possible, that it was. In my life before the monster uprising, I hated the reviewers of my novels for missing one of the most important points in my work: they looked for moral meaning where there wasn't any. You could find allusions to all of the great American catastrophes, from slavery and genocide to rising blackwaters and earthquakes, but at no point did I argue they were self-imposed; I treated them as accidents beyond the scope of the individual human, just as an ancient might have relegated them to the fates; they were accidents of geography and history and bumbling malevolence in people long dead; and that is all they were in my writing: swelling tides and tectonic faults bestowed upon us from the past, and, in my books, functional: color, detail, context. Surely amoral dross in narrative form was the smallest, pettiest thing we lost.

And knowing this, I chafed with regret for every word I had written. Fielding called critics "clerks": pencil-pushing bureaucrats in the literary supplement, lacking spirit, with peevishly-educated minds and a lack of imagination. What writer failed to inherit his contempt? The suckers and sycophants amongst the critics did as well, and wrote in embarrassment. But the critics had been right about me. The reviewers of my novels had been right all along. Their futile quest to find in my novels something to hold onto, something that spoke of consequence, something morally eerie and ethically uncanny, had been an attempt to save my writing from what it was: banal.

I had an excuse. I told myself that to be adored meant collaboration and appeasement, to be rejected meant oblivion. My role, as I saw it, was to forsake this spatial and temporal relationship, this hegemony of opinion; my job was to forsake the problem not as insoluble, but as the problem itself. Trying to solve the problem *was* the problem. The choice was either to become the problem by pretending to solve the problem, or to turn away and, instead, to write with integrity. To write with integrity. Integrity was what I strove for, and if it was morally banal, so be it.

But if my concepts of time, space, and humanity changed, so did my concept of morality itself. Lost in space but moving; alone but with love; compelled to write but wholly aware of my irrelevance; shedding myself of the half-baked idea of who I was, I underwent a conversion. It wasn't hallucinatory, it wasn't glorious. It was just a grim encounter with a reality that wasn't packaged in human space, human time, or humanity itself. And what did I see? That integrity was not an escape from banal morality; everything was moral. Because everything was fault. The greatest excuse humanity ever made was its never-ending cry of "it's not my fault." That was humanity's heartbeat: *it's not my fault, it's not my fault, it's not my fault, it's not my fault.* Yes, it was our fault. Every bit of it. Ours. Mine. *Mine.*

I had just been the most minor scribe, duly jotting down the precious, the cute, the whimsical, the fortuitous and the felicitous, whatever my muse—humanity at its most mediocre, immersed in reflexive stories, a dull storyteller half-wood, half-spit, all arrogance—told me to write, with a few references to events that might make the reader think, "yes, this is significant." I didn't follow damaged Achilles or perverse Odysseus, I chose petty despots who neither won battles nor lost them, but who survived, basking in a glory they did not deserve. The heroes founded not in significance but in fault were comical to me, and if I emulated them in my prose it was with an eye on pastiche, appealing to those who would see the ridiculous in them. What was it I said as a writer? I said yes. I said yes to integrity, to reflexive virtue, I said yes to narratives that did no harm, I said yes to human mediocrity, I said yes to history as background. But couldn't I justify myself? Couldn't I say that the integrity of "yes" is the root of morality? After all, isn't morality itself a resounding "yes" to the universe?

No.

Morality is not affirmation; it is not manifested in agreeing to abide by a law. Morality is about saying no; it's about saying no to those who stomp and kill in its name; it's about saying no to the options you think you've been given by a numinous deity or by its secular alternative, society. Morality is about saying no to what prevents you from living with real integrity: broken integrity, pitiable integrity. Giving a dollar to charity while stealing from the public purse is not living with integrity, writing hard while children die is not living with integrity, caring without doing is not living with integrity, bombing and extinguishing life and emptying the oceans is not living with integrity, lying about yourself in the belief that history will forget your lies is not living with integrity, justifying yourself when everything is fault is not living with integrity, letting yourself off the hook with pious self-congratulatory faith is not living with integrity, writing yes is not integrity, but what did people do? Did we say no over the course of our lives? No. We said yes, we said it—*yes, yes, yes*—however much our crass enthusiasm and petty zest for little flourishes and cheap kindnesses and the boo-hoos of compassion ate away at our souls. And finally the world said, "Alright then, have it your way: yes to everything. Yes to zombies, yes to your most stupid of nightmare fairytales, yes to blood-curdling stories your parents told you, yes to the absolute annihilation you've flirted with, yes to your cowardly, self-righteous emptiness, yes, yes, yes."

Huh. So that's what it sounded like to the rest of the universe when they had to watch us say "yes, yes, yes."

"Yes."

We had never worked the muscle of no. It was a withered strand of meat inside us, easily hacked; without real integrity, in our banal integrities, we shirked our responsibilities to ourselves, to space, and to time, in countless numberless ways, and when we were stranded, we had nothing left; and then we whimpered "no" to the monsters, and expected another outcome?

The drive was slow going. We went through a township of bungalows and two-story homes; no mansions, just a sprawl of cheap houses with aluminum siding, a few shopping centers with discount muffler shops and chain pizzerias and donut stores, a factory whose broken sign suggested it once made machine parts. It was harder hit than anything we had passed so far. The houses were burned out, corpses lay in grotesque angles in the gutters and on square lawns, stray dogs trotted with their heads down along the side streets. We went down a street that looked like the aftermath of a riot: an overturned fire truck with its enormous fat black wheels sticking in the air, police cars crunched up on the curbs, broken glass, smoldering fires. The rioters had apparently won.

Rafael said he was hungry again, in that chipper voice of his, as if we just passing through any old town on a road trip. I told him to shut up—we were all hungry, we were all tired. I didn't think much of it but Rafael grabbed the steering wheel.

We swerved, I slammed on the brakes, and we screeched to a halt.

"Stop telling me to shut up!" screamed Rafael.

"Christ, Rafael, you prick. You almost killed us with that stunt."

I punched his arm. He unstrapped his buckle and charged over the gear stick, grabbing at my shirt. Trish and Gammy jumped forward from the back seat, squeezing through into the front. Gammy held me against the driver's side door, Trish pinned Rafael back.

"Calm down," Gammy snapped.

Trish said, "Stop it, you two."

Rafael and I glared at each other around the women. Gammy's face was next to mine. She was straining to hold me. I could smell her sweet and sour breath, her soft cheek against my stubble, her hair tickling my forehead.

"Say you're sorry," she hissed.

"I'm supposed to say sorry!? He almost killed us!"

Trish was holding Rafael's wrists on the parking break. Her top button had popped in the struggle, and I could see most of her right breast, all the way to her pink raspberry nipple.

"Rafael," she said, with the same maternal tone of certainty, "say you're sorry too. You did almost kill us."

The stand-off lasted for one more resentful, dignity-preserving minute. Finally, I relented.

"Okay, I'm sorry I tapped your shoulder."

"You punched it," sniffed Rafael, rubbing his bicep, "and you told me to shut up."

"Say sorry for telling him to shut up," said Gammy.

"I'm sorry I told you to shut up."

Gammy and Trish relaxed and we loosened ourselves.

"I'm sorry I grabbed the steering wheel," said Rafael. He glowered at me and added, "But you've got to stop belittling us."

"Oh shut up!" I said.

"He said it again!" Rafael screamed victoriously. He lurched around Trish, poking my nose with his outstretched fingers.

I tried to swat him. "You little English rat!"

There was a tussle of bodies and then a blast that left our ears ringing. We went quiet and Gammy tensed against me—Rafael had shot her! I gasped with righteous agony as Gammy died in my arms. The smell of gun smoke filled the car.

"Everybody calm down." Praj held a smoking pistol out the window. "Let's find somewhere to stop and afterwards, when we've eaten, we'll all say sorry."

Gammy—still very much alive—and Trish slumped back. Rafael and I looked ahead. My nose hurt where he poked it. I opened my mouth to say how stupid it was for Praj to fire his gun but Gammy sensed my intention and sighed, "Drive, Jack. Just drive."

We left the township to the dogs and the wreckage and moved on through the suburbs festering on the edge of Chicago's wound. Some were worse off than others. To the extent that we noticed and judged them, that was how: the number of corpses in the streets, how many homes were reduced to smoking ruins, whether we saw a pack of zombies huddled over red and salty remains. We were getting low on gasoline, our nerves were threadbare.

Gammy hummed, a soft sound we could barely hear at first, but she got louder as if she knew we wanted to hear her. For the first time since the uprising, music made sense. The yo-yo of hope spun upwards. All wasn't lost.

We came to another forest preserve, a parcel of nature with rustic wooden signposts, tall trees, and tangled green foliage around a wide river, and stopped by a concrete dam where people spent their Sundays fishing for bass and drinking beers out of cans they carried home to recycle or tossed into the froth. Brown water seeped over the edge of the dam into scummy foam swarming with late-season mosquitoes.

We got out and stretched.

"Trish and I will prepare lunch," said Praj. "You three make sure everything's safe."

"Do you think they should be together?" asked Trish, as

though Rafael and I weren't even there. It was very infantilizing. I was about to tell her to go suck on her own tittie, but Praj answered.

"No," he said, "we're a team. They've got to learn that."

Chastened, Rafael and I set out under Gammy's supervision. We walked to the dam and along the river. I was quite glad I didn't say anything to Trish about her breasts; it was one of those moments in adulthood when only the intervention of another adult prevents you from being utterly childish. Larry, my agent, had tried to help me from being utterly childish about my writing. He saw the stagnation, he saw my temperament and cowardice, he saw where my career was going, and, when it was gone and I was trying to recover, he listened to me when I told him how I planned to start all over and write Young Adult fiction.

"Because my fiction *is* young adult," I said. "I *am* a young adult."

"Yeah," he said.

"No, it isn't," he said.

"No, you're not," he said.

But I wasn't listening.

Gammy walked between Rafael and me. We wandered over the carpet of leaves. Her hand brushed mine and I felt her fingers linger; I took her hand in mine and it felt right.

About a quarter of a mile in, I spotted a boy fishing along the banks of the river, framed by the hanging yellow threads of a willow. I stopped. Was he a vision? A hallucination?

But Gammy and Rafael stopped as well. Gammy let go of my hand. The boy was no more than a patch of fabric, a baseball cap, two skinny arms, and two toothpick legs kicking pebbles in the inch-deep water around his ankles. A rod poked over the water, held in place by stones.

Ten feet out, floating in the silver coins of reflected sunlight on the matte brown surface, was a red bobber. The bobber ducked below the water. The little Tom Sawyer didn't stir. His line went taut but he didn't jerk the rod to catch the fish or even put a hand on the reel. Whatever nibbled the hook was soon free and the bobber popped out, spun a few times, and righted itself. The boy still did not move.

Just in front of us, a man emerged from behind a tree, holding a bough out of his way. He had thin hair and round spectacles over ruddy cheeks and was wearing a blue business shirt untucked over gray slacks. The first impression he gave was of the calm but slight air of a banker or an accountant, accompanied by the creepy feeling that this pale, graceless, but stealthy man had been watching the boy as well; the second impression was of profound misery—not the slump of defeat but the awful compulsion to act against one's will, sketched in a look of terrible distaste on his face. I unslung my rifle. He took a few paces towards us. He held a carving knife in one hand—but his arm was limp by his side.

"Who are you?" he asked with dull curiosity.

"We're just passing through," I said. "Who are you?"

He placed the knife on the pine needles at his feet, as if it was just something he happened to have in his hand, and removed his spectacles with the unattractive, open-mouthed squint of the myopic. He wiped them on his shirttail, huffed on the lenses and wiped the fog away.

"Dr. Robbie Miller," he said, putting the glasses on and looking at us through them. "That's my son, Bobbie, by the water." He gestured towards the boy. "Robert Jr. He's ten. Small for his age but whip-smart and a good athlete."

"What are you doing out here?"

"Fishing," he said, stating the obvious. He went on, a man used to giving bad news, his voice soft and high, but he blinked back tears as he spoke: "We're staying a few miles away with one of his mother's relatives. His mother and brothers were in Chicago for the symphony. Last night, we were hiding in a basement. He looked at me and said, 'Dad, do you think we'll ever go fishing?' I always told him I'd take him fishing but I never did. I decided we'd go when the sun came up."

"That was a good thing to do," I said. The man needed comfort; we all needed comfort, but he was queasy with his need for comfort. His expression did not change, so I went on:

200

"We haven't seen much in the way of good parenting over the past week." The sorrow melted from his face and he looked at me like I was stupid.

"If there's one thing I'm not," he said, "it's a good father. I've been a good doctor—my patients say so—I was a good student, a good husband, a good son. At least I always thought I was good. But if I stopped to think about it, I saw that whenever I was tested, I failed. It's easy to be good when you're not being tested."

Rafael and Gammy shifted uncomfortably. There was something not right about this situation.

Miller looked down at his knife. We did as well.

"I was the enlightened one," he continued, "the one who became a family doctor to make the world a better place. I always thought I was better than everybody else. Turns out I was the worst."

"This is a bad time to be hard on yourself," I said. "We're all just trying to make it day by day."

"I was a mean dad to that boy there. Can you believe it? Look at him." We did. The boy kicked at the pebbles. "Who would be mean to a little guy like that?"

I had no idea how to answer. Rafael and Gammy were letting me take the lead.

"Kids can be shits," I said.

"Phuh. I said things no man should say to his son."

"Kids get over it," I said. My parents had been tough. They never liked me very much but I never doubted they loved me. Miller seemed overwhelmed by love for his son, not despite what he was saying but because of it. "You love him, right? That's what counts."

Miller ignored me. "I never knew what to do with him. With the two other boys, it all came naturally, but with him? You might not think so looking at him but he was a handful. I went to our pediatrician. He told me to wait it out. I took him to a child psychologist and she told me it was okay, things would get better, we were just . . . how did she put it? We were mismatched."

"Yeah, that happens," I said. "Parents and kids aren't

always on the same page. My parents never read a novel, let alone one written by me." Miller was not hearing anything I said, and didn't seemed particularly interested that I had written novels; he looked from the knife to his son beside the water and we followed his gaze.

"Thing is," said Miller, "that boy is my favorite. I've got an older son and a younger son, but Bobbie is my favorite. Maybe I knew it from the start. We named his older brother Alvie, after his mother's father, and made him Robert Jr."

"Parents love all their kids," I muttered. My words were swept away in the breeze like specks of dust. There was no connection between what I was saying and what this man was saying. I couldn't feel him out. We were, I suppose, mismatched.

"I had a dream," Miller said; his voice became stronger. "This is the apocalypse, isn't it?"

"I can see why you feel that way," I said helplessly. Again the words disappeared in the air.

"And I dreamed of a burning bush."

Gammy stepped around me towards Miller. "Don't do it," she said. Her words startled him. I had no idea what she was talking about—or what he was talking about for that matter. But he looked at her with a flash of anxiety like a man who had just been caught confessing in a code he did not expect anybody to understand.

"It was just a dream," said Gammy.

He shook his head. "I've had a lot of dreams but this was different. It was real."

"Don't do it." Gammy was pleading with him. "It won't solve anything."

"It won't solve what?" I said. Miller looked down at his knife. Gammy spoke to me, without taking her eyes from him: "He thinks that if he sacrifices his son, God will forgive us and make the monsters go away."

"*What?*"

I looked to Miller, expecting him to laugh off what she said as so much religious tomfoolery; he was a doctor, he wouldn't believe that kind of primitive claptrap. But he withdrew into a terrible confidence and conviction, his eyes steely behind their spectacles, his shoulders pulled back. He looked over at his son fishing beside the river much as one might look over at any stranger's child in the distance. Only his hand trembling at his side betrayed his horror.

"Pray with me," Gammy said. She held out a hand. "Pray with me, and you'll find that God did not have that in His plans for you."

I tried to catch Rafael's eye so we could share bemusement at the nonsense. The last thing the world needed was religious nuts holding hands and chanting to make things better. But Rafael did not look at me; he was imploring Miller with his eyes to take Gammy's hand.

"Pray with me," she said, "and—"

"If I'm right, then this will save the world—"

"You're not right—"

"If I'm right," he said, his voice rising, "then this will save the world." Beside the river, his son half-turned at the sound, then stopped himself and faced the river again. Miller continued quietly, conscious that his son might have heard him, but just as fervently: "And if I'm wrong, then at least this boy will die at the hands of someone who loves him, not from a vile monster; and either way, I die afterwards. The boy's suffering ends no matter what."

"It doesn't have to be that way," whispered Gammy.

"I've already committed the act in my heart. The deed is as good as done."

"If you haven't done it," I said, "it's not done."

Gammy scowled at me to be quiet. Miller shook his head and scoffed; he now knew he got the upper hand in this ridiculous argument. "You don't understand! Are you a Democrat?"

It felt like a trap; of course I was. "Yes?"

"Do you remember when Jimmy Carter confessed he sinned in his heart?"

"I'm too young," I replied. I was being disingenuous. I knew Carter said that, but I didn't want Gammy and Rafael thinking that I remembered the Carter years.

"I could never understand why people laughed at him

for confessing that he sinned in his heart. A sin isn't committed in the doing, it's in the desire. That's the sin." He pointed a finger at our guns. "You could shoot me to stop me but what I've already done in my heart has been done forever."

"Then pray with me," said Gammy, "don't ask for forgiveness, *pray* for forgiveness. You're repenting."

"I'm doubting!"

"You're *repenting*. God knows it. You're right, you've already done it in your heart but God is merciful."

"If He is merciful," Miller said, "He will spare that boy."

I lifted my rifle and pointed it at his chest. "I'll be the agent of mercy."

Miller let out a sob. "Do it," he whispered. "Do it."

"Daddy!"

The boy had come from the river without us noticing. He still held the rod, bent almost to breaking because the line was tangled on a branch. He dropped it, dashed between us, and threw his arms around his father's waist, looking at me in pale terror. He had his father's plain ruddy looks and thin hair.

"Daddy," he cried, "what's happening?"

Miller put a hand on the boy's shoulder, rubbing it, then patting it; he glanced down at the knife with a look of complete calm.

"Please," said Gammy.

"Oh no," I said. "Don't."

"Please!" shouted Gammy.

Miller lunged for the knife. In one quick move, he fell to his knees, grabbed the knife, and plunged it into the boy. The boy screeched and collapsed like a puppet with its strings cut. I fired. Miller came onto his feet, then fell alongside his son, a bloody hole in his forehead. The father rolled over and wrapped around his son on a bed of brown needles and pinecones. They shuddered and twitched against each other, father and son, then were motionless.

I danced around, kicking at the pine needles; Rafael sank and crawled to a tree and hugged its trunk, his head buried in the turf beside its buckled roots; and Gammy keened long and hard, pausing to take breaths between her screams.

When we got to the car, there was no sign of Trish and Praj. We stood on the tarmac, listening to the quiet rush of the river. From the underbrush on the other side of the road, Trish and Praj poked their heads up over the grasses, then scrambled out and rushed across the road. Praj stopped when he saw our faces but Trish came up to us.

"We heard the screams," she was saying, and then furiously: "What were you doing?" Her face was twisted in anguish. "We thought you were being murdered."

None of us said a thing.

Praj was watching our expressions. "Be quiet, Trish," he called to her and looked away.

"What happened?" she screeched and shoved my shoulder hard. "Don't do that to us!"

Praj came to put a hand on her shoulder; she shrugged it off, still glaring at us with a wretched look on her face.

Praj explained, his eyes still averted, "We were scared. We thought you were dead."

Trish burst into choked sobs and put her arms around my chest. I did not return her hug. Still crying, she unwrapped herself and hugged Gammy, who patted her stiffly on the back just once. She moved to Rafael, her shoulders heaving with her sobs. He held her loosely, staring without seeing.

"Are you okay?" asked Praj. He could tell that we were not.

"We just buried a father with his son," I said. "It was down by the river where the boy was fishing. I guess he always wanted to go fishing with his dad."

XI.

We went the wrong way when we left the forest preserve. Our decision to stay off the highways proved again to be the more reckless choice. We found ourselves leaving the suburbs, not a good indication that we were nearing Chicago. Houses disappeared. The spaces widened. The land undulated in low earthy waves towards the lake, which was now on the wrong side of the car. Up ahead we could see the sky-scratching machinery of refineries—Gary, Indiana. We headed back. At dusk, we pulled over onto the shoulder beside a cornfield.

Dinner was a somber affair. We sat in a circle in the grass, primitives with cold food in the feeble glow from the car's open doors, and ate the last of our rations, listening to the *whish* of the corn and the occasional snaps and scuffle of rodents in the stalks. Far across the fields was a farmhouse. As the sun set, a green light appeared in an upstairs window. It was like one of those stars that disappear when you look directly at it. None of us had any inclination to go to the farmhouse, nobody suggested we investigate the mysterious green light; it winked and blinked whenever we didn't look at it until we no longer even thought about it. Without speaking, we shared a more mundane but more powerful compulsion: we just wanted to be together.

Something happened. Something crept over us, as disquieting as a twig snapping in the dark, as unforeseen as a monster's silhouette passing against a whitewashed wall. We were not sure where it came from but we knew it was out there, pacing and snuffling, making tentative feints towards our tight circle, then pulling back to trot around us; pretty soon we could identify it: it was joy. And like a monster, once it revealed itself, it became something much more intense and real: euphoria. Nothing was said, no useless words uttered, we just succumbed to it, together, freed from the loathsome snide prickles, the bitching, the mockery, the vanities of society—we were alive.

Done with our last jar of pasta sauce, we were buoyed

by the presence and the vindication of life itself, and we became giddy. Do you ever wonder what life is like for an anchovy or an ant: a small life, a dash of life, a speck of life from the moment of spawning until it becomes a fully-grown meat version of a vegetable, grown to be gobbled? It's pure in its smallness, an ecstasy of life in its pure smallness, and then it ends. As we fell off the top of the food chain, we were finally allowed to return to a smallness and a purity and an ecstasy in life itself. Like the Brady Bunch, we looked at each other and caught each other's eyes in the light cast from the car's interior and smiled.

"I'm sorry," said Rafael eventually, "but I was just thinking of Ophelia. Now isn't the right time to be saying it, but I'm already beginning to forget her a little bit. And I'm not so bothered by that, it's just—I just wished I could have thanked her, that's all."

Praj waited a moment then said quietly, "She knew."

Gammy was next to me. I put my hand on her thigh. Her jeans were tight over her skin. She put her hand on top of mine, pressing it against her leg, her fingers laced through mine. Rafael and Praj beamed; Trish shook her head with a soundless laugh as though she had known all along and what had taken us so long?

It wasn't just me anymore; it was all of us, together. We were suspended in love and compassion. There was no need for lights. The sky was bright with stars. The big dipper scooped up millions of them, Orion's belt was pulled tight, the Milky Way was a creamy smudge. Time passed, uninterrupted or stopped.

A memory flickered just out of sight, a light in the attic that disappeared when I sought it out. When I was a kid, my dad took me to the lake one winter's night. The sky was icy clear and we looked up at the stars.

"Makes you feel small," he said.

Weird thing was, it didn't. It made me feel huge and lived in. Maybe because he was next to me and my Mom was waiting for us at home and I still believed in drama and fate and in myself.

But you take all those things away and when you're faced with the night sky, you become mighty small. I finally understood what my Dad was telling me and was struck by the bravery and cruelty of his words, and how sentimental I was about him. *It makes you feel small.* That's what growing up is. Not getting big; getting small. But he could teach it to his son and that's what made him big.

I had nobody; we had nobody but each other. And that was even better.

Praj's eyes sank, his head bobbed. Trish yawned and as the yawn ended she put her wrist across her mouth. They smiled sleepy-eyed goodnights and crawled to the car and into the back seat, leaving the door open to let in the cool air.

I wanted Rafael to join them but I also wanted him to stay. What was I supposed to do with Gammy? Would a kiss extinguish our joy like a puff of air across a lit wick? As long as Rafael was with us, we were safe, there was no need to answer any questions solitude might pose.

Gammy removed her hand from mine and yawned. I cursed; I'd missed my opportunity. She stroked the nape of my neck.

"Do you want to take a walk?" she said in a low voice.

"All of us?" I rasped.

Rafael rolled to his feet. "Actually, you two go alone. I'll stay and guard Praj and Trish."

We stood, close to one another, my arm against hers. She slid a hand around my waist.

"But don't go too far," said Rafael. "Stay within shouting distance." We set off down the road. "And if I hear anything worrying," he added, cheekily, "I'll come running. No disturbing noises please!"

We strolled along the edge of the field. I was breathing fast. She hugged my arm tight. I leaned down to whisper in her ear but no words came. My lips touched her cheek and she held her face against my mouth. My lips jogged up, to her hair, and then I looked forward, and we just kept moving. The world hushed around us, and we were watched only by countless blinking eyes in the heavens, who for once seemed to care.

There was no light in the farmhouse.

In the car, the doors were shut and locked. Praj watched the road behind the car with a rifle in his hands, trying to detect movement in the moonlight; Trish was squinting into the night, a gun on the dashboard.

A werewolf had come out of nowhere. It stopped to sniff the tires and bolted upright when it sensed live humans inside the car. It rubbed its black sticky jowls against the windowpanes leaving a smear of saliva, its teeth clacked against the glass, its fiery human eye stared at the people inside, huddled against the far door. It snuffled around to their side of the car and they scrabbled across the seats. It went back and sniffed where we sat for dinner and pawed at the empty jar of pasta sauce. And then it picked up a scent. With a look of contempt over its bristling shoulder, it trotted off, sweeping its nose across the gravel beside the road, heading towards Gammy and me.

Rafael waited a moment and then got out to pursue it.

Gammy and I found a clearing on a wind-flattened carpet of thatched stalks. The moon cast the corn in white lead. A breeze justified the contact between our legs, the one part of our bodies where we were warm.

With a rifle over his shoulder, Rafael crept through the stalks, doubled over, his hands flat and palm-down in front of him, every part the cartoon villain tiptoeing away from the scene of the crime. He was smart enough not to freeze every time a branch broke under his feet: a snap followed by silence was suspicious; a snap followed by ongoing rustles indicated animal life unworried about the occasional broken twig.

Under the stars, Gammy and I faced each other, cross-legged in our stalk-walled room. The earth was quiet, rustled by a tender, fond, and shy wind. She wrote on my thigh with her finger but I could not keep track of the letters; I enjoyed the feeling and, even more, how I had become a palimpsest for her, and not the other way around.

I'd once listened to a famous Japanese writer read one of his short stories at a bar in Wicker Park. He read it in Japanese. I didn't understand a word and yet I knew what he was saying, I knew where he was in the story, I could make sense of the shape of the narrative, I knew when he was coming to an end. I'd never enjoyed a short story as much. Until now. The story written on my thigh.

With my skin, I listened to Gammy's silent words, lost to the curves and lines of her touch, but following her—angry and peaceful, seductive and Christian—someone who could never be mine and yet was choosing me, if only for the duration of the story she was telling. She kept writing.

Rafael pricked his ears with every new sound. He triangulated noises and fixed in his mind's eye the location of every creeping raccoon and mouse and wild turkey in the field. And he kept going on, sweeping through the stalks, over silver-lit clods bursting from lockboxes in the shadows.

Gammy whispered something about the night. I don't remember what she said; it was sorrowful, it was melancholic. I touched her knee; she shifted her weight into my fingertip and leaned towards me, her face inches from my own.

"Are you going to—"

I kissed the word "kiss" in her mouth.

Her lips were firm, so firm that I thought I'd made a mistake; but they parted and, covering mine, her mouth opened and my whole being fell in. It was the first time I had kissed for love in more than a decade; it was the first time I had been lost in a kiss since I was a teenager. There was no urgency, there was no time, there was no space; we kissed and unfolded our bodies without separating our mouths and lay on the rustling leaves and stalks. She rolled onto me, covering me heavily, my hands slid over her smooth, rocking ass; the cross around her neck fell against my chin; we rolled again so I was on top, and we kissed until our lips tingled and the taste of our mouths took on the sourer hues of the morning.

210

"Do you want to?" she whispered. I trembled like I was fourteen, and she hugged me, burying her face in my neck, and I couldn't believe it but she was grateful, grateful that I was trembling, grateful to be wanted so much, maybe even grateful for me. I kissed her forehead. We shifted and settled, side by side, and we stared; her moonlit eyes were black oceans reflecting a thousand stars, her pupils were satellite images of night-shaded continents alive with cities, sparkling with lightprick invitations and unanswerable questions. I unbuttoned her jeans, the soft roll of her belly against the back of my fingers. She hefted her hips up, arching her back, fibrous corn leaves falling from her. I unpeeled her jeans and her underwear. She brought her bottom down and lifted up her feet, kicking off her boots. Without forgetting my etiquette, I left her underwear and her jeans around one ankle so they would be easy to find.

"Do I need a—?"

"It's alright," she said.

I almost came on the spot.

Rafael stopped. He thought it must be gone. It had been too long. But he heard something looping through the cornfield.

I kissed Gammy's neck, her breasts over her shirt, her exposed belly. Her bellybutton was deep-set in the softest expanse of skin I'd ever felt; my lower lip was tickled by a hair, curved and perfect, a miniscule St Louis arch. I followed the trail south, finding tinier hairs on a creamy-soft veldt cooled by the open air, and down until I reached the moist, humid, musty air caught in the wiry, tangled forest that my chin, my mouth and then my nose entered; it was thick and tough, rough against my face, it smelled like sweat. I slipped her thighs over my shoulder and followed the thicket down to the soft, pulpy folds below, a luscious bog in the forest; I kissed once, a lovely kiss, unreciprocated but welcomed; I licked, savoring the rusty taste, the sweetness that was not quite sweet, the sourness that was not quite sour. She tensed like she was going to cough, and I kissed harder; then we gave up pretense and she ground against my face. Her under-thighs rested on my shoulders. I put one hand around her leg to rest on her bellybutton (she put her hand over mine, and we interlaced fingers), my other hand reached up under her shirt to touch a beady nipple. And I licked at the folds of damp skin and sucked and danced my tongue, then mashed my tongue, against her.

Rafael whispered something but nobody heard. He waited, his head cocked for sounds. Nothing. He knelt and swung the gun from his back.

Gammy jerked and pulled her crotch away from my sticky, sore mouth. She reached down to my armpits and pulled me over her, fumbling to get me out of my jeans. I helped her, squirming my jeans and underpants off, and we lay still as she guided me in.

"Gammy."

"Oh," she coughed, her lips against my ear, and then said my name with each thrust. "Oh, Jack."

And we pushed so hard we pushed through each other, our legs burning and tight.

The wolf darted from behind. Rafael heard the flurry and the whisper of the stalks, he spun and punched at the leaping shadow, but the wolf didn't worry about the fist in its sinewy, sharp-haired neck. It snapped its jaws wherever it could find purchase: Rafael's shoulder. Rafael twisted. The wolf fell.

Gammy and I pushed and thrust until we came, our bodies as tense and rigid at metal, the grimaces in our cheeks hard against each other; I subsided a moment before she did, my toes curling, and, still bucking inside her and gasping, I looked at her in the moonlight, her face contorted with love or whatever was left of it.

With a searing pain in his shoulder, Rafael raised the gun in his good arm, its muzzle inches from the wolf's forehead.

He fired. The force of the bullet drove the werewolf's head into the broken stalks, its paws splayed out like it was a rug.

"What was that?"

We carried Rafael to the car.

XII.

When we woke, Rafael was gone. There was a dismal silence. It was not only a silence of recrimination and loss; it was the silence Rafael usually filled with his chatter.

I want to say that we behaved admirably, that we held him in the back of the car and soothed him, that we pushed the strands of hair from his forehead and clasped his hand tight, that we leaned in so he could whisper a few words to each of us, and that we spoke words of comfort in his ear; but who cares what I want to say?

What we did was desperate and hurried: we stuffed a t-shirt against the puncture wounds on his bruised shoulder and strapped the dressing down with belt-buckle cut from the car, tied in a knot across his thin, quaking chest. We laid him down, after which we stood in the starry night by the hood of the car like a gang of ashamed mechanics unable to fix a motor.

Whatever was going to happen to Rafael began. He swallowed hard as if trying to choke down a hairball; sweat beaded on his brow and thin nose, and dripped into the hollows of his cheeks around his dry lips; he shivered, turning his head to the left and to the right with sudden uneasy jerks. It was painful to watch so we didn't. We huddled in the darkness and the chill air.

As dawn painted a gray swathe over the black cornfield, Gammy leaned against me and fell asleep; she was heavy against me, and I buried my nose in her springy curls, savoring the tart smell, until I too nodded off; like cows, asleep on our feet. Trish and Praj were tucked next to each other by the bumper, the cheerleader and the philosopher at peace.

As the sun shot its first rays over the land, Gammy and I startled awake; I helped her down, kissed her cheek, and as she curled up next to Trish and Praj, I went to see how Rafael was doing.

He was gone. The door was open, the belt buckle and blood-stained t-shirt on the tarmac. Streaks of dried blood crusted the seat.

I looked around. Nothing.

"Ain't nobody here no how," I whispered. But if I tried, I could convince myself that far down the road, far away, beside the cornfield, stood a lone wolf, watching us; but whatever it was, it didn't move and may have just been grass, a post, a trick of the eye.

After a while, the others got to their feet. I took Gammy aside and asked what she saw down the road, without telling her what I saw. I watched her eyes as she scanned the horizon. They stopped where I thought I saw the wolf. Her mouth opened very slightly, maybe just the parting of her lips for a breath, and then closed.

She shook her head. "Nothing."

On the road, we languished in an uneasy silence and made our way to Chicago.

In Arlington Heights, we lost Praj. Unlike Rafael, Praj was taken as we watched.

It was at home. We got there not too long after we left the cornfields behind. He gave me directions—when to turn left, when to turn right— and as we got closer, he began mumbling the names of people who lived in the houses we passed.

We arrived at a wide, attractive street lined with fat-trunked trees and tilting mailboxes.

"Here, on the right."

Praj's home was a lovely, chunky, two-story brick house with a fine oak in the front lawn, a rope dangling from a branch. All the Chicago suburbs were once filled with these sturdy neo-colonial mansions, but they were being torn down for undistinguished six-bedroom McMansions, with multiple gables for want of anything else of architectural interest, and faux-Tudor three-car garages.

"Nice house," I murmured.

Praj opened the car door before I even parked. Shoving a pistol into his trousers, he raced up the driveway with the nerves and excitement of a student coming home for Thanksgiving. We checked our remaining weapons and scrutinized the quiet neighborhood for anything suspicious, then followed him. Praj threw open the unlocked front door and stomped upstairs with a boy's abandon.

We waited in the entrance hall, standing in a shadow outside a rectangle of daylight angling through the front door and establishing a bright skewed frame around a gilt-framed family portrait. Praj, appearing even younger in a blue blazer and tie, stood beside a boy who looked like an older, cooler version of Praj; their mother was stoic and seated, wearing an ochre and gold sari; grandly joining his sons behind their mother was a plump, mustachioed man with smile-creased, benevolent eyes, one hand on his wife's shoulder. The family glowed in front of a purple backdrop.

Praj came down the staircase. His eyes were lowered. He licked his lips, his hand on the bannister to steady himself.

"They're not here."

Trish went to meet him on the stairs and gave him a hug. She led him into the living room and sat him down on a sofa.

I looked over to Gammy and whispered, "No matter how old you are, you still think your parents will be at home waiting for you."

She half-nodded like a child pretending to understand an adult who'd just explained rainbows. I knew why she was so reluctant to accept the banal truth: she had the same hopes, didn't she? That her parents were safe at home in Texas, sitting by the phone, waiting to hear from their daughter. I felt much older than her until she looked imploringly at me and my gut heaved. She knew. I felt the same way they did. I assumed my parents were in their den on Oak Street in Gurnee, getting ready to scold me for not calling sooner. I'd spoken without any sense that what I was saying applied to me, much as if I had said "everybody dies" without believing that "everybody" included me. Gammy grabbed my hand, squeezed it, and let go. And for the first time in my life, I actually knew that I was going to die.

Gammy joined them in the living room. I went too. You don't really want to be alone right after you fully comprehend that you're going to die. That's what doctors were for. They were society's promise you won't die alone. But whether or not you die *well*? No promises there.

Trish slipped over. "What now?" she whispered.

We left Praj alone in his thoughts, went upstairs and opened doors. It could have been any suburban home: spacious rooms decorated with photographs of the children, an empty bamboo birdcage, exotic prints of delicately rendered lotuses, turbaned men, elephants with beaded caparisons. The beds were made, the bathrooms were clean, curtains hung over the windows. There was a kind of Midwestern, middle-class prurience in how neat it all was, like it would have been embarrassing if monsters invaded your home and discovered it was a mess.

But I felt odd as I opened drawers with neatly folded squares of underwear, sniffed glass bottles of perfume, and checked the medicine cabinets. There was nothing intrusive or stealthy about our actions. What felt so strange was how detached we were. Our exploration of Praj's home was just a proficient inspection by aliens checking for life on an abandoned planet without any particular interest in the former inhabitants, taking in just enough information to convince their tentacled overlords they'd really been there.

We found what we guessed was Praj's room: a bed, a desk, a rolling chair, and a bookshelf, the bottom row of which was filled with standard boys' adventures, hardbound copies of *Gulliver's Travels, King Solomon's Mines, Harry Potter*s; the middle shelf held High School and college textbooks, math, geography, history; the young philosopher's Wittgenstein, Plato, Bacon, and Foucault were stacked on the top shelf with novels by Mann, Baldwin, Forster, and thinner volumes of poetry, Dickinson, Eboule, Gunn. The cupboard was open and I peeked inside: clothing, shoeboxes, a pair of ice skates, and nestled in the bottom corner, a tiny black violin case.

We shut the door and went on.

In the master bedroom, I lay my rifle across the King Size bed and sat in a stuffed chair while Gammy and Trish tested the taps in the en-suite bathroom. The furniture was conventionally off-white, probably purchased one Saturday afternoon as a matching set from a mid-upscale home furnishing warehouse on Rand. The seat was not comfortable. It felt like nobody had ever broken it in. Praj's father probably used it to lay out his tie and his pants when he came home from work, for Praj's mother to whisk away and put with the dry-cleaning in a wicker basket. Or maybe not; maybe they straddled each other on the chair, making love when the kids were away at math camp, her sari around her waist, his ample moustache buried in her bosom; maybe late at night while his wife and children slept, Praj's father stroked his moustache and read Tolstoy and Melville, taking notes in the margins when he came across a passage he loved; maybe he sat in the chair as he heard the news of what was happening around the world and dragged his fingers through his moustache, while his wife shook, holding the phone to her ear as she tried to reach her sons.

Now that I knew I was going to die, my life took on a shape. With my eyes shut, I could see my entire life in the form of a long movie. And not a good one. I'd slept through much of it. One of the problems with seeing your life as a movie is that you always come in late. Nothing makes sense. The plot, the good guys, the bad guys, everything that's going to happen is established in the opening shots, and by the time you've settled down to watch, you're having to guess what happened and who's who. Entire professions evolved to explain what happened in the bits you missed—not just the psychologists; the historians, biologists, archeologists and novelists too—but they didn't do any good. At the end, when the lights come on and you stumble out of the cinema wondering what the hell it is you just saw, the best you can say is that it passed the time.

I had images to run with the opening credits. Snapshots as grainy and blurred as the 1970s photographs they were: me in knee-high white socks, a baseball glove tucked under my arm; me cross-legged on a lawn in tiny white shorts, grimacing into the camera; me on Santa's lap; me, my cheeks puffed to blow out seven candles on a cake. With each came an emotion: pride in a well-oiled baseball glove, excitement that summer would last forever; pain from looking into the sun—we had to, or else we would be photographed as our own shadows; the infinite excitement of Christmas; feeling special and loved by the world, with one whole day of the year devoted to me.

I would have gone past the credits, but Gammy gently pulled me from the seat and we went downstairs.

Praj remained on the sofa, running his fingers between the cushions like he was searching for lost car keys. He gave us instructions on where to look for food and tools; we checked but everything worth taking had been taken.

When we came back to report to him, he said, "The car's not here." He puzzled over the fact and then spoke in the calm manner of a logician who solved a problem: "They loaded up and moved on to the city. We'll find them there. Was anything written on the fridge?"

I went into the kitchen. There was a white board stuck to the freezer with a marker hanging from a thread: "milk, butter, cardamom, plumber" were scrawled in erasable blue. I told Praj, hoping against hope that it was a message. He was still searching with his fingertips between the sofa cushions, maybe in the hopes that his childhood was down there. He wouldn't meet our eyes. There was no way to interrupt his silence; we waited for it to end; finally he said, "I want to go somewhere." The lack of specificity did not invite questions. He tumbled into the hallway like he was about to burst into tears and ran through the kitchen. We heard the slap of a screen door shutting.

Gammy and I sat on opposite ends of the couch as though Praj was still between us.

"Poor boy," sighed Trish. She trailed her fingers along the mantle above a fireplace filled with a clutch of dried flowers in a ceramic jug. The mantle held a clock, a pair of candlesticks with no candles, and two photographs of the boys, taken when they were in their teens, or maybe younger, I still couldn't tell; they wore ties and perky smiles, their eyes finding a happy place in the far corner of the room.

"Poor boy," she said again. "This was his home."

Really, I thought, *really*? I was filled with a blast of hate: Trish was discovering empathy. The entire monster uprising occurred so that she could come to somebody's house and reveal to the world that she was a real person with real feelings. Trish was the princess in the gilded carriage who called for the driver to stop because she spotted a frail sooty urchin, whose stick-thin body she hugged despite his filth, despite the lice in his hair, without giving a damn for her clothes, which would have to be burned afterwards, and pressed a silver coin into his paw. She had a far-off look in her eyes, as if in this moment of empathic enlightenment she was deciding to become her sorority's community chair so she could organize lollipop collections for sick children and take brassieres and unwanted dresses to a homeless shelter, her eyes blurring with tears at her small act of grace.

"It's so . . ." she paused; I prepared to puke at whatever cloying sentimentality was about to come out of her mouth. "It's so bland."

"Trish, you—oh."

I frowned. She was right. That was exactly it. I had sensed it but couldn't put my finger on it. The house felt unlived-in; there was enough furniture to tell you that a family lived there, and there were enough photographs to tell you what the family looked like, and there were some well-chosen touches that suggested taste but without a commitment or an ideology; there were no personal touches, no messes, no strangenesses, nothing that gave you a sense of who they were, what they believed, where they came from. Trish gave an apologetic shrug; it was a pretty tough observation under the circumstances, I granted her that.

Gammy shifted onto the edge of the sofa and hunched over her knees. "Sometimes that's the way with other people's homes," she said, under her breath. She didn't want to upset me or Trish; she stared at the carpet but we could feel the sting of her rebuke. "You never know what you're seeing or whether you're even seeing the same thing they do."

Trish and I kept quiet. We knew there was more.

"Maybe they were trying to fit in. I don't know where they're from, I never asked. But maybe they didn't want anything unusual or too personal, they just wanted a home for a quiet family living a quiet life, successful while being . . .

careful. Some people have to be careful." She glanced up at us. "Some don't."

We had no response. Gammy was right. I wondered what her house looked like in Texas, if her family had a pick-up in the front drive, a state flag on a flagpole in the lawn, steer's horns over a brick fireplace.

We heard the distant snap of a pistol shot.

"Oh my God."

"He shot himself!" cried Trish.

There was another shot.

"He must have missed the first time," I said.

We grabbed the rifles, ran through the hall and kitchen, and clattered through the screen door, which smacked against the wall three times as each of us pushed through.

Behind the house was a prefabricated gray wooden porch overlooking a vast lawn shared with the neighboring houses. About the width of a football pitch away was a row of trees, marking the border of the lawn and the banks of a canal. With his pistols out, Praj was stumbling back from the tree line, not far from a wooden tree house with two square windows, a doorway, a rope ladder waving under its entrance, and probably a "girlz keep out" sign nailed to the tree—that was what Praj must have been visiting, the secret place his parents could keep an eye on, his childhood home away from home.

Crawling out of the canal was a horde of water creatures, gelatinous black shapes splashing through the water with graceless swings of their long rubbery legs; they disappeared into the dappled shadows of the riverbank then burst through the rushes and into the sunlight like an army of fast-moving slugs plopping out of a haystack.

And coming across the lawn on his other side were zombies, twenty corpses thrown up from the earth in ragged clothing, rotted faces on rotten bodies staggering across the grass.

Praj stopped. Running was hopeless. With pistols in both hands and his arms outstretched, he fired at the water creatures to his right and the zombies to his left, and with each shot a zombie or a water creature tumbled.

We ran across the lawn, stopping to fire into the masses of monsters bearing down on him. I could see Praj in slow motion, his face calm with concentration as he turned his head from side to side, taking aim and firing to his left, then his right, then his left again; everything was unhurried except for his blinks as the pistols went off.

But there were too many and they were coming too fast. We tripped and ran, shouting his name, pulling up to aim and shoot. He stopped looking from left to right; he looked straight out at us; we were too far away for him to look at us individually—he watched us run, stop, shoot, call his name, as pistols blazed and jumped in his hands; he watched us calmly, saying goodbye with his eyes, glad that he was, maybe for the first time, looking at friends.

I don't know which got to him first. Water creatures and zombies collided together like hands clapping with Praj in the middle, crashing in a frenzy like he was a loose little brown football in a scrimmage, and he disappeared into a mass of flailing arms. We fired at the fringes, careful not to shoot into the mass in the middle, until we were out of bullets, but it was hopeless. At the far end of the lawn to our right, another group of zombies had been attracted by the noise and jogged with loose limbs across the grass; and at the other end of the lawn, a werewolf prowled in the undergrowth, lolling its head from side to side.

I took my rifle and was preparing to use it as a club.

Gammy grabbed me by the collar. "Come on, Jack."

"It's no use," cried Trish. "Oh Praj! It's no use!" She ran screaming back to the house, her face in her hands.

Gammy pulled me back. The mound of monsters was thrashing over Praj.

We barreled through the screen door, which slapped behind us, and ran past the white board on the kitchen with its to-do list and past the family portrait in the front hallway, out the front door, down the front steps, and to the car.

More zombies were coming down the road. I reversed out of the driveway, jammed into forward, and we roared past them, their smoky eyes looking lifelessly at us.

And as we skidded away, I noticed that one of them was plump with long black hair and a tattered sari, and another, grasping at the air in front of him, had a thick black moustache.

Part III. The Windy City

I.

Chicago looked beautiful. It always did. Of all the cities in the world, Chicago was the most striking—a wave of glass and metal rising from the plains and crashing against the water's edge.

It wasn't cramped geography that spouted the city upwards but an organic autochthonous will, a unique composition of Gothicism and Modernism, a perverse celebration of divine space and secular reach. From the bloody work of cutting cattle throats and shipping grain under a thin endless sky, from the blood and the blues miscegenating in the city's high-storied history, from eye-level slaughter and lowdown grace, from somewhere and nowhere, Chicago rose in grandeur, in motion and permanence, as unsettling as the saltless sea lapping against its breakwaters; it was an ancient city-cathedral built on stockyards, slums, and abattoirs, the future of cities *avante la lettre.* In the fat body of a nation spread out from sea to drab sea, loafing across the hemisphere like a tourist in a chic resort it was rich enough to pay for but too classless to appreciate, the hard-tracked arteries all led to a crystal and steel heart housed like a locket against the vast ruffled breast of the Midwest.

The Second City: at its worst, a city of sloppy seconds, the second-to-last stepping stone for those on their way to New York or LA; it echoed with pathetic good cheer for those who left to become successful, like a hapless hooker proud of the clients who go on to get married and congratulating herself for teaching them a few tricks in bed, ones they would have discovered for themselves anyway. It was the greatest city in the world to have as its finest historical moments a fire, the murder of strikers, the legendary corruption of its politicians, a crooked sports team, a fat-assed gangster, and a police riot; it was the greatest city in the world not to have a literate newspaper; it was the greatest city in the world that was at no point ever the greatest city in the world.

But then again, the Second City: there was a wisecracking second-guessing in its nostalgic corruption, a wit to its proud local sleaze where nobody was the fool; there was humility in the brashness, and you saw it first when you saw it first: the skyscrapers didn't strut into the sky with arch phallic arrogance; the skyline wasn't the cock fight of New York or Shanghai, it wasn't spoiled by the tiredly stiff corporate machismo of Houston, London, or San Diego, and it definitely wasn't anxiously strident with the extravagant priapisms of theocratic oligarchies. No, it was a windy city where words and those who trafficked in them—writers, actors, comedians—passed through, carried through like dust and pollen, but the arts that stuck were architectures and sculptures too heavy to blow to the coasts.

It was the home I left because it was the last place I wanted as home; it was the place I ended up because I didn't make it anywhere else; it was my home.

We came in from the west.

I leaned over the steering wheel, willing the car on, pushing it into familiar neighborhoods whose ethnicity was marked by signs on the bakeries, cafés, and restaurants established by the Argonauts and draft-dodgers from Poland, Mexico, the Ukraine, Germany and Romania several generations back, and then by new ethnicities with new shop fronts and new restaurants, hanging new flags from third-story windows.

What did I expect on my return? Banners strung across Western like on Mexican Independence Day? Fireworks released into the sky for every human who made it to safety? No. Nothing fancy. But I thought there would at least be a roadblock, and armored vehicles like enormous beetles with American flags on their exoskeletons, and guns peeking like crickets' legs from behind sandbags, and tangled coils of barbed wire strewn across the streets, and helicopters beating the sky, and an imperious MP in a silver helmet who would take our names and direct us to the fortified zone, where we would leave the car with a grateful pat on its dusty, claw-marked, steaming hood, and a debriefing center where our clothes would be removed and taken away to be burned, and we'd be hosed down in sterile white-fabric cubicles, our blood drawn, and doctors would inspect our eyeballs and teeth and with a curt nod tell a pair of waiting soldiers, "These are humans, let 'em through"? Was this too much to expect?

Apparently.

I held onto this hope even though we saw no roadblocks or choppers or MPs. I held onto the hope even though the mists hanging in the streets were not a morning fog rolling off the lake but the smoke from fires burning themselves out. I held onto the hope when I saw there were no tanks lumbering down Ashland, no people in the streets at all, and that the signs hanging askew above smashed shop windows, the glass sprayed across the sidewalks like spilled diamonds, the abandoned oil change stations, and the empty restaurants were not charming affectations of tough working class neighborhoods but the aftermath of a terrible battle. I even allowed myself a moment of disappointment that there was no roadblock *before* my neighborhood, as if it was merely a nuisance that the safe-zone did not include my apartment.

We turned on Division and drove down the crumbling, smoking blocks to Hoyne. The sidewalks were thick with a yellow crust of leaves. Tempting fate, I drove the wrong way down Hoyne, a karmic plea for a cop to skid in behind me with blue lights whirring and an incredulous look when his face bent into the window to ask me what the hell I was doing. No such luck.

But if there was no policeman ready to ticket me, there was also no indication that anything much was wrong at all. Hoyne looked untouched by troubles, as hushed as Saturday mornings, the cars like giant dead cicadas around trees.

We parked in front of a three-story brick walk-up.

"Here we are."

I got out and looked around. What struck me first was the absence of faces. Even when the yuppies began buying all the houses in Ukrainian Village, much to the disgust of those of us who lived in the neighborhood for more than a year, you would still see scornful old Ukrainian faces, puckered and mottled like grapefruits that had begun to rot, peering from windows. When I first moved in, the flat taciturn faces creeped me out; but after a few months, I began to welcome the Eastern European moons rising and setting in their nightdark rectangular skies; I liked coming home, forging a path through the ancient brick jungle with the locals peeking through the lacy foliage, mostly invisible but occasionally letting themselves be seen because they wanted me to know they were watching.

The entrance was set in the side of the building because the front door led straight into the first floor apartment's living room. We walked along a tall wooden fence erected by the lawyer who bought the house next door. He didn't like the wire-mesh fence that separated his property from ours, even though it was knitted with the tendrils of a vine that burst with yellow flowers every summer.

There was a flurry of movement up ahead: an animal streak of fur at the end of the alley, a pelt skimming between the wood and wire. We braced for an attack.

A tawny-golden animal popped up on the fence.

"Argh!" I shouted, and then, recovering, "Cat! It's you!"

"Braaa," she let out a milky yawl.

Cat the cat belonged to the lady on the first floor. She mewed, showing us her tiny white teeth and prickly pink tongue, tiptoed along the fence, and tilted her head so I could scratch her ears. I did so and then sniffed my hand, a familiar reflex after petting her. My fingers smelled like damp fur. I had heard that cats were supposed to be clean, but this one wasn't. Cat the cat was one dirty housecat; that made me like her even more. I called her Cat the cat because she didn't belong to me; giving her a generic name maintained the mutual pretense that I didn't like cats and that she had no interest in me either. I thought her Ukrainian name—Koshenya or something—was elegant and lovely until a neighbor explained that it was Ukrainian for cat.

Cat the cat let out another trilling meow. She reached her paws out, her back arched and her tail poked up as straight as an exclamation point. Trish and Gammy cooed and held out their hands, which she sniffed and rubbed with her hard forehead, purring loudly. Satisfied and excited, she jumped down from the fence and pranced to the door.

I followed her and carefully, slowly opened the door. Cat squeezed inside before the gap looked wide enough for her to fit through. She sniffed the iron umbrella stand and then darted up to the first floor landing with a reassuring feline insouciance.

I called a hallo. The fusty hallway absorbed my voice.

I invited Gammy and Trish in. "We're going to the penthouse."

We followed Cat up, treading quietly in the dim light of a single bulb on the second floor. On the third floor landing, I knocked on the door opposite mine. I had never really known the woman who lived there, though we shared the floor for ten years. Every once in a while we came face to face on the landing with wordless nods over the brown oval rug she laid when she arrived in the United States, a welcome soon stamped into the ground. She was, as Trish would say, *old* old, with neat gray hair cut boyishly and a closed face with dull blue eyes. She kept to herself, protecting her privacy in the rarely-glimpsed confines of her apartment by pulling the door shut and looking into my eyes to watch me try to glance around her at the couch, the table, the lace curtains across a window glowing like a television, which gave the room a filtered light as if she was developing prints; the most we ever said was when she would come out to find me with my arms folded over the bannister in conversation with our landlord, looking up from the second floor with owlish glasses and pants buckled up over his bellybutton, and she roughly translated our platitudes. But I never knew much about her life, if she had any relatives, or where she was when I didn't see her. It felt good in a neighborly way to check in on her.

There was no answer, so I crossed to my front door and pushed. It held firm. I was surprised and relieved and insulted. The old faces in the windows watching the monsters invade the neighborhood must have commanded them, "Not in there, he's got nothing."

I took my keys out, unlocked the door and entered after Cat, who again slipped in before it seemed physically possible.

The front door opened straight into the kitchen, the biggest room in the apartment with an expanse of linoleum in a fake tile pattern, bubbled in the corners. I walked cautiously in. Everything was untouched, as rudimentary and thrown-together as when I left: a cabinet with bare upper shelves and a thin crack in the glass repaired with lines of yellowing tape, a magnificent sink and drying rack stained with the residue of pipe water, resting on pipes that dove and curled into the wall, a single Formica-topped table on tubular metal legs, a chunky fridge. The window beside the fridge used to look out at an orthodox church designed by Louis Sullivan, a few blocks away; during sunsets, the light hit the dome and blasted a blinding golden ray into my kitchen. New condos were built between us and ended that joy.

I kept going. The kitchen merged into a living room, its boundary demarcated by the stiff, cheap carpet—Cat ran over and sharpened her claws, plucking at the brown synthetic fibers. My television set, a fat squat machine with a square face, looked out at a tatty orange couch and a pair of cheap chairs with metal-tube limbs that also came with the apartment. I had eaten many a beef sandwich on that couch, my feet up on a chair, watching that screen.

Gammy came in but Trish remained in the hall, gaping at us like we were social klutzes who passed her favorite pop star in the street without spotting him.

"Uh, Jack?"

"Yes, Trish?"

"Uh, you didn't notice?"

"Notice what?"

"Duh," she said, "there's electricity? The light was on?"

She pointed down at the second floor landing.

I didn't quite believe her. I flicked at a light switch. The orb on the kitchen ceiling glowed. I switched it off and on again—it worked.

"Wait—if there's electricity . . ." We stared at each other, our eyes widening.

"The fridge!"

Trish and Gammy needed no invitation. They ran me over. Trish got there first, flung open the door and grabbed a carton of orange juice in the door; she sniffed it in a proprietary way and then took deep glugs from the spout. Gammy, positioned tactically in front of me, allowed herself the luxury of surveying the contents of my fridge, eyeing the two bruised pears, the opened jar of puttanesca pasta sauce, a mushy bag of spinach, a cellophane-wrapped brick of parmesan, and a yoghurt. She picked the yoghurt, tore open the foil lid and stared at the blueberry moon; rather cleverly and observantly, she went over to the cabinet and, guessing correctly, pulled out a drawer with my limited selection of mismatched cutlery; she removed a spoon and dug in, her eyes shut in quiet ecstasy.

If they thought I was being generous giving them first dibs, they were wrong. Trish sighed, her orange-sweet breath wafting over to me, and scanned the fridge for something else. Gammy scraped at the bottom of the yoghurt container. I casually removed a foil-wrapped package on the bottom shelf and slipped over to the table to unwrap it with my back to them.

However nonchalant I tried to be, they knew something was up. Trish hovered behind me, impatient, her breath coming out in hot orange blasts, as subtly and incongruously threatening as a koala bear being kept from eucalyptus; Gammy, the spoon still in her mouth, moved aggressively up against me, a hard breast like a gun in my back.

"Jack, that isn't—" A whiff of orange juice.

Gammy removed the spoon from her mouth. "Is that—?"

There was no need to hide now. I pulled the silver foil back and regarded them. All the power in the world was mine.

"Yes, ladies," I said. "Pizza."

There were two slices left. Two chilled, hardening triangles of pizza. A thick rind of cheese with moist puddles of oozing tomato sauce, speckled slices of pepperoni, precious black olive rings and green peppers. There was a lot of crust: the pizza was made at a venerable local shack where the pizzaioli threw the pies together with respect and love but without much interest in aesthetic effect, so the toppings and cheese and sauce were always unevenly distributed; naturally, I had eaten the best slices and left these behind for breakfast or in case of an emergency.

Well, this was an emergency.

Trish tried to maneuver around my newfound power. "It's not Chicago-style," she said primly.

"You want 'Chicago-style'? Go out and order one!" I shouted.

"No, no," she said, "I don't like Chicago-style. I like this kind."

A fugue-like part of me was trying to figure out how I could extend this moment of absolute authority, and whether it intimated a new world order, and if, in some primal way, my possession of the pizza with two beautiful young women by my side wasn't an auspicious new beginning for humanity itself; but my mouth was watering, I was almost literally starving, and, hell, we'd been through too much together. Gammy was close against me and her breast was rising and falling against my back; I had the truculent thought that she had been seducing me in anticipation of this very moment, when I could split the pizza with her, possibly after dispatching Trish.

"What's the plan, Jack?" she said huskily into my ear.

I thought hard. Complete power or pizza, complete power or pizza—neither would last. It was time for pizza.

"How do we divide two slices into three?" I asked.

Gammy and Trish relaxed behind me. I tried to do the math. Math was never my strongpoint. We stood in silence. I didn't know if they were doing the calculation or if, like me, they had been jolted by a memory of Praj, who would have had a rational answer right away, or Rafael, who would have had a bright idea that may not have made any sense but would have worked; or if they too had noticed how lonely the number three is when it should have been five.

"Let's cut each slice like this," Gammy traced a line from the point of one slice up to the center of the arc of crust, and then repeated the motion with the other slice. "Trish and I can each have one, and you can have two."

"But then why don't we just cut one in half?" asked Trish, astutely. "And Jack can have the whole other slice?"

"I thought of that," said Gammy. "But watch."

She went to the drawer and rooted around until she found a knife to her satisfaction. She returned to the table and bisected each slice, ensuring an equal portion of toppings, using the flat part of the blade to shift pepperoni, olive rings, peppers from one side to the other. She handed us a sliver and took a third.

"Cheers," she tapped her stiff slice against ours. With her eyes closed, she nibbled the point.

It may have been old and cold but it was everything a pizza could be: sweet and tangy and fatty, with pulses of pepperoni and pepper, the crunchy saltiness of olives, the chew of the cheese and crust. It took us as long to eat those slivers as it did for me to polish off half a pizza on my own. I gave Cat a shred of pepperoni with a strand of cheese. She gobbled it up and licked my finger with her raspy tongue.

The fourth sliver lay on the foil like a golden trowel. We stared. It was supposed to be all mine but Gammy had figured something out. She'd found a way for me to ask forgiveness for my power-play with the pizza: I picked it up and took a bite, then handed it to Trish, who took a bite, and then she passed it to Gammy. In this manner, cartoonishly paring it down, we finished the pizza.

Afterwards—well, you know how you felt after sex?

It's nothing compared to how we felt.

But we weren't done.

"I have another surprise."

I opened a drawer in the broken cabinet and from behind a bag of dried pasta, removed a package of chocolate chip cookies. Trish squealed and bounced; Gammy sighed profoundly.

Cat jumped onto the table and, after licking the pizza foil, found the yoghurt; while we ate the cookies, she put a paw on the pot to steady it and stuck her head in, licking it clean. We laughed when she got her head stuck, and we wiped away the cookie crumbs stuck to our lips by the pizza grease.

"And now," I said, as though I were a magician with an endless supply of tricks, "Another surprise." I paused cryptically. "Follow me."

The bathroom was inconveniently situated beside the front door, which meant padding across the apartment to get from the bedroom to the bathroom, a tribulation on cold winter mornings, an impossibility when blitzed. It was little more than a cubicle into which hulking Eastern European plumbers had ingeniously fixed a toilet, a sink, and a bathtub in such a way that you could pee into the toilet from the shower while checking your reflection in cabinet over the sink—if this doesn't sound like architectural ingenuity, bear in mind that this was true for men *and* women.

We crammed in and were shocked to see that we were accompanied by three gaunt, dirty, haunted tramps. They disappeared when I opened the mirrored cabinet above the sink.

Gammy and Trish crowded behind me. Knowing smiles spread across their faces. I removed my toothbrush. "Exhibit A." I found the half-rolled-up tube of toothpaste. "Exhibit B." I squeezed a slug of toothpaste onto the brush. "Now, go like so." With mechanical rigidity, I brushed my teeth. Gammy and Trish clapped.

It was magical. I fell into a reverie. moving the toothbrush around my mouth the way I had every day twice a day for four decades—across my upper teeth on the right-hand side, my lower teeth on the right-hand side, a switch and turn for the upper left, the lower left, up and down across the front, and finally over the biting surfaces. A week of fur was scoured from my teeth, a week of sour grime scrubbed from my mouth; the paste smarted in my gums, the mint burned my tongue. I opened my eyes, coming back into the world, pivoted over the sink, my mouth frothing and white, and said thickly, "Then one does this."

I turned on the tap with all the confidence in the world that it would work; there was a sarcastic hiss of air, a splutter, the faucet coughed, and a stream of cold water gushed out, splashing against the dry ceramic. I leaned down, spat voluptuously, and rinsed my mouth. I held the brush out: "Who's next?"

Shoulder to shoulder, they took turns with the toothbrush. I inspected my face. It was thin and tougher and my eyes were more alive than they had ever been—and more guarded, even to the point of being suspicious of the face looking back. A week's worth of salt-and-pepper beard was more salt than pepper. I had to admit, I looked like I could be in my fifties. I lathered my chin and my cheeks and dragged the blade down my face; it sounded like a city snowplow clearing the streets with each new stripe and every scratchy, pinpricking drag of the blade; I tapped the poppy-seed foam into the sink. With a tatty green flannel, I scrubbed dollops of soap from my nostrils and earlobes. When I was done, Gammy's eyes lit up and Trish laughed kindly.

"You look fifteen years younger!" Trish said.

I tilted my head towards the ceiling and placed the cold wet cloth over my face. It absorbed the stresses of the week and saturated each breath with a humid, cedar scent.

Things were looking better. And we hadn't even showered yet.

II.

Trish was looking summery and upbeat in my Northwestern sweatshirt. Gammy, squeaky clean, stood beside the phone. She was wearing one of my shirts.

"You've got messages," she said.

Nobody ever left me messages. She pointed to a red light blinking five times, pausing, then blinking five times again.

"People still have answering machines?" asked Trish, as though Gammy found a loom in my living room. "How does it work?"

I pushed the button hard, poking it into action. There was whir, a chirp, and then a voice.

"Jack? Jack? Are you back?"

"My friend Lance," I whispered. "He's a poet."

"Ja-ack," said Lance eerily, "more weird shit is happening. That ape has friends. I need a reality check, man. Call me, okay?"

Click.

"If I know Lance, he's holed up in his apartment with a bag of weed, writing poems. He's a cockroach. All poets are. They're always surviving shit then writing about it. Novelists— we just give up and die."

The next message was a long silence, the type of silence where you can hear the seconds ticking by, an anonymous and personal silence ending in a sharp click. Gammy and Trish were on either side of me, sharing the moment like prisoners of war reading a letter from home over my shoulder. I twitched with disappointment and embarrassment.

The next message was another silence, not quite as long, but long enough that we knew it would only be a silence. This time it felt crueler, more malicious. As we listened, it was hard not to imagine a vicious spirit erasing the voices from the past and leaving only a rustling, scarred passage of time.

The fourth began with a long silence and we sank into airless gloom like we were astronauts and the voices that connected us to the world had been erased, leaving us lost in space.

There was a faint cough.

"Hi Jack, it's me, Rory."

"My wife," I said. Gammy bristled. Trish perked up, thrilled and scandalized.

"I'm just calling to see if you're okay," Rory said. "Tony and the kids and I are safe, we think, but I didn't know if anybody was checking in on you. Anyway, I hope you're okay and your mom and dad too. Okay then. Goodbye, Jack."

Click.

"We got divorced a few years ago," I explained, avoiding their eyes. "She was a good person." The past tense sounded too convenient.

There was one more message. Despite myself, I leaned over the answering machine and cradled it. I knew what I was yearning to hear. I wanted it to be my parents. I wanted to hear my mother speaking into the answering machine with the self-consciousness of a woman who never got used to talking into a machine, not trusting it to convey the message and speaking to it like it was an official who might deign to relay the message in a garbled form and superciliously; and in the background, my father would look up from the back pages of the *Tribune* and shout to tell me that I should watch the next Bears game or whatever sporting event he was invested in at the time, because he still thought I followed them with him.

The message began with a crackling silence. I could see my mother biting her nails and wondering if the beep meant she was supposed to start speaking or if another somehow different, somehow clarifying beep would be the cue; I could see my father folding the paper on his lap, waiting for her to start speaking so he would know when to shout his message; the silence went on, crackling, and I whispered aloud, "Come on, Mom; come on, Dad."

Click.

Nothing.

Gammy and I sat on the bed.

My bedroom was basic and bare, a single unmade bed, a window overlooking the city, a bureau with a collection of half-read paperbacks in case of insomnia, and, on the walls, a movie poster for *Ladri di biciclette*, a postcard of Ernest Hemingway looking spoiled and fat, and a poster of Johnny Cash in Folsom Prison glancing sweatily over his shoulder. The decor may have seemed casual but it was a carefully curated collection of images: I wanted the young hipster chicks I intended to bed to know that I liked foreign films, that successful, studly authors could be fatter than me, and that I was a fan of Johnny Cash before Rick Rubin made him famous again, even though I only had the *American* recordings.

But Gammy was the first woman to sit on the bed with me.

She didn't know where to begin and looked moodily out the window. I had never put curtains up. A quirk of the local architecture was that my building faced a single-story bungalow, behind which was a church parking lot, which meant that my view of the downtown skyline was uninterrupted. Can you imagine how reassuring it was to watch the sun rising over the Chicago skyline from my bed, even on the mornings I didn't plan on getting up? Especially on those mornings?

I gave her time to speak. When she didn't, I decided to start.

"We had lives before this. Yes, I was married."

She looked at me like I had asked her to perform a perverted sexual act on our first date: her lips pulled back from her teeth with disgust, anger, annoyance. I waited for her to explain whether she was disgusted, angry, annoyed or all three, but she shook her head, closed her mouth, and went back to staring out the window, her eyes searching the thousands of windows in the distant skyscrapers. There was a dot of toothpaste on her lower lip; I wanted to kiss it off.

"I'm sorry—" I tried again.

"You're sorry?"

"Yes, I'm sorry. I should have told you about Rory."

She shook her head. "It's not that." Her big brown eyes glazed with tears and settled on something bleary and awful and poignant in the middle distance between us and the skyline. "I didn't tell you."

"You didn't tell me what?"

"My boyfriend is here."

"Oh," I said. And, for good measure, I said it again, "Oh."

I waited for more details but she was suddenly closed off.

"Remember, it's your turn," I said. "Truth or dare?"

She faced me. I wanted her to say "dare"; I'd say, "Kiss me."

"Truth," she said.

But I already knew the truth, didn't I?

Trish appeared in the doorway, fidgeting, poking at her wet hair. "Hey, guys?"

"Not a good time," I said, with the sickening realization that the problem wasn't Rory. The problem was that I was being dumped.

As if I could feel any worse.

Even when Rory and I split, after the final papers were signed and we half-waved goodbye in her lawyer's office, and I sat alone on the edge of what had been our bed in our apartment, a morbid sense of failure had me reaching for the bottle; that hopeless feeling, less an actual feeling than a way of not-being in the world, was far preferable to this. This didn't feel like a descent into oblivion, it felt like being killed. And there was no anesthesia—no whisky, no bourbon, no scotch, no beer.

I fell back on the bed with my hands over my eyes, ruefully aware that the bed had still not been tested by lovemaking. Gammy. Gammy. Oh god.

"Guys?" said Trish.

Gammy squirmed on the mattress, causing me to roll towards her; I think I wanted to begin to cry a little bit. Or throw up.

"Give us a minute," said Gammy. Her voice wasn't angry, disgusted or annoyed; there was softness in it, directed to me. She had more to say. It wasn't over yet.

But Trish remained in the doorway. She flapped her hands in front of her like a game show contestant asked to pick

238

between answer A and answer C.

"Guys, I'm sorry, you gotta listen."

"What is it? Can't you see this is important?"

"Cat just hissed at the front door and then ran and hid under the TV."

III.

Gammy wiped her eyes and whispered, "Did you bring a gun?"

I shook my head, no. My mouth was dry. I couldn't speak. I was scared, more scared than I had ever been. Why would I have brought a gun? I was just coming home. Back to my apartment. I was moving by habit, I wasn't thinking about a gun.

"Oh my God, oh my god, oh my god." Trish flapped her hands faster, stirring the air into a frenzy. Once she created enough power, she took off, racing around us with tiny doll steps, pitter-pattering like a wind-up propeller plane; she came to a rest beside me and we crouched on the edge of the bed, listening as hard as we could.

There was nothing, not a sound. We held our breaths. A cloud crossed the sky and the apartment plunged into a foul mood. The skyline several miles away was still in the sunlight, glistening sharp and clear.

The front door creaked. Gammy pressed against me, shivering and twitching. Trish edged away as if she meant to slip over into the space between the bed and the wall. I had the fleeting thought that we should roll backwards and pull the duvet over our heads and be very still and we wouldn't be noticed and it would just go away.

Something bumped into a chair in the kitchen. Knowing it had given itself away, it began moving swiftly with shuffling feet.

"*Hkkkkk. Hkkkkk.*"

It was Cat, hissing.

"*Hkkkkk.*"

A loud pounding of feet and a hideous yowl. Trish and Gammy screamed. Trish fell into the crevice between the bed and the wall, Gammy buried her face against my chest. Overcome by a wretched fury, I pushed her off and ran into the living room.

A huge gray figure was kneeling in the living room, one club-like hand on the television, the other holding Cat's neck down as it buried its lumpy head into her bloody fur. The thing reeked of clay and vomit. It lifted its head with red slop dripping from a cavity in the middle of its round head with malformed yellow teeth like pieces of candy corn. It looked at me with two pebbly black eyes in fist-print orbits. It had no other features.

Cat was bloodied but blinking. Still alive. The thing roared, a furnace blast that stank of hot meat. I grabbed a chair, raised it over my head, and brought it down as hard as I could on the creature's back. Its flesh absorbed the blow like I had slapped a branch in the mud; I pulled the chair back, leaving imprints of the legs in its back. The creature fell onto its haunches, its mouth working like it was trying to formulate its very first thought; it looked at cat in its hand, then it snapped around to look at me again. I wasn't going to win a war of attrition. With the legs of the chair pointing at its chest, I charged; it swung a huge hunk of a hand, but at the very last instant, I ducked and instead of aiming the chair at its torso, I lifted it, sending the bottom leg right into its hollow mouth; the blow from its fist clipped me on the back, knocking the breath out of me, and it chomped down on the chair leg; instead of pulling the chair out, I lurched up from the floor with all of my strength, thrusting the chair upwards. I felt something give in the back of the creature's throat; its arms dropped, and I pushed again, driving it as hard as I could, screaming with the effort to push the chair upwards until there was another give, and the chair leg slid smoothly through the back of the creature's head. The creature wrenched upwards. The chair was torn from my hands. The thing lurched to its feet with the chair stuck in its head; the chair leg that passed straight through its mouth and out the back of its head tapped against the ceiling. It held Cat like a filthy limp rag in its hand. The creature's beady black eyes moved—but not quite in sync, one crawling up while the other crawled down; the two eyes sank together, as if the thing was going cross-eyed. With its yellow teeth clamped around the chair leg, it collapsed, falling face first onto the chair, which buckled and snapped, driving the leg deeper into its face, shearing the top of its head off.

The cloud passed and the apartment lit up. A grainy and sandy liquid flooded out from its shorn head, like a waterlogged sandbag had been cut open. The thing did not move. It filled most of the room, holding Cat's corpse in its hand.

We had to leave. Death was going to keep coming at us until we found somewhere safe. Trish and Gammy stepped around the mud creature and Cat, trying not to look, and fled down the stairs. I brought up the rear, having taken a moment in the doorway to look back at the apartment where I had lived for almost ten years, most of my thirties. And what was I looking at? A mostly empty apartment. I owned nothing. There were no memories stored in the space, nobody had visited except my parents once or twice in the early years; the only affection and friendship was with Cat, stiffening next to a dissolving bag of sand and pus. There's never any point looking back, I thought. I left the door open and charged down the stairs after Gammy and Trish.

At the bottom of the stairs, I crashed into Trish, who was backing up step by step, panting with her hands to her mouth. Gammy was in front, holding her breath, also backing up the stairs. A man stood in the doorway, facing out. He was in a poorly fitting tweed jacket, pale slacks and sneakers, with yellowish hands and what looked like thick swirls of muddy hair pasted to his head.

"Who—?" I began.

He spun around in the doorway, a ridiculously fast movement.

He had no face. His head was a coiled and slabbed, a wasp's nest on top of a body. Gammy dove around Trish and picked up the umbrella stand with both hands and slashed it up like she was swinging for home. The foot of the umbrella stand, a curl of iron, caught the front of the head and tore a sheaf from it, revealing a sour, blackened honeycomb. Dead wasps dribbled from the exposed hexagonal cells, and landed on the floor with the hush of dried insects, then more and more fell out, and soon every pocket of honeycomb was spewing dead wasps; then a few live ones flew out—but they weren't wasps anymore, they were flies, and they were followed by the nodding pointed heads of maggots. The torn honeycomb became a sluggish marshmallowy white as maggots filled the hive head and popped out like moist globs of half-chewed popcorn.

Gammy jammed the umbrella into the thing's chest and pushed him back and out, giving Trish and me the chance to run behind her. Up against the mesh fence, the maggot man's chest collapsed, and flies streamed out. We raced back to the car, swatting at the air, scratching at our necks and faces in a cloud of flies.

At the car, frantically batting the bugs and waiting for Trish and Gammy to get in, I checked to see if there were any other monsters. Far down on Hoyne, maybe three blocks away, I thought I saw a dog or a wolf trotting in a straight line towards us; I didn't wait for confirmation and ducked into the car. We sped away, swatting stray flies in the car, past the taqueria on the corner.

It went without saying that I would never go home again.

There was, of course, no traffic on Ashland, just closed banks, Mexican restaurants, and auto repair shops. Someone had crashed into a newspaper dispenser on a street corner and knocked the front panel off; it was shedding newspapers sheet by sheet. A lake of newsprint expanded as pages slid over one another.

We drove north. The Kennedy Expressway was demolished where it crossed Ashland, as if a giant Monty Python hand had come down from the clouds and smashed it. All that remained was fat rounded pillar frayed with metal supporting rods, like it was a cement chia pets or vast minimalist bust of Malcolm Gladwell; it could have been transplanted into a downtown courtyard as another sculpture on the Picasso-Dubuffet-Miro walking tour.

Beyond the remnants of the Kennedy, the train track had collapsed into a twisted metal mess, barricaded for good

measure with a stack of streetlights crisscrossed like
barricades in a hypermodern Alamo.

I spun the car around and stopped. I caught Gammy's
eye. Her expression was tense and soft and apologetic, like she
wanted to say sorry to me.

"What?" I said. "*What?*"

The look on her face faded and I saw I had been half-
right: the look had been wistful regret—but not about me.

"He lives about two miles up Ashland," she said quietly,
looking past the barricades, "in Wrigleyville."

"Who?" I asked. I knew who. Her boyfriend. She was
trying to bring me into her life. She was allowing me to share
the moment with her. But I scraped together some dignity and
refused to be part of her emotional *ménage a trois*. I shrugged
like I didn't care.

"You mean Mike?" asked Trish, inserting herself
cheerfully into drama. I winced, because I realized she knew all
about it and always had.

"Yes," said Gammy.

Fuck, I thought. Now he had a name. Mike. She was
dating a guy called Mike. Who lived in Wrigleyville. Hold on, I
thought. A guy named Mike who lived in Wrigleyville? He had
to be white. There was no way he wasn't white. And probably
worked in computing or finances. And he was a Cubs fan for
sure. I don't know why, but when she told me her boyfriend
was in Chicago, I assumed he was a cool black guy named
DeShawn or Tejesus or Jamiroquoi, living on the South Side,
maybe on the University of Chicago football team, and
definitely a White Sox fan. Not weenie Mike from Wrigleyville.

Gammy could read me like a book.

"What?" I said, with angry innocence.

"No, you what?" she snapped.

"Does he collect comics?" I sneered. She *tsk*-ed me. "So,"
I went on, in a sing-song way, "What does he prefer: Batman or
Spider-Man?"

She looked out the window, folding her arms and
scrunching up her nose.

"Aha!" I said. "He does! So let me guess, my competition

is a scrawny white guy, not far out of college, who collects comic books and isn't even ashamed of it; he works in finances in the Loop; and he's a diehard Cubs fan." I said it in the gayest way possible. "In fact, on your second date, he took you to a Cubs game. Am I right? Am I right?"

She unfolded her arms and looked coldly at me. "What do you mean 'competition'?"

Silence. Words died in my throat. My massive victory was crushed. I thought I was an enormous tank, but as I tried to roll her over, she just stepped aside and, with a tap against my flank, caused me to collapse into a pile of broken machinery, springs boinging from my side.

I think I would have literally fallen apart if Trish had not poked between us with the undeterred optimism of a cheerleader whose side was down 45-0 in the last seconds of the game. "Guys," she implored, her lips twisted in a smile, "please don't say anything you'll regret."

"It's too late for that," Gammy and I said, together.

We said the same thing at the same time. I searched her face for a twitch of a smile in her lips, for a sparkle in her eyes, for anything that might trigger the same in me; but she gave away nothing. She looked at me without emotion and was beautiful in a new way, her face as elegantly shaped and expressionless as one of the wooden masks from the Gambia or Nigeria I had seen in museums: flawless, solid, perfect.

"You're beautiful," I said. Her lips parted but her expression did not change. I considered adding, "I hope Mike knows what a lucky guy he is", but I was not entirely convinced that she wanted to be with him; I then thought about saying, "I hope Mike told you that," but I struck that thought down: if he was a comic-book-collecting Caucasian Cubs fan, he had definitely said that, probably on the first date.

We were facing south on Ashland.

"It's three miles to the loop," I said. "We've got a quarter tank of gas, three rifles, there are monsters out there, and I'm with two beautiful women."

Trish swung a rifle to her chest, Gammy followed my stare south. "Hit it," she said.

IV.

On the corner of Milwaukee, we pulled over in front of the strangest sight we had encountered so far.

Now, let's face it, it had been a strange week. I had seen things I never expected to see. But this took the cake—this took the cake, it took the dessert, it took the whole meal. My mouth fell open and with both fists I rubbed my eyes like I was a goon in a 1930s studio comedy; the only thing I didn't do was say "ya-gubbity, ya-gubbity, ya-gubbity."

Trish perched between Gammy and me. I checked their faces to see if I had finally gone mad, but they were as freaked out as I was. If I'd gone nuts, we were having the same hallucination.

What we saw could best be described as a nightmare parade. Out in front were six gangly figures who looked like they might have been conjured into life from Walt Disney's long-forgotten racist drawings of a New Orleans jazz band: each figure was tall and skinny, with long spidery black limbs attached to anorexic bodies; they had tiny bowling-ball heads with big mouths, rolling white eyeballs, and delicate puffs of hair on top. They pranced and jived, they waved their limbs in the air like giant muppets, they shimmied to the side and skedaddled forward, they jiggled their long skinny bodies. We couldn't hear whatever they were dancing to, but they were mesmerizing: we leaned forward, straining to hear the music that got them moving in that delirious fashion, carrying them along in a crazed, ecstatic bop.

After them came the bowed heads and bared backs of a dozen people trudging ahead of a cart, which they pulled like slaves, straining to drag it over the crunched glass. Their faces were smeared black, their foreheads nearly scraping the ground as they leaned into the yoke. Lumbering beside them was a gray mud creature, like the thing that killed Cat, chained by the neck to the cart. It held a whip, which it cracked across their backs.

Standing on the cart were women, maybe twenty of them, lounging and laughing, reaching out to touch one another's hair, and waving at the imaginary crowds collecting on the sidewalks.

"What the hell?" I said.

Gammy pointed down the street. Coming from the entrances of buildings on Milwaukee were the last survivors, the ones who had remained hiding all this time, trembling in attics, huddled in basements; some crawled, others limped, some came out as families holding hands; they were bedraggled, scabby, dirty and skinny but they had beatific smiles on their faces, the happiness of salvation sparkling in their eyes. As they staggered into formation behind the cart, their eyes seeking out the women, their faces beaming with deliverance, another gray creature with a chain around its neck slew them, one by one, pummeling them into the street, and stomping them like it was swatting moths fluttering towards the light. Milwaukee Avenue was stained with flattened people.

"Don't get out," I whispered between gritted teeth.

The skinny dancers boogied to within a few feet of the car but they were oblivious to our presence—and it was still so quiet. Then came the people pulling the cart, bowing under the weight; there was something weird about their heads, which were like bruised and bloodied melons, but I couldn't make it out. They drew the cart closer. The women on the cart were a multicultural mix: black, white, Asian, other; younger, older; skinny, flighty, hefty; Goths with black dreads, prim Mormons or Amish with straight hair bound under a kerchief—but their mouths opened and closed in unison.

"What the—?"

Gammy put her hand to her mouth and scrunched up her face. In a flash, she whipped her belt out of her pants, shifted over to straddle the gear stick, and ran the belt through the steering wheel, under my belt, and through a pair of loops on her own pants. She pulled the belt tight and buckled it.

The cart came alongside us. A pretty woman in a blue bandana with black curls bursting down the back of her neck looked down at us, smiled prettily, and beckoned us. Gammy wrapped my head up in a hug, her arms tight around my neck, our bodies linked by the belt to each other and the car; it was like we were bracing for a collision after she had tied us to the crashing vehicle—and then I heard it.

Their singing wasn't like any music I knew; all the music I'd ever heard before sounded like the noise a five year old without much talent and with no instinctive love for melody would make if given a piano and a mallet and told to be as loud and mean as possible. Compared to what was coming from the women on the cart, Beethoven's music was the mindless lowing of a herd of cows as they lumbered towards grain spilled by the farmer into their trough; the music of the Beatles or the Beach Boys was the gurgling of stupid boys who ate their hot dogs too quickly and had to be given the Heimlich maneuver; this was beyond next level shit, this was having a Goddess rub her crotch against your ears, coming into your entire body and bringing you to a state of divine ecstasy.

Gammy and I bucked and shook like we were having fits; with faint inklings of rationality, we snatched and clawed at the buckle to get out of the car—all we wanted was to hear more beautiful music; we cried, we screamed, we gagged as the music came out of their mouths like a vaudeville hook and pulled us to them. Being unable to follow was like being stretched on the rack, like they had reached into our mouths and were pulling us up the trachea and lungs; the pain of being held back from them was like every single hair in our body and the nails in our fingers and toes were being slowly plucked out by plyers.

The cart kept moving, the music began to fade, and then, with a snap, we were released. We could hear the echoes of their voices, like we were in the hallway outside an auditorium, but the music no longer pulled us; Gammy and I collapsed against each other, panting—when we checked afterwards, our waists were mottled with bruises, our jeans were torn and the belt was frayed: if the music had gone on for much longer, we might have freed ourselves.

As my mind began to clear, the first thing I realized was what was so odd about the people dragging the cart: their ears had been cut off.

And the second thing . . .

"Trish?" I gasped. The back seat was empty, the door open. "Oh no, oh no."

We looked at the procession. Trish had fallen into position behind the cart. We could not see her face, her back was to us, but she was sashaying in her black overcoat, her hands wafting in the melody, as alive and content as she had ever been; I think she began to skip, and for a moment, Gammy and I melted with jealousy, because she was awash in beauty, oblivious to the great creature lumbering over to her.

"Move," I said, inaudibly.

"Oh no," hushed Gammy.

We were so jealous and so scared and we couldn't look away. The creature with beady unblinking black eyes lifted its huge hand and brought it down on her head like a mallet, driving her blonde skull into Ashland Avenue.

"Trish," hissed Gammy, making a sound like tissue paper was removed from the back of her throat.

"Oh Trish" I said. Her name came out of my mouth like a bloodied wad of gauze after dental surgery, salty and squishily solid—it was almost a relief.

V.

The chess pavilion on North Avenue Beach was empty. A gull pecked at something stringy and black on one of the cement boards. On Navy Pier, the Ferris wheel was bent and mangled like a bicycle wheel run over by a car. The boats were gone from the lake. White masts jutted out of the waves like bones in an unearthed graveyard. No more summers of boating, fishing, and diving into the cold waters a mile out from shore. A mat of what looked like algae pulsed with the waves against the cement breakwater. Bodies.

"Should we rest?"

"No. Keep going."

Gammy and I stumbled through the parking lots and taco stalls, past a burned-out police car and the wreckage of a helicopter—mangled metal, fins, blades twisted along a sooty trail of burned grass and dirt. Chipmunks and squirrels watched us from the safety of trees, chewing nuts like popcorn, waiting to see what would happen next. A squirrel jerked its head to look past us and I followed its sciuridian gaze.

"Here they come," I said.

We'd lost the car about a mile north, not far from the Lincoln Park Zoo, on Lake Shore Drive. We came across a throng of zombies in the road and before we knew it, we were driving through them. They were in front of us, behind us, clawing at the car, rubbing their faces and hands against the window, sloughing off layers of skin and black smears of coagulated blood on the paint. I accelerated. It was like driving through a chicken and beef satay forest, with orange and red meat sheared from the broken bamboo toothpicks of their bones; the windscreen was messy with a paste of yellowish chunky zombie flesh like peanut sauce; inside the car, in the ochre light, we could tell by a sudden lack of thumps and a lurch forward that we had passed the zombies, but I couldn't see where we were going and I just kept driving, screaming, with the windshield wipers smearing zombie-satay sauce, and every second we were moving we were moving away from the zombies. We crashed into an abandoned car in the middle of the road. We barely managed to get out with a single pistol each. We were hurt.

Gammy put an arm around my waist.

"We're almost there," she said.

We'd come into the city on Kinzie, past the Merchandise Mart, which looked like a drunkard who had his teeth punched in. Smoke was coming from Lake Point Tower, the Sears Tower—as I will always call it—and everything Trump had built. Down the river, the Marina City exuded thick reams of what appeared to be peach-colored foam rubber; the two towers looked like a pair of the bad-assest wasp's nests ever. We turned up LaSalle, keeping our eyes peeled for any sign of resistance or an open Al's Beef. We weren't too far from the Original Pancake House. Gammy wouldn't let me check to see if it was the center of the resistance. I'd come to trust her instincts, even if all I could think about was a plate of thin, chewy 49ers with extra whipped butter and maple syrup.

We went up Clark and then switched back at Fullerton, coming down Lake Shore Drive. And then we saw it. Maybe a quarter mile away. From the top floor in a glassy condo on Walton or Delaware came staccato blasts of white light. A sheet hung from the window; something was written in blue paint, the words indiscernible. There were people there; they had a plan; they were calling us together to safety. We had found the safe zone.

There was just one problem: we'd lost the car, we were almost out of bullets, my ankle was swollen, each step was a pinch of agony, Gammy wasn't losing any more blood from her arm but she was pallid and weak, we were both sore, tired, ready to give up, and there were hundreds of zombies chasing us. The problem was a single problem, but it had a lot of parts, and just about all of them pointed to the same solution.

We sat in the shadow of an overturned taxi skewed across the grass by the Lakefront Trail. Coming down the lawn was the mass of zombies with muddy blood-jeweled faces and ragged claws groping through the air. The squirrels darted higher in the trees for a better view. The zombies were rambling, they were even cheerful. Were they hungry or just excited that their work was almost done?

"I have three bullets," said Gammy, checking her pistol then shifting across the bruised lawn so she was right up next to me. "How about you?"

"Three."

She pretended to count the zombies: "More than six," she said. We both managed a smile. She went on: "If we killed six, we'd have no bullets left. And they'd eat us."

"A few days ago, I would have said let's kill six of them and suffer the consequences. But I'm too old for this."

"You're not, Jack." She elbowed me in the side and we both winced.

Then we laughed a bit.

"Should we kill four and then use one bullet on each other?"

They were getting closer, a throng of rotting limbs, tongueless mouths, empty white eyes, we could hear the air whistling through their dry necks. We knew it didn't matter what we decided, or how many of them we shot. We were just drawing out the conversation before saying goodbye.

"So you think we should shoot a few and then . . .?" She was resting her head on my shoulder; I stroked her hair, springy under my fingers.

"It would suck," I said, "if after wasting four bullets on them, we shot each other but only wounded each other, and would therefore suffer the fate of being eaten alive after being shot, but not *fatally*, by the person we love most in the world."

I bit my lip. The L-word. Talk about killing a conversation.

"I'm sorry," I said.

"You love me?"

There didn't seem much reason to play hard-to-get. "Oh hell, yes, I do, Gammy. I know it's not a romantic time to say it but I love you."

Her eyes glazed with tears. I couldn't tell if they were the same tears she was shedding when she was thinking about Mike a few hours before. But I wasn't in the mood for playing games.

252

"And just so you know, Gammy, I'd be proud to kill you, because you're the bravest woman—the bravest *person*—I've ever met. It's a tribute to how much I love you that I could even consider shooting you in the head."

She smiled coldly at me. "It's easy for you, falling in love."

She saw me blink. I was hoping she would tell me she loved me too, though I was ready if she didn't; but I have to admit, the worst I expected was affection. A lecture? Not so much.

"I'm not saying it's cheap, but I mean it's easy because you can fall in love even with this happening." She pointed at the zombies, stinking and rotting, now only a few feet away. "All your life, you've been taught that you can fall in love outside of history. That's what your love stories tell you. But that's a kind of dream you could have. I never could."

"I just want to be clear," I said, looking at the zombies shuffling towards us. "It's like, being killed by zombies isn't enough for Jack Forbes. First, I have to see my career end in ruins, then I have to be humiliated when I say 'I love you' to a woman half my age who then lectures me about the narrative construction love in its sociohistorical context, and *then* I get eaten by zombies. This is how *Lolita* should have ended."

She laughed, but not in a good way. "Funny thing is, Jack, if you knew what love was, you wouldn't feel bad for *yourself* right now."

"Oh, the lecture's not over? You're going to keep going until the zombies are actually eating me? The last thing I'm going to hear as I'm eaten alive is that my selfishness is so profound that even my love is selfish? You know, I thought I knew what rock bottom was like, but . . ."

She leaned up, gasping at the pain, and kissed me hard, lingering against my face. It was the sweetest kiss of my life.

"I'm sorry, baby, I shouldn't have said what I said." Gammy smiled. "This isn't the worst way I could have died."

Okay, I thought. It wasn't the highest praise I'd ever been given, but this was going to be my last choice, so I chose forgiveness and let myself love her. I drew my pistol and held it against her head. I felt something hard against my own temple. Her gun. With our free arms, we righted ourselves so that we were kneeling, our bodies pressed up against each other, her breasts against my chest, her thighs against mine.

"On three," I said, and kissed her.

"Jack, wait!"

"Yes?" I could taste her breath in my mouth. I knew I'd made the right choice. If this was my time to die, if I was going to die with her taste in my mouth, her lips against mine, then I was going to be one of the lucky ones; but I also hoped she might have a better idea.

"This time let's count all the way to three. We'll begin with 'one', okay? Let's make this last."

The zombies were grunting, tilting towards us, slobbering, scrabbling faster.

"Okay." With my free hand, I held her face, trying not to see the muzzle I was pressing into her temple. Something occurred to me: "I won't jump the gun this time." She smiled kindly at my joke.

"You go first," I said.

"One." She kissed me hard, pushing her lips against mine.

I pulled back.

"Two," I said, pressing my forehead against hers, breathing in her breath.

"Oh, Jack," she sighed and tensed. "Thr—"

VI.

We didn't get through three. We were interrupted by a hideous, rasping screech, like a recently-spayed tomcat was being declawed with plyers in an alley. The sound came from a zombie whose head above its lower jaw had been torn off. It fell to its knees, a monstrous whoopee cushion releasing a whistling sepulchral fart through its neck. It collapsed at the feet of a werewolf spitting skull and flesh.

"Oh that's just dandy. A werewolf is joining in the fun."

The werewolf twisted to peer at us from under its haunches. There was something oddly familiar about the wolf. It was slender, fair-haired, green-eyed, and the lupine features could not disguise a long thin nose. With a paw, it clawed at its forehead as though hair was falling into its eyes.

"It's Rafael!" cried Gammy.

Rafael faced the oncoming zombies. His tail swished, he feinted. Zombies stopped in their tracks and even tried to back up, but the mass behind them pushed onwards. Rafael snapped at their fetid ankles and darted back, spitting out torn clothing and rotted meat. Four or five zombies collapsed without their shins. The rest kept coming, weakly clawing the air. If they had hearts, you'd say they were getting half-hearted.

"He's giving us time!" said Gammy.

She groped up the side of the taxi and pulled me to my feet. We began hobbling across the lawn. On Lake Shore Drive, our feet crunched on broken glass and spent casings and we shimmied over what looked like a barbed wire fence. I didn't turn back to look, as if doing so might condemn us never to escape. When we made it to the far side of the drive, we collapsed against a light pole.

And then I looked.

The crowd of zombies, ravaged forms, man's final stage of existence, the undead schoolyard bullies, the unthinking masses, a tidal swell of decomposed violence moved in on the darting and biting wolf. Rafael barked. They weren't interested in us anymore.

"Get out of there," I shouted.

Rafael sat bolt upright and snarled. And then with great strides he vaulted across the meridian and bore down on us, his eyes sparkling in his scrunched-up bristled features.

"He's coming for us," I shouted, trying to stand.

Gammy held my back. "No, he's not."

Rafael slid along the asphalt, coming to a stop about fifteen feet away; he panted once, twice in our direction.

"He's telling us to run," said Gammy.

"Rafael, come on, come with us!"

He woofed, inspected the ground, and then woofed again, obviously not entirely aware that we couldn't understand him. It was quite frustrating, especially because the zombies were flooding across the street and I wasn't sure how long he was going to continue his woofing monologue. But with a paw Rafael pushed the invisible hair from out of his eyes, swiveled around and charged into the zombies. He didn't snap at their ankles, he didn't feint; he bore right into them, slashing with his claws, biting whatever he could get his jaws on. Twenty zombies oozing guts and blood collapsed and died again but there were a hundred more and a hundred more after that.

They crushed around Rafael. And tore him to bits.

We made it to the Gold Coast and scrambled past old money mansions, the tough tiled buildings with mansard roofs on Schiller, Goethe and Elm, the brick aristocrats that survived the Depression and the next one and the one after that, getting sootier and more dignified. Behind them, the buildings were flattened and gouged black. The place looked like it had been hit by a bomb.

We came to a 1970s lake front condo, where the light had been coming from. Glass frosted the tarmac and coated the shrubs in the formal cement garden like snow. The wintry feel was not inapt—a cold wind came tripping off the lake. In the chilly air, with the sunlight sparkling on the glass, it was like visiting the Christmas light show at the Botanical Gardens.

The Christmas theme didn't end there. A once-jolly fat man with a bushy white beard slumped against a pillar like

Santa after an all-night bender. I kicked his foot. He was as dead as Santa, too.

"Let's go in."

Gammy studied the corpse. "You sure?"

"Other than the dead guy," I said, "which is quite a big exception, I'm feeling good about three things. Number one: check out the glass. It's everywhere. On the road, the sidewalk, the plants. It didn't fall by accident. Whoever's inside, they blasted out the windows and made a glass moat. Effective against zombies, werewolves, water creatures, anything bare-footed, bare-pawed, or bare-flippered. They knew what they were doing. And now they're up there, calling us in."

"Okay," she said, unsure. "What else?"

"Number two: the zombies didn't follow us after killing Raf—anyway, zombies, they're not smart. In fact, they're mindless. They're driven by instinct. Something's telling them not to come here. I don't know what it is but it's a good bet we want to find out."

"What's the third thing?"

"I shouldn't say."

"Let me guess. You got aroused when we kissed?"

That *was* the third thing, but she made it sound cheap. "I know you pretty well, don't I?" she said.

I put my arm under her moist armpit and we entered the smashed lobby together.

"Let's find the others."

We didn't expect the elevators to work but were disappointed that they didn't. If that isn't a defining feature of humanity, I don't know what is.

For over an hour we trudged upwards, moving in total darkness, thirsty, sore, discovering new burning pains in our thighs and calves. A week before, I'd have been whining and stopping for a break before we got to the third floor. But I'd changed. I pushed on, glad when my ankle went numb, letting Gammy encourage me with a hand on my shoulder or a soft "c'mon on."

One thought kept me going: we're not done yet. There's

a reason, there's hope, there's a point to all of this. At the end, we would find others—the resistance, the survivors, the heroes who put the sign out, calling for us to come.

At last, trembling and sore, we reached the top floor. We caught our breath and pushed through a stiff door. Slabs of light came into the hall through open doors. At the far end, a man poked his head out.

"Hallo!" I shouted. "Hallo there!"

He ducked back.

"We're humans," I called after him; they wouldn't have survived this long without being cautious.

"Is that you, Ralphie?" a voice called down the hall.

My legs seized up in cramps and I doubled over. Gammy answered, "We're alone, just the two of us."

"Is Ralphie with you?" the voice hollered.

"No," replied Gammy. "We're coming."

I stretched the cramps out. Gammy put her arm around my waist and helped me down the hall and into a muggy apartment.

Our reception party consisted of an old black man, standing helplessly in the middle of a living room, slouched like he was carrying two heavy buckets in his hands. He had white-flecked sideburns with several days of stubble, and was balding on top with messy black and white curls retreating from a high, furrowed forehead. Bits of paper stuck in his hair.

I shrugged off Gammy and gave him a crisp salute. "Where are the others, sir?"

He looked around as if they might have been there all along and maybe he hadn't noticed them. When he didn't find anybody else, he turned back to us.

"Just been me and Ralphie up here for the week. We drank the last of the water buffalo"— a twiggy finger pointed in the direction of a water cooler—"and Ralphie went to get more."

I laughed politely. "Yes, but where's the rest of the resistance? The others?"

Gammy looked sadly at me.

"Ain't no resistance here."

"I know, but the others," I persisted. "With the guns. And the grenades. And the vaccines."

The man looked to Gammy to interpret.

"You don't have to hide them from us, sir," I said. "We're on your side. We're reporting for duty. For God's sake, we came because you called us."

"Didn't call nobody."

"What about your sign?" I demanded.

"What sign?"

"The one you hung on the window, telling humans it was safe to come here."

"You mean the sheet?"

"Yes, of course I mean your fucking sheet!"

"Did you read what Ralphie wrote on it?" he asked; he could tell we hadn't. He swallowed unhappily and said, "Ralphie wrote 'Help Us.' Like—" He searched for a synonym. "Like, 'Rescue Us.' Not like, 'Help Us Fight.'"

Nothing he was saying computed. "What about the lights?" I challenged, getting sharp and lawerly. "What about the signals?"

"That was Ralphie with the flashlight. Day or night, he'd sit at the window and flash: dot-dot-dot, dash-dash-dash, dot-dot-dot."

"What the godfuck does that mean?" I screamed.

"Morse code for SOS," he explained. "Save Our Souls."

I looked around wildly. "Who's in charge here?"

The man pondered this for a moment, then said, "Sometimes me, sometimes Ralphie."

Gammy knew this had to end. She put a hand on my forearm and steered me over to a white sofa, once expensive and beautiful but now grungy with a stain where one of them had been laying his head. I sat and tried to make my mind intercalate with the information accumulating in my brain. Gammy put an arm on my shoulder and massaged my neck.

I shook my head. "I'm sorry, Gammy, I'm fine. I'm fine."

I knew what I was seeing: we hadn't climbed all those steps to find a Gandhi-Che Guevara figure and thirty musclebound young people with weapons and a plan. I now believed it too. I fully believed that I was fundamentally alone in the world and doomed, worth no more than a mosquito, a swirling glob of plankton, an intestinal parasite, or a kind of bacteria that grows in the plump folds of an intestinal parasite's skin. I knew what my senses were telling me and I believed my senses.

But my mind kept going.

I shot to my feet.

"Okay, but where's the command center? And the radio? There's got to be a radio. And the fridge works, right? It'll have cheesecake in it." I giggled. "Yes, it'll have blueberry cheesecake." I began to shake with laughter. "Cheesecake. *Cheesecake?* Cheesecake!"

The man took a step back.

"Hey, Gammy, have you ever heard a funnier word than 'cheesecake'?"

I bawled with laughter.

The laughter became tears, I fell onto the couch and wept on Gammy's shoulder, and she wiped my face with her stained hoodie.

About half an hour later, when I calmed down, the man introduced himself as Mac. He sat in a reclining chair. It was obvious that he had spent a lot of time in that chair.

"So," he said, "Did you see Ralphie?"

"Who?"

"My buddy. Big guy, white beard. I sent him down for the water."

"Does he look like Santa?"

"Yes, that's Ralphie."

"We saw Ralphie," I said.

"Oh, that doesn't sound good."

"It isn't good."

"What got him?"

"We don't know," said Gammy.

Mac threw his arms up in frustration and rolled out of the chair. He went to the window and studied the glass itself then returned to his chair in a well-worn circuit. "Did you send him on?"

"What do you mean?"

"You didn't leave him there, did you?" His eyes bulged and he scratched his scalp. "Oh man, oh man, I promised Ralphie if he died, I'd send him on."

"How do you 'send someone on'?"

He looked at me like I was an idiot. "You cut his damned head off. That way he can't become a zombie or a vampire or a nightcritter or nothing. Aw, shit."

Mumbling curses and shaking his head mournfully, Mac went down to check on his friend. He came back about an hour later, surprisingly fast for an old man. He was still shaking his head.

"He's gone, he ain't down there. Must've become a zombie. Gobdarnit. I promised I would send him on if he died an' he promised the same to me. Poor Ralphie!" He threw himself against the wall, slid down, and put his head between his knees, letting out big male sobs. "Aw shit."

Amidst the blubbing, he retrieved a cigar with a soggy chewed end from his shirt pocket and stuck it in his mouth.

"Aw shit."

Mac told us about how he and Ralphie got to be there. They'd come to do freelance plumbing work on an apartment on the sixteenth floor. When the monsters struck, everybody in the building fled but he and Ralphie stayed put; neither had the imagination or energy to go anywhere else so they decided to wait it out. They camped out on the sixteenth floor for a night or two but monsters invaded the building. The only way to go was up, so they climbed to the top, set out their help signal, chewed stogies and argued baseball.

While Mac was telling his story, I sat on the sofa, idly stroking a throw pillow. Gammy excused herself and went into the bathroom. It smelled foul because Mac and Ralphie had been using it relentlessly and without any apparent concern for the plumbing. She found a pair of scissors and cut her hair, leaving a mat of damp curls in the bathtub. In the bedroom closet, she found clean clothes. When she came out in a blue dress shirt and slacks that were baggy and too long, Mac gaped at her like he was surprised we smuggled in a third person. The cuts on her arm from the car crash were seeping, leaving black stains on the shirtsleeves. She brought another shirt and the scissors over to the table to make a bandage.

Mac, accepting that new folks had shown up, went on with his story. "Sitting up here night after night, Ralphie and I agreed on one thing. We were sure of it, more sure than we'd been of anything: this year it was gonna be the Cubs." He gulped back tears. I thought he was about to eulogize Ralphie, but he blubbered, "The Cubs ain't ever gonna win the World Series now."

"You're a Cubs fan? Jesus, really?"

Gammy busied herself with tearing strips for bandages; I felt a twinge of jealousy as Mike's phantom appeared in the room.

"Hell yeah," said Mac, reinvigorated, "I've been a bleacher bum for thirty years. Still don't like the night games."

"I'm a Sox fan," I said.

Mac shrugged generously. That was one of the worst things about Cubs fans. Whenever it suited them they could become White Sox fans, like we were competitive brothers, not sworn enemies. It gave them a ghastly, almost-Christian magnanimity.

"Hey," said Mac. "Do you read?"

I hadn't seen any bookshelves in the apartment, which was efficient and spartan, if somewhat abused by Mac and Ralphie—a businessman's pad as was evident from the clothes Gammy found.

"You like books?" asked Mac.

"Sure," I said. "Especially my own."

Mac failed to pick up the cue, but he pointed to corner table with a big lamp and a silver-framed photograph of a blonde woman who looked like a middle-aged Trish. Next to her was a stack of newspapers.

"I read 'em," said Mac. He looked over at Gammy as if still trying to figure out where the other black girl went.

I went over to the table. The newspapers were from all over the world, dated the day before the monster uprising. I took them to the polished pecan dining table where Gammy was making bandages. With her hair cut short, she looked gorgeous and younger except in her eyes. I didn't ask why she cut her hair but she knew I liked it.

I laid out the papers and sat across from her. It could have been a lazy Sunday morning; all we needed were coffees in matching White Sox mugs and we could sit at the table and pass sections of the New York *Times* to each other, fighting playfully over who got the book review section first (she would let me have it), but I wouldn't open it until we'd read the Weddings/Celebrations section and discussed how our announcement would look—I would secretly be sure they'd publish our photo because of our race difference, and she would secretly be sure they'd publish it because of our age difference.

Gammy stood unsteadily and walked to the window with a view of the city to the west. I got up and followed her, the newspapers under my arm. We looked at the hazy smashed grid of high smoking ruins. Gammy recited something under her breath. I asked what she said.

"And the Lord said, 'You had pity on the plant for which you have not labored, nor made it grow, which came up in a night and perished in a night.'"

I put an arm around her and held her close. "Amen."

She rested her head on my shoulder and I kissed her forehead. Mac shifted in his seat and coughed to remind us he was there, although I couldn't imagine why he wouldn't prefer to watch us make love to spending another hour chewing his sodden cigar. At least it would be different.

I led Gammy back to the table and placed the newspapers between us, but she put her head in her arms, pushing them away—she was young; it was possible she didn't know what they were.

I picked one up and unfolded it. The *Hindu Times*. On page two: a semi-comical article from Rajasthan where villagers claimed they had been overrun by demons bounding out of the river, hopping like frogs with fanged teeth. On page seven: a paragraph about a village in Ladakh destroyed by an avalanche—but a strange one. A local Sherpa said it looked like an iceman as big as a tower flung itself from a cliff and crushed the village underneath. And, apparently, Indians love cricket.

I flicked through the *New York Daily News* ('Al Kong!') and the *New York Post* ('King Qaeda!') and the *International Herald Tribune*—nothing except CIA-censored claptrap and *Doonesbury*. Zonker had no idea what was coming.

I opened the *Telegraph* from England. It was hard not to read it without Rafael's accent in my head, explaining boring details with perky excitement. On page six, they reported a mass murder in County Kilkenny: a half-naked geriatric madman covered in filth and scabs had terrorized a market, killing more than a dozen shoppers. He grabbed them by the hair, dragged them to a sixteenth-century stone watering trough, and drowned them. It took a whole regiment of police to overpower him. Two coppers were drowned in the effort. And there was a lot of coverage of a 'test' match with India.

I moved onto a newspaper from Toronto carrying a bemused item on a spate of yeti sightings in Saskatchewan and Nova Scotia, and a one-paragraph report on an exorcism in a First People village that left someone and a moose dead; then a paper from Los Angeles with a Spanish language insert that I couldn't decipher, though there was a front page image of a chupacabra, which looked quite amusing until I realized that the grainy, distorted cartoon wasn't a cartoon but a photograph; and finally the *Christian Science Monitor*. The same thing: politics, economics, sports, editorials, nothing— nothing except for amused reports about legends and myths coming true, odd murders, wild mystical sightings that belonged in the *National Enquirer* or in an advertisement for lower car rates on a webpage. Nobody put it together. The first rumors of something awful and nobody heeded them. I felt like God, not in an all-powerful, all-loving way, but with a curious divine spectatorship, half-watching as a bumbling, not particularly well-meaning species finally faced extinction without being aware that it was truly facing extinction. We had smirked at death as something that was always happening somewhere else, but that was because we weren't paying attention. We had no idea that the person beside us, who we were elbowing and trying to make notice the amusing catastrophes, was the Grim Reaper.

When I was done, I pushed the papers away.

"That was fast," said Mac. Another thought, maybe a memory of what I said, struck him. "Did you like to write things?" He saw the expression on my face: the desperation and hurt pride that the question "Do you like to write things?" induces in every writer's face. He jutted his chin at the kitchen behind the sofa. "There's a computer."

Gammy shot up, startled.

"We found it in the closet," said Mac, who had not bothered to use any of the clothes he found there.

"Where is it?" said Gammy. "Is there—"

"No internet," Mac said despondently. Ah, I thought, I get it now. He was a porn connoisseur: innocuous half-witted grandfatherly figure by day, rabid masturbator by night. Gammy sank back into her arms.

I found the computer under a tatty lumberjack's jacket—from the size of it, Ralphie's. It was an outdated laptop, about an inch and a half thick and heavy. I muttered a quick prayer—*O holy machine, O great portal to the global mind, conduit of consciousness and light, please work that I may write*—hit the on-button, and the screen lit up blue.

"Halle-fucking-lujah."

"But there's no internet," said Mac, shaking his head. A lot of big breasts were jiggling unwatched in the last electric twitches of microchips embedded in forlorn satellites wondering what was happening on an earth no longer responding to their mechanical blips. I wondered if Rafael's video was up there too, a ghostly spurting, humanity's symbolic immortality, running out of batteries.

The desktop was sparse with an icon for an empty garbage can and the dispiriting blue 'W' in a blue box that I knew so well. I clicked. An empty page appeared before my eyes with a blinking black line at the top left hand corner. My instinct for procrastination compelled me to click on 'File' and examine the list of recently opened documents, but the computer could not find them.

I ran my fingers over the key pad like a concert pianist who has been on holiday and on the last day notices a piano in the hotel lobby and runs his fingers down the ivories, curious if any of the old familiarity had been lost, not quite willing to make music, just making contact. With a last ditch effort at procrastination, I tapped the cursor over the 'x' in the right corner, and then opened a new document. A clean start.

With a deep breath, I started typing: "It all began in New York."

I've typed through the night, through the darkness of a city that has no lights, keeping an eye on the battery icon in the top right hand corner: 9 hours left, 7 hours, 4 hours, 2 hours.

After kissing me goodnight, Gammy curled up on the sofa, letting Ralphie's head-stained pillow fall to the floor. Mac lay on his reclining seat and snored through a slack mouth. Every once in a while his breathing stopped and I'd pause, wondering if he had died; when I was sure he'd passed into heaven, he'd gasp, splutter, mumble a few unintelligible words, and the snoring would begin again. I got up only once. To put a blanket over him. He was shivering.

Other than attending to Mac, I didn't stop writing, I didn't stop to stretch or crack my neck, I just let the words tumble out. Thousands of them.

More than once somebody said to me with the reticent admiration one has for people who like getting fisted or who win hot dog eating competitions, "How do you do it?" How could I write so many words? I never knew what to say. I couldn't even answer why I wrote at all let alone so much. Maybe the two were connected.

But after settling into a rhythm, chasing time against the dwindling battery, I realized why I had been writing: all my life had been leading to this. It was all going to end with me. I was going to be the one who had the last say. I sure as hell wasn't the first and I sure as hell wasn't the best, but I would be the last. I was going to be the novelist in the doorway taking a last look and switching the light off on my way out.

I wrote all night long because that was what I was supposed to do. I wrote until my fingers were numb. And it all came back to me. The schoolroom in Ohio, the conversation with Lance, the rainbow, picking up the kids outside of South Bend, the warden and Zachary, Jerome, Ophelia and Starshine, making love with Gammy.

No, not all of it.

Trish said something funny about Praj but I couldn't remember what it was, except that it made his face light up, like he was finally happy to be with people whose jokes about him were the jokes of friends; and something happened between Rafael and Trish that suggested they had been amorous, but nothing was said, and I couldn't recall what it was that made me sure they had kissed but then done nothing else; and one afternoon when everybody was sleeping in the car, Gammy and I had a conversation about films we liked, but I couldn't remember which day it was, or which were the films we both liked and which were the ones we disagreed about— the only thing I could remember was how much fun the conversation was; and I forgot to mention the time we pulled over for a pee, and it turned out to be a meeting place for shapeshifters, squat animals like something you'd see on a totem pole, who rolled out from the pines. Praj and Rafael and I raced from the trees where we had been urinating, shoving ourselves into our trousers and tumbling into the car while Gammy and Trish provided covering fire.

And so much else. Gone, gone with my bad memory, gone forever.

But then, it's not so bad. That is where gratitude begins, in forgetting.

And now, illuminated by a clear dawn, the battery icon blinking, I hit save for the first time. I spent the night tempting fate.

Mac has come out of the bathroom where he stuttered out a piss. Gammy is on the sofa, her lips dry and cracked, but she comes over, and her lips are still nice to kiss.

"Did you sleep?" she asks. She strokes my cheek and I kiss her hand as she reads this sentence over my shoulder.

"No."

And then she whispers, "Write that you love me." And I do, with all the passion of a broken vow.

She doesn't say anything; but I'll write it, if not for her, then for me: "Thank you."

Mac is at the window. He makes a muffled sound and bangs lightly on the glass with his fists.

"It's all over," he says, a smile spreading across his face; it is the first time I see him smile. He looks at us with this sappy pathetic grin, his eyes twinkling. "They're coming."

Gammy limps over to the window. Mac is tapping the glass.

He says, chuckling, "Down there."

Gammy and Mac press their faces to the window.

"Oh Lord," says Gammy.

"Who's coming?" I ask.

"All of them," says Mac, joyously. "All of them."

-FIN-

JACK FORBES will not be back in any future adventures.

Books by Saul Wheelock

Human Sushi

Tricia Lifton

10.32, 10.33, 10.34

An Ethnography of the Spirit World

Questions, comments, compliments, critiques:

saulspinners@gmail.com

www.ingramcontent.com/pod-product-compliance
Lightning Source LLC
Chambersburg PA
CBHW070333260626
47160CB00003B/1030